Charles Shafer

ON CABRINI GREEN

CT Publishing

First published in Great Britain 2000
This edition 2000 CT Publishing.
Copyright © Charles Shafer 2000
The right of Charles Shafer to be identified as author of this
work has been asserted by him in accordance with the
Copyright, Designs & Patents Act 1988.

This book is fiction. All characters and incidents are entirely
imaginary.

www.crimetime.co.uk

A CIP catalogue record for this book is
available from the British Library.

ISBN 1-902002-14-8

9 8 7 6 5 4 3 2 1

Book design and typography by DP Fact & Fiction
Printed and bound in Great Britain by
Omnia Books Limited, Glasgow.

To Betty. Whatta babe!
Thanks to Dave Firks. Way back when, he took a
chance. Even more thanks to Peter Dillon-Parkin.
He took even a bigger chance.
Until then, I thought they were a couple of fairly
bright men. For editors, that is.

ON CABRINI GREEN

ON CABRINI GREEN
CHARLES SHAFER

Sergeant Paul Kostovic is sitting at the window of Millie's Deli, chomping on a pastrami sandwich, when he spots small time street thieves Dittybop Caldwell and his trusty sidekick Shoestring Tolliver apparently at a job of work. As he watches they commit a robbery worth a cool $250,000, and when he tries to stop them they get away with both the money and his gun—disappearing into the projects—into Cabrini Green.

Kostovic searches the projects for them, not knowing that their unusually efficient criminal career has taken an upswing due to a shadowy figure who is using street thieves to commit increasingly elaborate robberies, and that his pursuit of them will bring him into direct conflict with a criminal mastermind, who like Kostovic himself is an ex-marine. Kostovic increasingly finds himself falling back on marine combat tactics in a war of attrition with his unseen adversary.

CHARLES SHAFER was a Marine and served for 28 years as a Chicago cop. He retired in 1996 and is now a part-time golfer and full-time writer. His short fiction has won world-wide acclaim. ON CABRINI GREEN is his first novel

Chapter 1

SERGEANT PAUL KOSTOVIC sat at the window of Millie's Deli, chomping on a pastrami sandwich, when he spotted a couple of old friends on the corner. Gulping the last bite down, he said, "Hey, Millie, get out from behind that counter and come over here by the window. This, you gotta see."

"Jesus, Pauly. I got work..."

"Dammit! Get your skinny ass over here before it's too late."

"Okay, already." Millie, tiny Millie, with her apron hanging down around her ankles, scooted over to the front door. "Okay, what?" she said, eyeing up the street.

"Over on the corner. See those two black kids cleaning car windows?"

"So what's wrong with that? A couple'a teenagers see a chance at earning a buck, good for them."

"Not these two. That's Dittybop Caldwell and his trusty sidekick Shoestring Tolliver. Dedicated street thieves, the both of them."

Millie shook her head. "Ever since you made sergeant, got transferred back to uniform, everybody you see is a wrongdoer. Whatta you, thirty, thirty one? Lighten up, or you ain't gonna make forty."

"They're up to no good. Just you wait and see." He kept watch as Ditty and Shoestring, in T-shirts and floppy gym shoes, ran into the street, picked out a car, splashed its windshield with water from plastic bottles, then took paper towels and gave it a quick wipe. The car they've favored with their attentions was not necessarily left clean.

Millie laughed. "Yeah. Go on out there and shoot those dastardly bastards before they clean every windshield in Chicago."

"I'm telling you," Paul said, with eyes only for Ditty and Shoestring. They sure had picked out an excellent neighborhood to set up in. The Gold Coast District, with it's ritzy boutiques and shops.

"Well you have fun," Millie said. "Me, I gotta lock the place up so I can use the crapper before the lunch crowd shows."

"Okay."

"Are you going, or staying?"

"Whatever," Paul said, but he hadn't been listening. He scrunched down, recalling the time Shoestring had tried snatching some old lady's purse up in Old Town. Shoes would have got clean away except the goof tripped over his own loose shoestrings. And Ditty. All you had to do was open your eyes to see how he'd got his name. The way he walked, shoving one leg out, skipping to the other, dipping, then back to first leg. One supreme dittybopper, this kid.

Like right now, out into traffic, splashing a new car's windshield. Shoes right behind, trying to emulate his older pal, only stumbling now and again. Still with untied shoes, the dunce.

Maybe Paul had been wrong and Ditty and Shoes were actually working a semi-honest living. Nah, no way. Gotta have something up their sleeves.

Uh-oh, what's this? Ditty hanging back on the curb, looking in the direction of the Drake Hotel. Of course, the Drake. All the high class businessmen stayed there. Just Ditty and Shoestring's style, grab some rich dude's attaché case and run like hell.

Paul rubbernecked at the hotel. Nothing particularly interesting, just one or two strollers. A jogger too, who looked to be cooling off after a run along the beach.

He switched back to Ditty who was crossing over to the opposite side of Michigan Avenue, bopping at a determined pace to the exit ramp of the Drake Hotel's auto garage. Right next to the jogger. Almost looked like they were talking. But for what? And Paul took a good look at the jogger. Built like a prizefighter, this guy, with muscles everywhere, and hair cut down to the scalp. Didn't look like any kind of wrongdoer Paul had ever seen. Besides that he was white. Paul had never heard of Ditty and Shoes working with a white guy. Hell, they never took on *any* partner as far as he knew. Well, maybe if an especially good job presented itself, but still, never with a white guy.

He checked back to Shoestring, who had stopped the

window washing scam altogether, and was staring toward Ditty as if he were waiting for orders. Quick, back to Ditty. Only where was he? Paul raced his eyes up and down the sidewalk, searching for that distinguishing walk. Wait, there he was, in the street. In the street? And running behind— what? A Cadillac, and waving like a Michigan Avenue traffic cop at Shoestring.

Paul had to get out there, right now, and reached for the door. Only it wouldn't open. He hollered, "What'd you do, lock the damn door?"

Millie's muffled voice. "It's nineteen-seventy-eight, Pauly. Women have the right to lock the door when they use the crapper."

Paul, rattling the door, hoping its lock would break loose. "Not that door, dammit. Come on out here, will ya? It's going down out there."

Where everything was happening in quick time. Shoestring directly in the path of the Cadillac, beckoning with his water bottle and paper towels. And the Cadillac, screeching to a halt, its driver, a middle aged man in a business suit, shaking his fist through the windshield.

Paul yelled, "Jeezz-us! I gotta break this thing down, or what?"

Finally there Millie was. No hurry though, retying her apron as she came to the door. "You were sitting right there when I locked this thing, dopey." Using her key, she eyed the street. "What'sa matter? Your naughty little boys squirt somebody in the face?" Chuckling.

Paul hollered, "Call for help!" He burst out the door, pushing through a crowd of onlookers.

Cars were stopped bumper to bumper and he zigzagged through, trying to get a glimpse up ahead. There they were, Ditty and Shoes, with the Cadillac's door open and—here we go—with its driver out on the pavement. Shoestring holding the poor slob down while Ditty was removing, Paul couldn't tell what, from around his waist.

"Help, murder, save me, save me!" the driver screamed, curled into a fetal position.

Paul yelled, "I'm coming, I'm coming!" and charged onward,

grappling to get his service revolver out of his holster. Damn being in uniform and having to deal with these stupid contraptions.

Both Ditty and Shoestring spun around, giving Paul one of those 'uh-oh' looks. Shoestring jumped behind the Cadillac's wheel, hollering, "Gotta go, gotta go!"

Paul, closing in now, only still unable to free his service revolver. To hell with it, and at full stride he narrowed his eyes on Ditty who was scrambling to get into the Cadillac's rear seat. Couldn't let that happen. Paul dove headlong at Ditty's mid section. Just as Paul braced himself for impact, he was met with a brown-skinned forearm, and careened sideways. Out of control, he crunched into the side of the Cadillac, and fell stunned to the pavement, his service revolver clanking down at his feet.

"Go!" he heard Ditty yell, and saw through foggy eyes a pair of floppy gym shoes climb into the Cadillac's rear seat.

Tires lay rubber only inches from his head and he heard, more than saw, the Cadillac crash off one car, then another as it sped away.

Then gun shots; two, two more, and what sounded like six or seven in succession.

Other cops must have arrived, and were shooting at the fleeing Cadillac. Determined to get into the action, Paul grabbed for his gun.

Only little white dots began swirling in front of his eyes.

Chapter 2

SMEDLEY STOOD IN THE CROWD, in his jogging suit, trying to keep from laughing as he watched cop cars come streaming in from every direction. Had to be at least a dozen all told. Little late, weren't they?

The cop sergeant who had just about screwed up the robbery, still dizzy looking, was standing on the curb with another cop; a lieutenant, who was kind of a short guy, with a half-eaten cigar sticking out the side of his mouth. Both had TF patches on their shoulders. Meaning Task Force, Smedley figured. From his research, they were supposed to be the hardest working cops in Chicago. He'd see about that, and elbowed his way to the front of the crowd.

First things first, and he checked the name plates on their shirts. The sergeant, Kostovic. The lieutenant, Matthews. He'd store that information for future reference.

Matthews said, "You okay, Pauly?"

Paul, with his hand on his ear. "Just bumped my head is all. I'm still trying to sort out what happened." He pointed at a body laying in the gutter. "I still don't know how that got there."

Smedley could tell him. He could tell him a whole lot, but wasn't going to.

Some old biddy in a white apron came out of the crowd carrying a wet towel. She said, "Here, for your head," and handed the towel to Paul. Then to Matthews, "Come on, get after those assholes before they get away."

"Yeah, do something!" Smedley hollered. This was getting to be fun.

Paul gave the crowd, not necessarily Smedley, an angry stare, saying, "We ain't gonna get nothing done long as we gotta put up with Mister John Q. Bigmouth."

Matthews said, "You work the crime scene. I'll handle the crowd." He and four or five other cops waded into the crowd, effectively shoving them, and Smedley, to the curb.

Smedley couldn't have that. He stepped forward. "I'm a doctor. Can I be of help here?" Giving them an official type voice.

"Thanks, doc," the biddy said. She waved Smedley on like she was in charge.

"Dammit, Millie," Paul said, looking frustrated. He went to the opposite side of the patrol car. "Doc, I'm okay. But Mister Shakleford here could use some attention." He pointed at a man who was sitting on the curb, head down, vomit dripping from his lips.

Smedley had a hard time holding back from laughing. He'd already given Shakleford a good share of attention. Days in fact, counting all the time he'd stalked the man. "Of course," he said, and went down on one knee. So what would a real doctor do? He took Shakleford's arm, making like he was taking a pulse. Just that easy.

From over his shoulder, Paul said, "Mister Shakleford. You up to talking now?"

Shakleford, a rotund guy, said, "Thank God you showed up or they would've killed me." He gulped. "Only they took my diamonds. Over a quarter-million's worth."

Paul, typical cop, looked suspicious. "You mean to tell me you just happened to be driving down the street, your pockets stuffed with diamonds, and outta the blue get yourself robbed?"

Smedley fiddled with Shakleford's arms like he was looking for injuries as Shakleford said, "No, no, it wasn't like that." He gave his head a violent shake. "I do know my diamonds are gone. Yeah, they took my diamonds, over a quarter-million's worth."

"He needs this thing more than I do," Paul said. He handed Smedley the wet towel.

Smedley was loving this, and patted Shakleford's head with the towel.

"You know your license number?" Paul said, "so we can get after them."

"My diamonds," was all Shakleford could say.

Two more cops came out of the crowd, one saying, "Looky what I got, Sarge," bracing up the other cop.

Smedley had been wondering where that cop had gone to, and gave him a good look. Young, not more than twenty-two, twenty-three, with a baby face.

"Covello," Paul said. "How'd you get involved in this?"

"Pure accident," Covello answered, barely audible.

Smedley had everything he could do to keep from falling down, this was so funny.

Millie said, "You were flat out on the pavement so you didn't see him trying to shoot the robbers when they were getting away."

"No kidding," Paul said, and his face turned pessimistic. "I don't suppose you hit them?"

"To tell the truth, I dunno. I come up the tunnel. You know, from the beach. There you were lying in the street, this Cadillac racing down the sidewalk right at me. I thought they'd killed you. Man, I started shooting and whoever was in the Cadillac, they shot back." He looked at the body laying in the gutter. "That guy. He was standing right next to me." Covello's eyes went wide. "Know what? I heard the bullet hit him. Was like a splat. I'm telling you, he went straight down. Scared the shit outta me. I ran back down the tunnel. Been down there ever since." He sat down alongside Shakleford, dangling his gun between his legs.

What a bunch of idiots. No wonder Smedley had been getting away with this kind of stuff for so long.

Matthews came back from the crowd, saying, "How you doing?"

"Same old story," Paul said. "But I know who the bad guys are. Two kids from the projects. I know them from when I was a detective. Dittybop Caldwell and Shoestring Tolliver."

This, Smedley *didn't* like. The cops already knowing about Ditty and Shoestring. He should go. Yeah, find those two idiots and see if he could speed up getting the goods. No. He was here now. He'd play it out to the end.

Matthews pointed at Paul's gun belt. "Where's your service revolver?"

Paul flashed at his empty holster. "Jesus, I don't know."

Millie, leaning against a patrol car, arms crossed over her apron, said, "You guys are too much. The robbers took it with them. Where else you think it went?"

"Oh, Christ." Paul slumped against the patrol car.

"Yeah. What'd you think they were using when they were taking potshots at Tommy."

15

Paul said, "Only place they can go is the projects and I'm the only one who knows them on sight." He went face to face with Matthews. "How about giving me a car so I can try heading them off?"

"Hold on a minute. You run over there the way you are now, hell, who knows what'll happen?"

"Boss. They got my gun, for God's sake. And once they get in the projects, it'll be like pulling teeth trying to get them out."

Matthews rubbed his jaw. "I know how you feel, but…"

A detective car came screaming around the corner. Sirens blaring, lights flashing, it screeched to a halt in the middle of the intersection. Some fat ass lumbered out of the driver's seat, announcing, "Detective Kyle Debolt, Homicide. I'll take over from here." All the while straightening his tie in the reflection of the nearest patrol car window.

"Oh, man," Paul said, looking disgusted.

And Smedley congratulated himself for staying.

Paul pushed wiry blond hair out of his eyes. "Debolt, you dumbass. We all know who the hell you are. I rode with you for three damned years, didn't I?"

Looking wounded, Debolt moved up close on Paul. "I know *you* know me. Only it's standard operating procedure. The detective in charge's gotta report to the ranking supervisor so he can get a preliminary report on the crime scene." He made a quick look about, lingering on the body laying in the gutter. "Got any leads?"

"No, nothing just yet," Paul said, his eyes straying to Matthews.

Who said, "Guess you got a mystery on your hands, Kyle."

Some dope, this Debolt. Hadn't even caught on he was being snookered. Just nodded confidently, and said, "No problem. I'll get to the bottom of this in no time."

"Yeah, sure," Smedley heard Paul whisper to Matthews.

"You ain't kidding," Matthews answered, and heading away, said to Debolt, "I gotta go see if I can't clean up this traffic. You and Paul can sort out the murder-robbery stuff."

"Count on it," Debolt said, and turned to Millie. "Homicide Detective Kyle Debolt, ma'am. Uh, did you see which way the perps went?"

She laughed out loud. "Where'd you get this guy, Pauly?"

Paul looked down at his toes as if he was trying to hold back from laughing. Smedley, too. These cops. How they caught anybody was beyond me.

Then one of the traffic cops came up with a lady who appeared to be in her mid-thirties. With short cropped red hair and olive skin, she looked Latin to Smedley. With gold bracelets on both wrists and a diamond necklace over a silk blouse, she also looked like she had a few bucks.

"Sarge," the cops said, "this is Mrs Andujar. She and her husband just flew in on a private jet. He had some business so she went did some shopping. They were supposed to meet on Michigan Avenue this afternoon." The cop flicked at the body in the gutter. "She showed me a picture."

"I'll take care of this," Debolt said, and pushed in front of Paul. "Ma'am, I'm Homicide Detective Kyle Debolt, in charge here." He pointed at the body. "I'd like you to take a look at…"

She covered her face with her hands, her entire body convulsing. Paul embraced her in his arms, saying nothing, just hugging her, and giving Debolt the evil eye.

Debolt, fiddling with his tie again. "I promise you, Mrs— uh. I promise whoever did this will be brought to justice. I'll make the collar myself."

She stepped away, and with tears streaming looked up at Paul. "Who?" she said.

Paul started to answer when Debolt broke in. "Mrs Andujar. What you mean, 'Who?'"

"I talkink to him," she said, and pointed at Paul. "Who for to keel me Eduardo, Meester Sargente?"

Smedley was impressed. Firstly with the way this lady conducted herself under the worst of circumstances. Secondly with how she had quickly perceived Debolt to be a numbskull.

And Numbskull said, "We're sorry for your loss, Mrs Andujar."

"No for to be sorry," she said flatly, still with eyes only for Paul. "You juz tell me who the keeler ez. I finish wit him."

Debolt, back in between Mrs Andujar and Paul. "But we don't know…"

17

She pushed him aside, and stared at Paul. "But you will gonna know. Right, Meester Sargente?"

Paul said, "Yes, sooner or later."

She shifted from Paul to Debolt, and back to Paul. "And when you do, you," touching a finger to Paul's chest, "not him, call me Uncle Benito."

"Uncle Benito?"

"Si, Benito Cisneros, Vice Presidente de Colombia. From him, I will know." Not waiting for Paul's reply, she stepped into a waiting taxi.

Debolt, scratching his head with his clipboard. "Man, this thing could get messy. You know, with a big shot politician involved and all. I better go report in to my boss." He dragged his fat self into his car, and drove off with its siren blaring.

Lieutenant Matthews returned, saying to Paul, "How'd you put up with three years of that guy?"

Paul shrugged. "You gonna give me a chance to run Ditty and Shoestring down?"

Matthews' cigar flopped about in his mouth, and he said, "You ain't even got a gun. No, uh-uh."

Paul pulled a snubnose from his rear pocket. "Still got my Detective Special."

Matthews, nodding. "Okay, already. Take my car. But you see those two wrongdoers, don't go chasing after them without back up." He looked around. "Listen, I need every man I got to clean up this mess so take the kid with you. You know, just in case."

Covello's head popped up. "Me? No, not me."

Paul released an exasperated, "Humph." He grabbed Covello, and shoved him into Matthews' car. "See you back at the office, boss," and off they went.

Time for Smedley to fade out. He started away, then heard, "Hey, doc!" And stopped cold. "Uh, thanks for stepping up, only we need your name. You know, for the report."

And Smedley had been worrying. "Any time, Lieutenant. It's Dr Butler."

What a day! Couldn't have been better!

Chapter 3

"I DON'T KNOW WHY I gotta go chasing after these guys," Tommy said for the third time. "I mean, I work the beach, Sarge."

"You work nowhere, far as I can see."

"But..."

"Just keep your damned mouth shut!"

Tommy slumped down in his seat.

"Good, and while you're at it keep your eyes open for the bad guys." Paul went back to the surveillance. He figured he had a good spot to hide the lieutenant's patrol car. In an alley, between a Mission Baptist Church and an abandoned pool hall.

He scanned over the Cabrini Green Housing Project, specifically the 1160 Sedgwick building, where Ditty and Shoestring operated out of. The outside the building looked innocent enough; fifteen-sixteen stories, red-brick walls, with white trim. The windows were the give away. Some bare, others with rags for curtains. And the parking lot at the base of the building, about half full. Only two or three of the vehicles there looked to be in running condition. The rest were better suited for a junkyard; doors missing, hoods and trunk lids ajar, windows busted out.

But no white Cadillac, which was a good sign.

A good sign, that's what Paul needed with Debolt working the case. That class A fool, with his perps this, collar that. Got that phony stuff from watching all those cop shows on TV. And another thing. The robbery. Had to be a planned kinda thing. Which didn't make sense, Ditty and Shoestring involved. Them plan a diamond robbery. Never happen. Someone else had to be involved. Who? That he'd find out when he got his hands on Ditty and Shoestring.

Which might not be today, because they'd probably made it inside before he could get there, Cadillac or no Cadillac. Damn that Debolt, taking all that time playing the big time homicide dick.

He'd give it another ten minutes, and let his eyes wander to a group of children playing in front of the Mission Baptist church. The front door swung open, and out walked a white woman. Surprised Paul, seeing anybody white in this neighborhood who wasn't a cop, and he looked closer. She was tiny, not much taller than some of the kids. Maybe a couple years younger than he was. And had the shiniest black hair, which was combed straight back over her shoulders. Had on an ankle length, flowery print dress. A looker, this one, which made Paul nervous. Never had been entirely at ease around girls he'd found attractive.

The kids ran up to her, and one at a time she gave them a big hug. Then she looked toward the patrol car, and in a snap made a face which Paul was used to seeing in horror movies. Now she was marching directly at him, like some kinda storm trooper.

Tommy said, "Where'd Katie come from?"

"You know her?" Paul said, and offered his hand out the window. "Uh, I'm Sergeant Kostovic." Still wondering why she was so upset.

Ignoring him, she said, "Well, if it isn't Officer Covello."

"Hi, honey," Tommy said. "Long time no see."

Katie spat right back, "You just love calling me honey, don't you? Well I'm not your honey, honey."

Tommy, almost singing. "Honey, you miss me and you know it. So how come I never see you at the beach anymore?"

"Because of you, Covello. Hitting on me day after day."

"Yeah, sure. Was you hitting on me, and you know it. Honey."

She looked like she was about to attack, the way her eyes were raging, and Paul said, "Can you two settle this some other time? I mean, we got police work to get done here."

She showed Paul a sneer. Pulling attitude on Tommy was one thing, but no way was she going to play that game with Paul. "Go on, beat it," he said. "You've made a big enough fool outta yourself today."

And Tommy, "Give it to her, Sarge."

As soon as Tommy spoke, Paul wished he hadn't opened his big mouth.

Especially when Katie said, "Looky here, the big dumb

looking one can talk too. What are you doing anyway, picking on some innocent project kid?" Like that, smartalecky.

This just wasn't worth it. Paul turned back to the street—Jesus, about a block down, Ditty and Shoestring! He grabbed the radio's microphone. "This is Sixty-six-seventy, Squad. I've got the suspects from today's robbery in view at the Eleven-sixty Sedgwick building in the Cabrini. Send me back up."

Paul looked back out the windshield but Katie was in front of the car, blocking his view. Katie waving, and yelling, "Run, boys, run!"

Paul hollered, "What'sa matter with you? We're trying to make an arrest here!"

Which was a huge mistake, because now she was back in his face, hollering, "Those boys haven't done a thing. I'm a witness. So you better leave them alone."

All while Ditty and Shoestring were making good another escape. No other choice, Paul gunned across the street into Eleven-sixty's parking lot. Ditty was just disappearing into the entranceway with Shoestring right on his tail. Paul couldn't let them get away, and bumped the patrol car over the curb, sliding to a stop on the mostly dirt frontage.

Tommy, bracing himself against the windshield. "Whatta you, trying to get me killed, or what?"

Paul, out of the car and racing toward the entranceway. "Come on, they're getting away."

"Like I give a shit," Tommy yelled, and remained in the car.

No time to argue. Paul climbed the front steps, passing a crowd of defiant looking gangbangers. To hell with them. Without breaking stride, he found the stairs and sprinted up to the second floor landing. Vacant, less one old man lying in a corner sound asleep, an empty wine bottle gripped in a limp hand.

Paul realized just how futile this was; Ditty and Shoes could have entered any one of the many apartments or continued up the staircase. A dozen men would be needed to conduct a thorough search, and they still probably wouldn't be able to find them.

A crash came from down below, echoing up the staircase. Sounded like glass breaking. Uh-oh, the gangbangers. And

Tommy alone in the patrol car. Paul rushed back down the stairs, finding the gangbangers throwing bricks at the patrol car, Tommy all hunched down inside.

Paul tackled the nearest kid, bringing him to the cement floor. Holding him there, Paul looked up at the others, who were staring back at him as if trying to decide if they should help their buddy or run for it. Sirens whined from off in the distance. First one gangbanger ran, then another, like frightened birds from a telephone pole.

A line of patrol cars came around the corner, some chasing after the gangbangers, others stopping and emptying into the parking lot. Lieutenant Matthews jumped out of the lead car and came running into the entranceway. "Didn't I tell you not to do anything by yourself?" he said, trying to catch his breath.

"No choice. At least I got one of the gangbangers." Paul raised the kid up, and shoved him toward the patrol car.

"No, uh-uh," the kid protested, and scurried back under the entranceway.

Paul started to give the kid another shove. Matthews held him back, saying, "You've been working Homicide so long, you forgot what it is to be a real cop." He peeked up the outside wall of the building. Then snapped his head back. A flowerpot passed where his head had been. Clay and dirt splashed in every direction. Next came a rain of books, old shoes, dishes, bottles. An old television set crunched into the cement.

Matthews chomped on his cigar. "I guess maybe now you get it, huh?" And not waiting for an answer, grabbed the gangbanger. "You got two choices, kid. Make a run for it, or end up at the home away from home."

"Hey, I just arrested that kid." Paul said.

Matthews waved Paul off, saying to the kid, "Make up your mind." He pulled out his handcuffs, ratcheting them in the kid's face.

The kid leaned out of the entranceway, yelling, "I'm coming out, I'm coming out!" And raced across the parking lot, heading for the nearest alley.

"Now's our chance," Matthews said. He shoved Paul into the parking lot, and ran after him, jumping in alongside Paul as he got the car started.

Crouched down in the back seat, Tommy yelled, "Get me outta here, and now."

The downpour returned, and Paul gaped as a black sphere came arching down from one of the top floors. Looked like it was coming straight at his head, and just as it was about to land, he backed the patrol car off. The sphere crashed into the hood, rocking the patrol car to the front and then rolling it to the rear like a boat hit by a tidal wave. Only when they got to the street did Paul see the sphere was a bowling ball, and that it was now embedded into the car's hood.

Once safely away from the projects he pulled over, and turning to Tommy, said, "You okay?"

"Man, we're lucky we ain't all dead."

Matthews, with a half grin. "Hate to say it, but the kid's right."

"I didn't have any choice," Paul said. "When Ditty and Shoes showed up, some dogooder broad yelled at them to run. I hadda go after them."

"Choice?" Tommy said. "Yeah, right. We never shoulda come over here, that's the choice."

Paul gave Tommy his best mean stare.

And Matthews gave Paul a violent shove on the shoulder. "Goddammit. You're one big pain in the ass, you are." He got out of the car, going to the front end. He yanked the bowling ball from the hood, and threw it down on the pavement. Getting back in, he said, "Those gangbangers, you gotta admit they did a hell of a job." As if they had been a crew of carpenters who had just painted his house.

Two fists began rapping on the glass next to Paul's head. Thinking the gangbangers were back, he brought his arms up to guard against the broken glass that was sure to be flying into his face.

The window held, apparently not happily for the owner of the fists. "Let me in there!" came a screech.

Paul ventured a look around his elbow. It was the girl from the Mission Baptist Church, and her teeth were bared like an alley cat. "Come out here, you coward you!" she screamed.

"Ignore her," Matthews said. "Come on, let's just beat it."

Paul wasn't going to argue with his lieutenant, but it wasn't easy. And he couldn't very well drive off, not with her hanging on the car. Good Lord, she was trying to break down his door. And now she had her nose against the window, yelling, "You coming, or do I have to drag you out of there?"

"Don't do it," Tommy said. "Believe me, don't do it."

Both of them, Matthews and Tommy, acted as if they didn't care what this goofy girl did. Well, Paul cared. He'd witnessed a brutal robbery, his gun had been taken, he'd been attacked with a damned bowling ball, and now some crazy know-it-all was accusing him of being a child beater and an animal. The real animals were back at the Cabrini Green, didn't she know that?

He shoved the door open, intending to jump out and set this obnoxious broad straight once and for all. The door hit Katie squarely in the forehead, knocking her flat on her back.

"Oh, Christ," Paul said, forgetting his mission. Not knowing what to do next, he tried to help her up.

She slapped his arms away, and rubbed at a welt which was beginning to form above her right eye. "Don't you dare touch me," she hollered. She scratched her way to her feet, and before Paul could react, snatched the name tag from his uniform shirt. "There, now I've got your name whether you like it or not. Wait and see. I'll have you charged with assault. Causing a riot, too." The hell with this. Paul ripped the name plate from her hand. "You won't be needing this," he hollered, "because I'll tell you my name. It's Paul Kostovic." He spelled it out. "I work at Area Six Task Force." He got back in the patrol car and slammed the door on her screams.

As he pulled away, Matthews said, "Nice job. So when's the wedding?"

Paul, peering out the rearview mirror. "What a nutcase. Imagine living with that every day for the rest of your life."

Chapter 4

THERE SHAKLEFORD WAS, on the payphone, cleaned up and in a new suit. Looked pretty good for a man who'd just been beaten and robbed. And Smedley had been ready to feel sorry for the poor slob. Almost. He removed the phone in the adjacent booth from its hook and listened.

Shakleford saying, "Hey, babe. Thought you'd never answer—I'm at the airport. My plane takes off within the hour. I'll be there, say about midnight. You can't believe what happened. I was robbed—yeah, of my diamonds. No, no. Not to worry." He giggled like all little fat guys do. "I already called the insurance company. They say I'm fully covered." Making a quick check over his shoulder. "It's gonna come out extra good. I told the insurance company the loss was twice what really was taken. You're going to get a nice homecoming present out of this, babe—okay, see you soon."

Smedley was about to give Shakleford a tap on the shoulder when, oops, there he was dialing again.

"Hi, Essie," he said. "Got bad news. I was robbed this afternoon—No, I'm okay, but it's the cops. They want me to stay over a couple of days—Why? Hey, I don't know. To help them, you know, in case they run across my diamonds—yeah, sure, I'll take care of myself. So how's the girls doing in school?—Good, good. What hotel? Uh, don't know just yet. The cops, they're putting me up. Tell you what, when I'm settled I'll give you a call—yeah, say tomorrow night. That okay?—Okay. Love and kisses. Bye."

Smedley couldn't hold back any longer, and whispered into Shakleford's ear. "You're a naughty boy, Henry."

Who spun around, looking startled.

Exactly how Smedley wanted him. "That's your name, ain't it? Of course it is. I guess I oughta know after all the work I put in on you."

Henry's face brightened. "Now I remember. The doctor from today, right? Hey, I never got a chance to say thanks."

Smedley gave him a smile, the scary one, and said, "Yeah,

25

the doctor. Only I ain't no doctor. I'm your worst dream come true, is what I am."

"Uh, if this is supposed to be a joke…"

"Oh, no joke. Deadly serious." Showing another smile. This time the witty one. Oh, man, *loving* it.

Henry took a step back, looking like he was ready to run. "I got a plane to catch, so…"

Smedley pushed Henry down in the nearest chair, slipping in alongside. "Sloppy, talking right out in public. You know, on the phone to your sweet piece. What's her name? I wrote it down somewhere. Her phone number, too. Yeah, couldn't help but hear. But don't you worry none. I wouldn't tell a soul. That babe, though. With her, I wouldn't be so generous with information."

Little beads of perpetration popped out of Henry's forehead, and he gulped like a bullfrog in heat.

Smedley knew he had his mark and grabbed Henry's hand, saying, "You can call me Smedley. I suppose you got lots'a questions. I know I would. Go ahead, shoot. I'm all ears." Smedley looked at Henry's swollen ear. "Oh, and sorry about that. I don't condone violence, you know."

Henry looked like he was having a hard time believing what was happening, and looked around. People were walking past, minding their own business, not giving Smedley and Henry so much as a sideways glance.

Smedley gave Henry an even brighter smile. "To the cops, you said your loss was a quarter mil. The take was only about, oh—" He leered into Henry's eyes. "—little more than a hundred thou. That right, Henry?"

"I'm calling the cops," Henry said, but not very convincingly.

Smedley laughed out loud. "Come on, Henry," he said. "We both know that ain't gonna happen."

"Oh, no? Why not? I…" Henry's voice cracked, and he was left with his mouth hanging open.

Smedley said, "Shame on you. That's a bad thing, trying to defraud an insurance company. Kinda like stealing, I'd say."

"I didn't…"

The dope couldn't finish a simple sentence without making a

complete fool out of himself. Smedley said, "That's all right. You're nervous. I can understand that. It ain't like you're a pro or anything. Which makes me wonder. You got yourself a nice family waiting back in the Big Apple. Not to mention the babe. A walk on the wild side, huh? Anyway, so you got a nice life going and what do you do? Go out and pad the loss on the robbery. Money, Henry, it's only money. Are you crazy? You could lose everything, maybe even go to the shithouse for awhile."

Looked like old Henry was about to cry. Stifling a laugh, Smedley said, "Yeah, jail. Only maybe there's a way you can avoid all that. Sure, you listen to me, 'cause could be I got an idea that'll save your skin. You'll see, I'm good with ideas."

A flicker of hope came to Henry's eyes as if he were a child waiting for his mommy to take him into her arms, tell him everything was going to be all right.

Smedley put a friendly hand on Henry's shoulder. "You want me to tell you my idea, don't you?"

Henry produced a glazed look.

Which was just fine, and Smedley said, "Good, 'cause you're gonna like this. Here's how it'll work. About your goods. No problem, I'm willing to give them up. All I need is fifty grand. Sound fair? You get your diamonds, and for half what they're worth. And once I get my bread I'm in the wind. You can go back to New York, start back up where you left off, nobody the wiser."

A flicker of confidence shown on Henry's face, and he said, "I'll give you twenty-five. That's a good offer. You'll never get a better one. Not anywhere."

Smedley was caught off guard for a second, Henry trying to dicker with him. He said, "What you think this is, a used car lot? Fifty, that's the price. Take it or leave it."

"Thirty," Henry said, "and I'll throw in any single diamond you want as my own personal present."

Smedley rubbed his chin, amused by Henry's offer. "Man, you're gonna get almost a quarter-mil outta the insurance company. From me, you get your diamonds, and all it's gonna cost you is a measly fifty donuts. Figure it out. Even with my tariff you still just about triple what you started with. Nah, I need my fifty."

"Forty," Henry said, gulping.

Smedley shook his head out of appreciation for Henry's tenacity under pressure. "Okay," he said. "I like your style so I'll come down a bit. Forty-five, but that's the end of the line. So don't go pissing me off with another one of your low-ball bids."

Forty-two appeared on Henry's lips, but never materialized. Smedley knew why, because he'd just shown Henry his best intimidating smile.

Henry said, "Okay, you got a deal. Forty-five it is, but I want you to know you're cheating the blood right out of my heart."

"Please, Henry. We both know better than that, don't we?"

Henry smiled for the first time since Smedley had tapped him on the shoulder. "You're good," he said. "You'd make a killing hawking diamonds instead of stealing them. So how we going to do this? I mean, I don't carry that kind of cash on me?"

"Glad you asked," Smedley pulled a plain white envelope out of his shirt pocket. From it he produced a hand-sized booklet and handed it to Henry. The cover read,

FIRST BANK OF CHICAGO

"Take a look inside," he said.

Henry opened the booklet. "So you've got five hundred. What's that got to do with me?"

"Look at the names on the account."

Henry paged back to the front of the booklet. "In my name?" he said, looking up at Smedley.

"Yeah, and mine. See: S. Butler."

Henry studied the booklet. "Hey, this account was taken out two days ago. How'd you get my name?"

"I'm good, huh?"

Henry nodded, but looked like he needed an answer.

So Smedley said, "You and me, we're partners, have been from the first day I saw you at the diamond sales convention."

Henry held up the bank book. "So what's this got to do with anything? I mean, you still haven't told me how I get my diamonds and you get your money."

"Always the businessman, huh?" Smedley stepped over to the payphone. "That's easy. You call your bank in New York, have them wire the bread to our account here in Chicago. Soon as I know the money's there I'll hand over the diamonds. You'll be on your way back to New York three times richer. Me, I'll be in the woods, never to be seen again."

Henry took the phone, but instead of dialing stared at Smedley's smiling face. "One question before I call. What's to stop you from removing the cash and keeping the diamonds to boot?"

"That's a good one, Hen. I was wondering when you were gonna ask." Smedley pointed at bold printing on the bank book's inside cover. "Look at that."

Henry read out loud, "Account requires signatures of both joint holders for all transactions." He looked up. "Got it all figured, don't you?"

"To a tee. You and me, we'll do the final deal right there at the First National. No place safer. For you and for me."

Something deep inside Henry's eyes flashed a warning signal, so Smedley said, "I know what you're thinking. Once you get your diamonds, would it be possible for you to call the cops and turn me in? Don't even think it. I'm much too good for the cops. And remember, I know about the babe." Then word by word. "And your daughters, too. Both of them."

Henry's knees buckled. "No, no. That's not it at all. It's just that I was thinking maybe you'd like to hear an idea I just thought up."

"Yeah, sure." Smedley shook his head. "I'm the idea man around here. You just get that money transferred. I'll get the diamonds. We make the deal. Plain and simple."

Henry held up his hand like a traffic cop. "Doggone it. Listen for a second. I know this guy. He's a diamond salesman, just like me. Only he does twice, three times the business."

Smedley let his smile disappear for the briefest moment, saying, "Sounds interesting enough. So…"

Henry, the words pouring out. "This salesman, he comes to Chicago all the time. Has a big load with him, too. A good half million at least. Name's Randolph Laidlaw. If somebody was to rob old Randy, without hurting him of course. Well, a guy like me'd be more than happy to deal with whoever ended up with his goods."

Smedley glared through squinted eyes. "I'm tempted by your proposal," he said. "Only it'd mean changing plans in midstream. Very dangerous for a guy like me. Sorry, just not interested."

Henry started again, but Smedley held the phone to his face. Henry began dialing.

Meanwhile Smedley played with the Ka-bar knife secreted deep in his jacket pocket, and shot glances up and down the concourse. Looked good. Just had to wait until the cash was transferred, then—

And Henry said, "I don't get it. Just think about it. Your share would be a cool two-fifty."

Just like that a plan played through Smedley's head. Amazed him sometimes, how he got these great ideas, and he dropped his hand away from his jacket. "Know what? Up until now I've always kept to my agendas. But there's a soft spot in my heart for a man who can come up with a good idea. So if you can guarantee that quarter mil, I guess you got yourself a partner."

"Guaranteed for sure," Henry said. "We'll close both deals at the same time. As soon as you get Randy's diamonds, of course."

"Okay, so when can I expect your buddy in town?"

"Don't know exactly. Could be any time. One thing I do know, he'll be staying at the Drake. Always does. You give me a phone number, I'll call you from New York, let you know."

Another smile, just for accent. "That won't be necessary. I'll call you."

"Okay. You got my number?" Henry said.

Smedley looked at him.

Henry laughed. "That's right. Of course you do."

The airport intercom came on. "American Airlines Flight Six-two-zero, non-stop to La Guardia. Now boarding gate seven."

Smedley said, "That's your plane, Henry. Have a good trip." He spun away, and stepped into the crowd.

Chapter 5

COMING UP FOR AIR, Tommy said to the bartender, "I'm telling ya, wasn't for Matthews and the rest of those Task Force rangers, I'd be one dead cookie."

Paul, standing inside the doorway. "For you to get dead, those gangbangers would've had to blow up the lieutenant's patrol car, 'cause that's where you were hiding the whole time."

Tommy rolled bloodshot eyes in Paul's direction. Looking back at the bartender, he said, "Run, save yourself, Woody, 'cause wherever Sergeant Kostovic goes, goes disaster." He took another swig.

Paul rested himself against the bar. "Gimme one, Wood." And to Tommy, "I've spent the last four hours writing reports, and here I find you across the street, drinking yourself stupid. Stupider. About par for the course, when it comes to you."

"Wouldn't be no reports, you hadn't gone chasing into the Cabrini after those two."

Paul emitted a frustrated, "errrr." Taking up his beer, he said, "Happens I'm a cop. And that's what cops do, chase after murderers. You oughta try it out some time." He took a long pull, letting the coolness soothe his tired body.

"I do, it sure as hell won't be with you," Tommy said, giving Woody a wink.

Woody scratched his pointed nose. "Kid's been doing me like this the whole damned evening. Get him outta here before I go nuts."

Not part of Paul's plan. But why not? At least he'd have a witness. A drunken witness, but a witness just the same. "Okay, Wood. I just stopped in for one anyway. Come on, kid. Let's go."

"I can drive my own self," Tommy said, and focusing on Woody. "One for the road, huh?"

"You can hardly sit up straight, let alone drive," Paul said, and pushed Tommy toward the door. He hadn't thought Tommy would go so easily until the kid hugged the nearest tree, and retched into the gutter. "Having fun?" Paul said, and headed for his pickup.

31

Tommy wiped his face on his uniform shirt, and straggled after Paul, saying, "I hate being seen with the biggest screw up on the Chicago Police Department. But under the circumstances—well, maybe just this once."

"Back off with the lip, boy, unless you think you can walk all the way home."

Which seemed to do the trick, because Tommy settled into the passenger seat, quiet for a change.

Just as Paul inserted the ignition key, thunder clapped and a downpour pelted the windshield. Paul started for home, the rain reminding him of better days, and his pop. How on warm spring afternoons they'd sit on the back porch of the family farm, quietly watching a steady rain fill the neighboring corn fields. Pop would take a sip of his homemade wine, and invariably say in his native Croatian tongue, "Paval, back in the old country your granddaddy told me God had a job all lined up for him when he got up to heaven. He was gonna be the rainmaker. So remember when there's a good wetting, that's your Dede up in heaven doing for all the poor souls down here trying to make the corn grow."

Paul looked skyward, silently telling his Dede, you must've got hold of some of that Croatian vino, even up there in heaven. 'Cause ain't no farmers around here.

"Hey, watch it, will you?" Tommy shouted.

Paul popped out of his dreams to see he had wandered over the center line. Jerking the steering wheel, he got back in lane.

"Good God! A guy can't even ride home with you without taking his life in his hands." Tommy squinted. "Hey, how you even know where I live?"

"Ain't taking you home. Not just yet, anyhow."

"Huh?" Tommy searched out the windshield where the upper floors of the Cabrini Green Housing Project were emerging above the warehouses and factories. "Oh, shit. I shoulda known."

"Stay alert," Paul said. "I just might need your worthless ass."

"Bullshit! I seen you in action. You can screw up just fine all by your lonesome."

"Not to help." Paul had to laugh. "I know better than that. As a witness, so nobody can accuse me of brutality, stuff like that."

"Lemme outta this damned truck," Tommy said, watching out the window with anxious eyes.

"Just relax. I don't plan on doing anything stupid."

Tommy, showing more and more sobriety, "Excuse me, but coming from you that don't make me feel any better." He pulled out his service revolver, checked its action, then replaced it, leaving the safety strap off.

Paul moved along at a crawl, scanning the projects left and right, glancing at Tommy now and again, just to be safe. Tommy's eyes darted from one potential danger zone to the next, which there were many, and pushed down in his seat so that his head barely showed above the windows.

Paul stayed upright. He didn't know why, but he himself didn't have the slightest concern. If he got shot, so be it. At least he'd be out of his misery.

They passed a crowd of toughs, who gave them a collective hate-filled stare. "Look at me," Tommy said, spitting his words, "riding around with a raving maniac, and in the worst hell hole in all creation."

Paul kept his eyes on the projects. The rain was still coming down at a steady pace, but the crowd didn't seem to mind. For the most part they were teenage boys, some looked a bit older. A few girls stood off by themselves. What surprised Paul was the presence of so many children, some not more than eight or nine. What were little kids doing out in the middle of the night? Where were their mothers and fathers?

For all the times he had been down here as a detective, he'd never seen it like this, and then it came to him why. After a shooting, or any kind of job homicide got called in on, the place was always teaming with cops. Normal flow taking a sabbatical, until they were finished. Lieutenant Matthews had been right on when he said Paul had been a detective so long he'd forgotten what is was to be a real cop.

Tommy said, "Well, I guess that's that, huh?"

Which popped Paul out of his thoughts. "What you mean?" he said.

Tommy inched up in his seat, and put the safety strap on his service revolver. "We looked the place over. Found nothing. Case closed. Let's head for home."

Paul made a U-turn. "Let's give it some time. You never know, we might get lucky."

Tommy cursed under his breath. "No way you're gonna be satisfied 'til I'm dead and buried." He pushed back down in his seat, and regripped his gun.

Paul was rapidly learning the lay of the land, and noted that while gangbangers were scattered all over the complex, sooner or later they all seemed to end up by the 1160 building parking lot. Ditty and Shoestring's home base. He kept circling the complex, with the 1160 building his main objective, trying to get close enough to make out faces, yet far enough away not to draw too much attention.

But not successfully.

Over the next hour the rain began to subside. Now it was barely dripping, and the streets and walkways were rapidly drying. As they did, mist rose from the cooling pavement, lingering like tiny clouds. Condensation developed on the pickup's windows, and Paul had to roll down his side window in order to see. A pleasant breeze filtered into the compartment, gently blowing through his hair. He peeled his sweat-soaked shirt away from his chest, and flopped it against the cooling air. But he wasn't refreshed, and it hit him that he'd been up and on the go for almost twenty-four hours. He was completely spent and knew it.

Tommy said, "Come on, Sarge. Give it up. There's hardly anybody left out there."

Disappointed, Paul gave a nod of his head, and turned the pickup away. As he approached the first main intersection, the light flicked from green to yellow. Too exhausted to care, he put his foot to the floor.

A bus was just starting away from the curb when Paul hit the middle of the intersection. The bus driver slammed on his brakes, but Paul still had to swerve in order to avoid a collision. The bus driver gave Paul a long beep, and carried on.

Paul pulled over, and looked over his shoulder. "Did you see that guy back there?" he said, still craning his neck at the back window.

Sounding sober now, Tommy said, "Are you kidding? Now you wanna start a fight with a bus driver?"

"No, not him. The guy walking down the street." Paul got the pickup turned around, and drove back to the intersection. He pointed down the sidewalk on the other side of the street. "Look, there he goes right there."

"So what? Come on, take me home. I'm beat."

"Look again. See what I mean?" Paul studied on a lone figure, who passed under a streetlight, taking a long stride with one foot, buckled slightly, brought the other foot up, dipped, and started with the first foot again.

"See the way he's walking? That's Shoestring, one of the robbers from Michigan Avenue. God! I'd like to run over there right now and squeeze the life outta him."

Tommy leaned close to the windshield, for once showing some interest. "You can tell just by the way he walks?"

"Uh-huh. At first I thought it was Ditty Caldwell, but now that I got a better look… no, too short. It's Shoestring, all right. That's okay, though. Right now, I'll take either one of those two rats."

He spun the pickup around, drove up a half block, and pulled into an all night service station. "This time I do it by the book, so nobody can blame me if something goes wrong."

Tommy said, "What the hell you know about the book? Unless it's a comic book. Come on. If we gotta do it, let's just plain grab the guy."

Paul was not going to let himself be deterred. He dug into his pocket and came up with a handful of coins. "Here, go inside and call for help. Tell them to have a uniform car meet us here. Once we've got reinforcements, we can swoop down from both sides. Won't be any escape this time."

"I got my own damn quarter," Tommy said, and flung open his door, again cursing under his breath as he walked into the service station.

Paul didn't give a damn. He was totally consumed with keeping up his surveillance. Oh, man, now what? A BMW pulling over to the curb in front of Shoestring. Shoes rubbernecked up and down the street, and jumped into its passenger's side. Shoestring, in a BMW? Didn't make sense.

This had to be something important. Thank God Paul had had the good sense to wait. But what if they left? Paul would have to chase them down, reinforcements be damned.

Then the BMW's headlights went out. Paul was in luck because it looked like they were gonna be there for a while. Maybe he should get closer, enough to see the BMW's license number. No, he was in a perfect position right where he was.

Tommy got back into the car. "What happened? I don't see our guy."

"He's there all right. See the BMW. He's in it. Did you get hold of communications?"

"Yeah, help's on the way," Tommy said, squinting at the BMW. "That car. You ever seen it before?"

"No, why? What about it?"

"Now I remember. It looks like the same BMW that, for the past week or so, has been parked next to the Drake Hotel, right on the other side of the fence from the beach. All the girls been ogling it, telling me if I had a BMW convertible, they'd stay with me forever."

Tommy flinched.

"What's the matter now?" Paul said, thinking maybe Tommy wasn't quite as sober as he had thought.

Tommy, with his eyes glued to the BMW. "You didn't see that?"

Paul snapped around. Nothing different that he could see. "See what?" he said.

Tommy blinked his eyes shut, then open again. "I swear I saw a couple'a flashes."

Paul tried to figure what this could mean. Probably nothing, considering Tommy's half-drunken state. Then the BMW's headlights came on, and it turned the corner, leaving Paul with more pressing problems. He started after the BMW, but a paddy wagon pulled up, blocking his exit. At least he had help, and he leaned out his window, intending to explain what was going on.

Oh, Christ, who does he get for help but Joe Holloway and Volly Dickman? Two of the biggest sluffoffs on the job. But he couldn't worry about that now, and yelled, "Follow us, guys. We got a murderer under surveillance."

He pulled onto the street, briefly genuflecting at the red light, then blew through the intersection. Shifting into high gear, he raced to the corner where the BMW had disappeared. Now back to low. The pickup lurched forward, Paul getting as much as he could out of its old straight-six engine. He swung hard left, his rear tires squealing as he aimed for the near curb. The pickup slid sideways, and when they were pointed straight up the street, popped the gear shift back into high.

Only where was the BMW? They were only seconds behind it, and racing while it had been traveling at normal speed. Paul screeched to a halt at the next cross street, flicking right and left. Okay, there it was, a block down and heading away. He wrenched the gear shift into low and slammed the accelerator to the floor. He was just about to shift into high again, when his headlights illuminated a body lying in the middle of the street.

He jerked the steering wheel hard left, sending the pickup sideways on the wet pavement. Its front tires skimmed safely past, and for a fleeting moment Paul thought the rear tires would miss too. But then he heard a "ka-thump, ka-thump," and knew all was lost.

They spun to a stop not twenty-five feet down the street. Paul looked back, gaping as the paddy wagon came cruising around the corner, and bumped over what was left of the body.

"Damn-damn-damn!" he said, and ran to the body, turning it over, hoping to see some sign of life. The face was gone, no eyes, no nose, not a mouth or anything else of distinction, except blurry tire tracks, which ran from ear to ear.

Tommy came strolling up. Leaning over the body, he said, "Hey, you black-assed piece'a shit. I guess that'll teach you to fool with the C-P-D."

Paul looked up to see Joe Holloway out of the paddy wagon, moving up on Tommy. His whiskey voice bellowing, "Ordinarily I wouldn't get ruffled over minor agitations such as rookie coppers with big mouths." He pointed at a black cop standing by the paddy wagon. "But seeing as Volly is my partner I gotta make an exception." With this he swung a fierce forearm, sending Tommy straight down on his back.

Joe stood over Tommy, showing a smug grin on his craggy complexion. "So how's about your ass, kid? Feeling kinda black-and blue-right about now, ain't it?"

Paul pushed Joe aside. "What'sa matter with you? I know the kid's got a stupid mouth, but we're all on the same side, ain't we?"

Joe retreated to the paddy wagon, and lifted himself onto the hood. Sitting so that he was looking back at Paul, he said matter-of-factly, "You talking to me, right?"

"Yeah, I'm talking to you," Paul said, angry enough he'd like a piece of Joe himself. "Who else would I be talking to?"

Joe gave his partner a proud smile and turned back to Paul. "First you call for help. Then you make it so's we run over some poor slob so's nothing's left but a pile'a mush. After all that, your buddy starts in with his black-ass shit. So's I give him what for. And then you come round, telling me I'm on your side." He snickered. "I don't think so."

"You and Volly ain't no prize," Paul said. "Ain't never done one lick'a work. And look at you, Joe, with your shirt out, trousers all wrinkled. Don't take much to tell you two been parked up some dark alley, crapped out like always."

"That's okay, Sarge," Tommy said. He pushed himself up on one arm, focusing in on Volly.

Jesus, this kid was more than Paul could take. He switched to Volly, to get his reaction. Volly's checkerboard police hat was pushed back on his head, long gangling arms folded over a barrel chest. Body language saying, bring it on, kid.

Uh-oh. On top of everything else Paul was going to have a race riot on his hands. He put a hand on Tommy's chest. "Stay there, I'll handle this."

Tommy looked up at Paul with a benign half grin. "Relax. I know I done wrong." He got up, and offered his hand to Volly. "Sorry about that," he said. "I was talking about that black-ass piece'a shit what got squooshed. Not your black-ass, you no-good nigger, you."

As Tommy said, 'nigger,' he lashed out with his free hand.

He would have scored a direct hit on the side of Volly's head had it not been for Joe throwing himself in between. Joe got the brunt of the punishment, and all three cops crashed to the street, arms flailing, legs kicking, mouths cursing.

Paul tried to pry them loose, but all he got for his efforts was a kick to the groin, which could have been delivered from any one of them. His knees buckled, and he sank to the ground, all the while picturing Lieutenant Matthews shaking a sad face at him.

Chapter 6

SMEDLEY PARKED THE BMW behind a vacant warehouse, and approached the Cabrini Green Housing project on foot. He crouched in the shadows of an alley, knowing attack was always best in early morning hours. Not missing the slightest detail, he scanned the sixth floor windows of the 1160 Sedgwick building. He'd done this kind of thing dozens of times before, and knew exactly what it took. Patience was the secret, and durability. He'd learned that lesson in the Marines, in the jungles of South East Asia, where success or failure was the difference between life and death.

The Marines stayed put for however long it took to develop the intelligence required to carry out their mission. Then, and only then, did they attack, without mercy. There would be no mercy on this night, either.

As the rain began again, there in a sixth floor window, his target finally showed himself. Smedley's perseverance had paid off. Still he didn't move, not for another twenty minutes, until he was sure the Cabrini Green grounds were totally unoccupied. Then, dressed totally in black, with grease to camouflage his face and hands, he slipped out of the alley and across the grounds like a cat after its prey, passing through the parking lot and into Ditty's building completely unnoticed. Forgoing the elevator, too much noise, Smedley found the stairs, and taking two with each stride, made a rapid climb to the sixth floor.

No panting either. In perfect shape. Wouldn't have it any other way.

He pressed his ear to Ditty's apartment door, listening for any telltale sound that might indicate the presence of danger. Which paid off. Once, then again, and then a third time, a pleasurable snore was heard from within. Wasn't something that could have been fabricated, not three times, not by an untrained street kid.

Smedley was ready, yet remained in place for another full ten minutes, taking time to rethink the design of the rooms he would have to secure before making his final assault.

Okay, now.

The door was no obstacle, its lock hanging loose. He eased it away from the jamb; an inch, then another. Then it stopped. He tried forcing it, but to no avail. He ran his hand along the opening, expecting to find a chain lock. No. He reached inside, feeling, search, and—Ha! A chair. A simple wooden chair, jammed against the inside doorknob. Taking care, he shoved the blade of his Ka-bar knife through the opening, and applied pressure on the chair. Not much. Just enough. The chair began to shift, and fraction by fraction, he opened the door until he finally had a view of the interior. He ran his eyes across the bare floor. There by the window was his objective, back to the door, asleep and completely defenseless.

His heart pounded as he slid through the doorway. One last cursory check of his surroundings. Yes, they were alone. Two quick steps, a skip, and he dropped on Ditty's back, straddling him with his legs, simultaneously clamping one hand around his neck, eliminating any possibility of a cry for help.

He made a satisfied hiss, and said, "I told you don't try hiding on me, boy. Didn't I say whatever you did, wherever you went, wouldn't make no difference?"

No answer. Only whimpering.

He yanked Ditty around so that he was lying face up, then readjusted himself on his chest, at the same time clamped Ditty's arms to the floor with his knees. He held his Ka-bar so that the tip hovered over Ditty's nose.

Two beady eyes mesmerized by the Ka-bar. If they could speak, they'd be pleading. Smedley bent forward so that he and Ditty were face to face, and whispered, "Terrifying, ain't I?" Loving the moment.

Ditty's lips moved, producing a broken gurgle.

Smedley said, "I know, you can't believe I ain't stuck you. You're right, too. I oughta. But we still can do good things together, you and me. Only it takes trust. Cooperation. Teamwork. So are we partners, or what?"

Ditty finally croaked, "Partners."

Smedley sat back on his heels, but kept the Ka-bar in place. He reached into his pants pocket, and pulled out a handful of Henry's diamonds. Holding them over Ditty's head, he said,

"I got your end right here."

As Smedley spoke, he let one diamond go at a time so they sprinkled down on Ditty's face. Was another of his spur of the moment ideas. A bit more agony would do the boy good. Didn't want to be too generous, though. When the tenth diamond hit its target, he said, "All you had to do was follow orders. But no, you sent your pal, and with the cop's gun in his pocket. That was wrong, Ditty my boy. Shoestring'd be alive right now if you'd only listened."

Ditty gulped. "You kilt him?"

Smedley nodded, smiling.

"Aw, man. You didn't have to go and do that. I mean, he brought the goods, didn't he? And you seen what happened during the heist, that cop jumping us and all."

Smedley could feel Ditty's body trembling between his legs, and kept up the pressure. "Yeah, I saw. I was there, remember? What's that got to do with Shoestring bringing the diamonds instead of you?"

Tears appeared in the corners of Ditty's eyes. "The cops made us, man. I know, 'cause later on when we got back to the Cabrini, they were waiting. After that, no way was I gonna show my face on the street. The cops don't know Shoestring hardly like they do me, so I sent him in my place. Why'd you go and kill him?"

Smedley swiveled his head back and forth, making it deliberate for Ditty's benefit. "Sorry, but I don't buy it. You disappointed me, showed me no respect. So when Shoestring got into the car, I showed him some respect of my own, with my Ka-bar. The fool went for the gun, as if I didn't know he had it. You should've seen me. I was magnificent. One quick flick of the wrist, a little pressure at the right place, and bingo, I had him pointing the barrel right back between his eyes. If you only could've seen the look on his face. It was awesome."

Ditty stared at Smedley with hate-filled eyes.

Smedley smiled. "You don't like my story, huh? Try this on for size. While I had that gun twisted at Shoestring's head, I figured what better time to have some quality time together? I told him I'd let him live. All he had to do was tell me where you were hiding. Hell, he couldn't get it out fast enough."

"But you shot him anyway."

"Yeah, well we both did. Easy, when you know how. I made him shoot himself, by putting my finger over his and giving it a squeeze. I almost creamed my trousers, it was so much fun."

Ditty's face raged, and he said, "But me, if I throw in with you, I ain't gonna get killed, that it?" Saying it like he had a choice.

Smedley liked this kid's guts, but he had control now and couldn't let it slip away. He made his voice sound as if he were talking about the weather instead of murder. "You keep missing the basic point, Ditty boy. You damn well better throw in with me or that's exactly what's gonna happen."

Ditty peeked around the tip of the Ka-bar, saying, "Guess I ain't got much choice, do I?" More smartaleckly all the time.

Smedley laughed, and said, "Feeling ballsy all of a sudden huh, kid?"

Ditty sneered like Clark Gable in *Mutiny on the Bounty*.

That was it. Smedley had to teach the kid a lesson he'd not soon forget, and tapped the Ka-bar on Ditty's nose. "Never, but never, show yourself like that, boy. 'Specially when a man like me is sitting on your chest with a Ka-bar in his hand." He lifted his right knee, releasing Ditty's arm. "Give me your hand."

Ditty balked.

"I'm tellin' you," Smedley said, "put it out, and now if you know what's good for you."

Hesitating, Ditty finally stuck his hand in the air, and as he did Smedley took a swipe with his Ka-bar. Blood spurted from the tip of Ditty's baby finger.

"Oh, God!" Ditty wailed. "You didn't have to go and cut me."

Smedley snipped off a portion of his shoestring, and with quick, self assured moves, applied a tourniquet on what was left of Ditty's finger. Getting to his feet, he said, "That was nothing compared to what'll happen if you try crossing me again."

Ditty was curled up in a ball at Smedley's feet, staring wide-eyed at his hand. Whimpering, he said, "Just tell me what you want and you'll get it."

Smedley wiped the Ka-bar across the front of his shirt, and replaced it in its scabbard. "That's better," he said. "Here's how it's gonna go. I don't want you to move outta this apartment, not once, until I give the order. Be looking for me after dark. Let's make it eleven… eleven sharp, you hear? I'll be in a limo, parked across from your window. Gonna be there for five minutes and five minutes only. After that, I'm gonna pull into the alley, outta sight. That's where I want you to meet me. Remember, it might be two days, it might be a week, but I'll be there."

Smedley heaved Ditty up, and lowering his voice to an evil growl, said, "Don't make me come after you, 'cause there ain't nowhere to hide, not from me." Staring into Ditty's eyes. "But you already know that, don't you?"

Before Ditty could answer, if he was still capable, Smedley shoved him into a corner, saying, "Oh, and just to show you I'm righteous, that was about a good two-three thousand dollars worth of diamonds I sprinkled on you before. Maybe it ain't the twenty thousand we agreed on, but I figure you forfeited that when you tried crossing me."

And slipped out the door.

Chapter 7

PAUL LEANED AGAINST A WALL in the tiny Task Force office, trying to avoid Lieutenant Matthews' scornful look.

"I just figured something out," Matthews said, looking like a poor man's George Burns, his pajama tops hanging out of his trousers, and puffing on a half-eaten Parodi.

Paul cringed, expecting the worst.

And Matthews said, "You're one of those damned ex-type-marines, ain't you? Yeah, gotta be out front, where the action is. Damn the consequences."

"Hey, this time I did everything by the rules and still I come up the loser."

Matthews, pointing into the outer office. "Got yourself a couple'a topnotch screw ups to help too, didn't ya?"

Paul looked at the two paddy wagon men. Joe, with elbows on knees, a towel applied to his cheekbone. Volly alongside, his uniform shirt reduced to shreds. Volly with a mean stare on. Which was meant for Tommy, who was sitting on the opposite side of the room, under a series of pigeonhole mail boxes for the 60 odd Task Force men. Even with blood seeping from Tommy's nose, he managed to return Volly's stare with a proud grimace.

Matthews puffed once on his parodi. "How'm I gonna get all of you out from under without putting my own self in the trick bag?"

Paul said, "Shoestring getting killed, it was an accident. Why can't we just plain tell the truth?"

Matthews looked like he wanted to laugh and cry at the same time. "The truth. You mean like you were out all night looking for the dude that robbed your gun, and oops, run over the same son-of-a-bitch?" He made an incredulous face. "And then two old friends of yours run him over, too."

"But…"

"But nothing. Nobody's gonna believe it. Hell, I don't believe it, and I know it's the truth. We gotta figure something that sounds good. Yeah, a lie. Downtown always eats up a good lie."

Paul said, "Ain't no way getting around we run over the guy."

"No shit, Marine," Matthews said. "What if, instead of you spending the whole night searching for Shoestring, you just happened to run across him on your way home? The kid was a wanted murderer. You had no choice but to take action." He stopped for a puff. "Yeah, and the one thing you did right was call in for help. Communications has it on tape. We can play it for the brass, if they ask."

"I don't know…"

"No. I like it," Matthews said. "And the hell with waiting for downtown to ask. We'll get a copy from communications, have it played for them. Tell them look, see, these coppers were doing everything according to regulations."

"I still don't know…"

"You sure got a lot of I don't knows. How bouts one or two I knows. Couldn't hurt, I know. I mean, you know. Hell, I don't know what I mean anymore."

Paul still didn't know, but kept it to himself.

"Yeah, I'm calling downtown right now," Matthews said, and picked up the phone. But stopped, because Kyle Debolt had just walked into the office.

Debolt saying, "They filled you in on what happened, right?"

"I'm filled in," Matthews said.

Debolt, giving Paul a look. "About my shit head partner running over the robbery suspect?"

And Paul, "Why you—I saved your ass so many times—I oughta beat your silly right here and now." He started for Debolt, until Matthews put a hand on his chest.

Matthews saying to Debolt, "So, what's your point?"

His voice wavering, Debolt said, "Uh, right. Anyway, Paul shoulda known better than to be out there looking for the bad guy by himself. Look what happened."

Matthews bore down on Debolt. "Paul wasn't looking for Shoestring. So happens he lucked across him on the way home. He called it in, exactly according to procedure. And took action only after help arrived."

Tommy, Joe and Volly's heads snapped up like a trio of trained monkeys. Debolt saw their reaction, and said, "Loot, you can't…"

46

"That's how it went down, Debolt. Plain and simple." Matthews smiled. "And that's how it's gonna get wrote up, too."

Debolt stood openmouthed. Paul knew how his old partner's muddled brain worked, how he was trying to figure out why one cop would try to save another. Even if Matthews sat Debolt down and explained word for word, which was not about to happen.

"Kyle," Paul said, less agitated now, "go ahead on. We'll write it up. I'll make sure you get a copy."

Looking relieved, Debolt said, "Okay, only there's things gotta get done. You know, statements and all." His eyes flashed at Matthews.

Paul said, "I'll do that, too. You'll have it all before end of watch."

Debolt pondered for a second. "Well, okay. It don't make no difference, I guess. I mean, it's obvious who was in the BMW, and all."

"Obvious?" Paul said. "Why so obvious?"

"Dittybop Caldwell. Who else? Way I got it figured, Dittybop and Shoestring must'a stashed the diamonds around there someplace, and were going back when you spotted them." Again flashing at Matthews. "I mean while Pauly was on his way home, of course."

Matthews' stare was steady, unyielding.

Still eyeing Matthews, Debolt said, "Yeah, well anyway, there must'a been a fight over the goods. Dittybop, being the bigger of the two, dumped Shoestring outta the car. Along comes Paul, squoosh, no more Shoestring. Makes sense, don't it?"

Paul wanted to laugh. No, it didn't make a bit of sense. Ditty didn't kill Shoestring, they were buddies, tight buddies. If Paul was working the case, a half dozen major questions would have to be answered before he came to any conclusions. First, where would a couple of street thieves get a BMW, and for what? Ditty and Shoes could easily walk the few blocks from the Cabrini to where the BMW was, and it would be a lot safer, too. Also, was there somebody else involved, and if so, who? Paul didn't know, but suspected there was. Diamond robberies just weren't Ditty and Shoestring's thing, not by

47

themselves anyway. Well, Debolt's stupidity wasn't Paul's problem. Let the fool think whatever he wanted, just as long as Paul wasn't going to be the fall guy.

Debolt, going on. "Last night, before I went home, I got a warrant for Dittybop and Shoestring for robbery and murder. Don't have to worry about Shoestring anymore, do we?" He cast a smile at Matthews, receiving more deadpan in return. "Uh, anyway, as far as Dittybop goes, no problem. I'll just add a second murder charge." Again he smiled at Matthews. "This one gets easier as it goes along, Loot."

The phone rang, and Matthews picked up. "Matthews," he said "Yeah, what is it?" He listened. "Can you tell what kind?" and waited for a reply. "You're sure?" He gave Debolt a look. "He's right here—yeah, I'll tell him. You can be sure I'll tell him—okay, thanks," and hung up.

"Tell me what, Loot?" Debolt asked like a child who was sure he'd been caught wrong, only didn't have the capacity to know exactly what he'd done.

Matthews plopped down alongside Tommy, and lay his head against the pigeon-holed wall. Looking up at Debolt, he said, "This one gets easier as it goes along, huh?"

All eyes turned to Debolt. "Who was that?" he said.

Matthews twirled his thumbs. As if speaking to them rather than Debolt, he said, "Just wait a minute, will you? I'm thinking." Finally he looked up, but not at Debolt. "Joe, Volly, either of you men hear any gun shots out there tonight?"

Joe and Volly gave each other confused glances. "Uh-uh," Volly said. "What happened? They up and find another body?"

"That's all we'd need," Matthews said, and let out a short laugh. "No, no other bodies. You're sure, though. No shots?".

Volly said, "If you're talking bout these two." He pointed a stubby finger at Paul and Tommy. "Nope, they never had a chance to shoot their guns. Not while we were there."

Matthews nodded at Volly as if trying to weigh something in his mind. He jumped up, and stood in front of Tommy. Holding his hand out, he said, "Gimme your service revolver, Covello."

Tommy peered up with speculative eyes. "He just told you I never shot my gun."

"Just give it to me."

Tommy removed his service revolver from its holster, and handed it to Matthews. "I ain't never shot nobody in my whole life," he said. "Yesterday, when those nig—" He looked at Volly. "—I mean those robbers. When they were getting away I took some potshots." His eyes went wide. "You mean I hit one of them?"

"Ha. That'd be the day." Matthews sniffed the barrel of Tommy's gun. He flicked the release on its cylinder, and opened it into the palm of his hand. Then checked the chambers, and mumbled, "All six full." to Paul he said, "Yours, too. The snubnose."

"I wouldn't lie to you," Paul said, and watched as Matthews repeated the same procedure with his snubnose.

Matthews smiled, more to himself than to Paul. "I know that. This is for our detective friend, here." He turned to Debolt. "That was the medical examiner on the phone. He's at the morgue. Guess what?"

Debolt made a blank stare, and just as Matthews was about to reveal his mystery, Paul said, "They found bullet wounds on Shoestring, right?"

Matthews gawked at Paul.

Paul shrugged, "Hell, you asked, boss."

Matthews gave Paul a silent rebuke, then looked at Debolt. "Yeah, one in the side of the neck, the other in the ear. How'd you miss something as easy as that, Detective?"

Debolt faltered. He finally blurted out, "How was I supposed to know?"

Paul, conditioned to protect his old partner, said, "Take it easy, boss. That body was tore all to hell, being run over by a pickup truck and a paddy wagon too. Hell, who'd be looking for bullet wounds?"

"A homicide dick, that's who," Matthews said. "So, by the time our boys came around that corner, Shoestring was already dead."

Tommy said, "So that's what those flashes were."

Everybody turned to Tommy, and Matthews said, "What flashes? You never said anything about flashes."

"I forgot. Well, not really, but I didn't think it meant anything

49

until now." Tommy looked at Paul. "Remember? Was right after the nig—" Tommy looked at Volly. "—The black dude got into the BMW. You were doing something, talking on the radio, I don't know. Anyway, I saw these flashes—or I thought I did. Hadda be when Shoestring got plugged."

Paul had been thinking right along with Tommy, and said, "It all fits. After that, the shooter drove around the corner, found a dark spot, and dumped the body. We come after him, and having our eyes painted on the BMW, don't see what's lying in the middle of the street until it's too late."

"That's the way I see it," Matthews said. "Here's how we'll do it. Paul, you sit down with Tommy. Get it all straight, then put it on paper. Downtown'll eat it up."

Paul looked at Debolt, waiting for him to say what Paul was thinking. But Debolt just stood there, hands limp at his sides, as if in a daze.

Having no other choice, Paul said, "We're missing one little thing, ain't we? I mean, what if somebody comes along and suggests the whole story is bullshit? Says we found Shoestring earlier, killed him, then made up this story to cover our asses?"

Matthews smiled. "That's what the gun inspection was for. I want everybody's gun, that's yours, too, Joe and Volly. They gotta go down to the crime lab for comparisons. It's the only way we can prove none of you guys did the shooting."

"Loot," Debolt said, "there'll be a copy of my report on your desk by this evening." He winked. "Won't be no problem for Pauly, either." He made his exit.

Matthews, looking after Debolt, said, "Can we trust him?"

"Kyle's stupid, but he ain't dumb enough to cross you, boss. Yeah, we can trust him."

"Okay, if you say so. Go ahead, write it up like we said."

50

Chapter 8

THE PHONE RANG but once before Henry picked up. "Hi, lover," he said. "I was just sitting here thinking about you… if you know what I mean?"

"That's nice to hear, Henry, only you're not my type. Anyway, I ain't never been to New York. And from what I've heard about all the crazies there, I ain't hardly coming."

"Smedley, that you? I've been waiting for your call."

"Yeah, I can tell."

"I mean it. Okay, and my girl. Her's too."

Henry sounded vulnerable, which was just what Smedley had expected, and he said, "Just checking in, pal."

Henry whispered into the phone like he was a spy on a secret mission. "The man we talked about, Randolph Laidlaw. He left for Chicago this afternoon. Should be there by now."

"He's here all right. At the Drake, hanging out in the lounge, just like you said he'd be. I picked him out easy, what with the bow tie you said he always wears."

"Good, then everything's set, right?"

"You bet, pal. You and me, we're gonna be a whole lot richer right quick. By the way, where's old Randy keep his stuff."

"He doesn't trust anybody. Keeps them tied around his belly, in a money belt. Just remember, though. Randolph gets hurt, no deal."

"Come on, Henry. I told you I'm not that kinda guy."

"Yeah, you did, but, well, you know…"

"Sure, I know. You and Randy, you're buddies, right?" Smedley laughed.

Henry laughed too, but it was a feeble attempt, Smedley could tell. He said, "So listen, I need you in town the day after tomorrow. You know, to complete the deal."

A long pause, and then, "I wasn't counting on coming back. I mean, why can't you send the diamonds registered mail? Soon as I get them, I'll wire you the cash."

"You gotta be kidding," Smedley said, picturing Henry holding his breath on the other end of the line. "At the airport,

I told you how it hadda be. Meeting at the bank, and all."

"I know. But… You can trust me."

"Henry, old pal. No way I'm gonna send you the diamonds without seeing my money. No more than you'd send me the cash without seeing your stones. Unless that's what you wanna do, send me the cash first. Sure, that'll work for me."

"But…"

"See what I mean?"

"Yeah, I guess. Only I'm not real cool on the bank idea. I want to do it out in the open, someplace where I can feel a little safer."

Which Smedley only expected. "Sure, if that's how you want it. How about right there in the lobby of the Drake? Say 8 a.m. day after tomorrow. You have the cash, I'll have the diamonds."

"Uh—I'm not sure…"

"What'sa matter? I thought you'd like the idea of us meeting at the Drake. What safer place than that?"

"Okay, the Drake it is," Henry finally said.

"A quarter mil, that right?"

"That's right, two-fifty."

"You got it together?"

"Yeah, all set."

"No surprises, you hear me, Henry?"

"I hear you," Henry said. "And I'll want to see the diamonds, too," his voice wavering.

"You're smart," Smedley said with a dead serious voice. "I like doing business with smart people. They don't make mistakes. This is gonna come off nice and smooth, clean like."

"Clean, that's how I want it," Henry said.

"See you soon, pal. Gotta get to work."

"Excuse me, but you're Mister Randolph Laidlaw, aren't you?"

The man in the bow tie spun on his barstool, saying in an uppity tone, "First off, just who the hell are you?"

"Uh, don't make any difference really. I'm looking for Mister Henry Shakleford. The front desk says he's checked out, but that you and him are associates. I thought maybe you could get a message to him." Smedley kept his voice low, and bent forward like one of those coolies he'd seen when the 9th Marines stopped

52

off in Honk Kong for R&R.

Which worked, because Laidlaw eyed him like a king to his slave. "Okay, so your name's Smedley. But that doesn't really tell me who you are, does it?" He flicked a smile at his drinking mate, some oldster in a loud sports coat.

Still the coolie, Smedley wrung his hands. "Like I said, it don't mat…"

"Pal, unless you tell me exactly who you are—well, then maybe you'd just better get yourself out of here."

Going good, but needed a few extra touches. Smedley spied over his shoulder, then blinked back to Laidlaw. "All I am is a limo driver, okay? So look, I need to talk to Mister Shakleford."

Laidlaw sipped at his drink, spying over the rim as if almost interested. "What about?"

Smedley forced a gulp. "I'm sorry. It's confidential. If you have his address, I'll send him a letter."

This Laidlaw just adored playing the big shot, adjusting his bow tie, lighting a Marlboro 100, exhaling a long stream of smoke directly into Smedley's face. "Can't help you, friend. Well, I could, but my buddy Henry, he wouldn't like it if I were to give out his address to somebody I don't even know."

"It's real important," Smedley said. "It's about the other day, on Michigan Avenue… I'm pretty sure." Noting the bulge around Laidlaw's belt line.

Laidlaw, with his royal highness attitude. "What do you mean, 'You're pretty sure?'" Sharing a laugh with the loud sports coat.

"Listen," Smedley said, looking left and right. "Not here, okay. It's about—the robbery—you know."

Laidlaw said, "What'd you do, find Henry's stones?" And looked around, as if he'd had enough amusement for one night.

Smedley made his best poker face, and waited.

Laidlaw's pompous sneer faded to a blank stare. "Jesus," he said, pulling Smedley to a quiet corner. He went nose to nose, whispering, "You didn't, did you?"

Perfect.

Smedley spun on his heels, hurrying out of the lounge.

"Wait!" Laidlaw hollered.

Not now. No, and Smedley carried on, knowing he'd done a good night's work.

Chapter 9

PAUL STOOD OVER the tiny gas range in his third floor efficiency apartment. Wearing only a pair of boxer shorts, he stared sleepy-eyed at his bacon and eggs as they sizzled in a deep layer of grease. Gently he flipped them, biting his tongue, and hoping just this once the yolks would not break.

A yellow ooze crept from beneath.

His hand strayed to the telephone, fingers wavering over the receiver before finally dialing.

One ring and a light, airy voice said, "*Dobra dan.*"

"*Baba,*" Paul said, "how is it you never break your eggs?"

"Huh," said the confused voice.

"*Kako ti, Baba,*" he said to his mother.

"Paval, what's wrong?" Catherine Kostovic said, switching to English.

"Nothing, Mom. Can't your favorite son call home without you thinking something's wrong?"

"You're hurt, aren't you?"

"No, I'm okay."

"Jesus, Mary and Joseph! You're in the hospital, aren't you?"

"No, Mom. I'm right here in my apartment. Why won't you believe me?"

Paul listened for a reply and finally his mother spoke, but not to him. "Paval's in the hospital," she said in Croatian.

Paul pressed the phone close in order to hear his father's answer, but his mother was still talking. "You don't believe me? Then get over here and see for yourself," she said.

Paul hollered into the receiver. "For crying out loud, Mom. Why won't you list…?"

"Paval, Paval, calm down. It's your father."

Paul released an exasperated "Humph," and said, "Yes, Cace."

"How come you're in the hospital?" his father said in Croatian.

"I'm not in the hospital. I'm at my apartment. What's the matter, you people won't believe me?"

"Wait a minute," Paul heard his father say. And then, "What's the matter with you, woman? He's not in the hospital."

Paul heard a clank, then another, followed by unintelligible screaming. He pictured the chaos going on in the Kostovic kitchen and had to laugh. He was still laughing when his mother came back on the line.

"Oh, so you think it's a big joke, making believe you're in the hospital."

"Baba," he said, thinking the Croatian term of endearment might help appease his mother, "I never said I was in the hospital."

"This is your mother you're talking to, boy. Why I'll come up there and slap that smart mouth right off your face. And I don't care how old you are. Then we'll see who's laughing."

"God!" Paul said in exasperation. "Baba, please listen to me. I just called, that's all. I wanted to tell you—tell you—to say hello."

A long silence.

"Paul, can you hear me?" she said.

"Yes, Baba."

"Explain."

"Nothing to explain, Mom. Just wanted to hear your voice, is all."

"Well, now you have. Tell me, why is it I haven't been able to get hold of you for two whole days?"

Not wanting to tell his mother about the loss of his gun and the rest at the Cabrini Green Housing Project, he said, "Let's just say I was involved in something… something unfortunate, and let it go at that."

"Are you gonna tell me? Or do I have to come up there and pry it out of you?"

"Mom, It's a long story. The main thing is… I'm okay."

"You're sure?"

Paul smiled at his broken eggs. "Yes, I'm sure."

He waited for his mother's answer, knowing she always saw through his lies. And wasn't surprised when she said, "Why is it you sound so tired?"

"I'm not tired, Mom. Maybe a little disappointed, that's all."

"Disappointed! About what?"

"It's everything. Since I made sergeant, and got put back in uniform, well, it just hasn't been the same. I don't know, maybe

Chicago ain't for me anymore."

Using Croatian again, his mother said, "So now you want to quit?"

"Baba, it's hard."

She emitted a short laugh, saying, "What do you know about hard?"

"Mom, list…"

"Be quiet! Your mother's talking. Hard, you wanna talk about hard? I've got a sixty-year old man standing next to me. He works a ten hour shift, six days a week, and in a hole in the ground. I'll put him on. He can tell you about hard."

"Mom…"

"Shut up, I said. You get your head up and go back to work. You hear me?"

"Mom, you don't understand."

"I understand only too well. Things get a little tough and now you wanna quit. Sorry, it don't work that way. Not for you, it don't." Her voice lowered to a hissing kind of whisper. "I'm gonna hang up now. When I do, you pull yourself together. Remember who you are, Paval Kostovic, where you come from." A pause and then she said, "Paval?"

"Yeah, Mom." Paul felt his voice cracking.

"I love you," and the line went dead.

Paul stared at the telephone, knowing exactly what his mother had been referring to. The old country, the terrible wars, and how his father had fled to America in order to make a better life. How he'd had to save for years before getting enough together to send for his young wife. At first they couldn't even speak the language, his Baba and Cace. But somehow they found their way. Paul's mother's voice echoed in his ears, "And we did it without whining every time something went wrong."

Tears filled Paul's eyes, because even though a large part of him still wanted to quit the police department and head for home, nothing this city had in store for him could come close to the wrath of that squat woman and her wooden spoon.

Whatever remaining part of Paul Kostovic that questioned

why he was still a Chicago policeman was long dispelled before he arrived in front of Tommy Covello's house in Little Italy.

"Come on, Tommy. Let's go get em," he said as Tommy got into his pickup.

Tommy made a suspicious face. "What's got into you? You know something I don't, or what?"

Paul grinned as he headed for the Task Force Offices. "All of a sudden life ain't so bad," he said.

Tommy opened a copy of the *Chicago Tribune*. "See if that don't change your mind."

Paul glanced at the mug shot-like pictures of himself and Tommy. Alongside were the headlines.

COPS BUNGLE ARREST
COLUMBIAN DIPLOMAT SLAIN
MURDER SUSPECT KILLED UNDER SUSPICIOUS
CIRCUMSTANCES

Paul pushed the paper aside. "Horseshit, all of it. I'll show them."

Tommy closed one eye, and squinted the other at Paul. "What you mean, show them? Who the hell's them?"

Paul's grin remained as he said, "Them? Them's everybody. This whole town's got me made out for a fool." He took a quick glance at Tommy to get his reaction, which was a disbelieving stare.

Then Tommy took off his police hat, put his hand on his forehead, and ran it through the curly locks on the top of his head. "All of a sudden I feel a splitting headache coming on."

Paul turned into the Task Force parking lot. As they got out of the pickup, Tommy said, "Okay now, promise me you're gonna be cool. 'Cause I don't want you screwing up me getting my job back at the beach."

"Don't worry," Paul said. He strode toward the side entrance. Trying to act confident. Not so sure he was.

Tommy ran after, finally catching up at the top of second floor landing. Paul marched past the Task Force office, never once making a sideways glance. "That works for me," Tommy whispered. He stepped in front of Paul, leading the way to their lockers.

Paul fidgeted with the combination on his lock, saying, "Did you see in the office? The lieutenant, and some detective I ain't never seen before, they were huddled around Matthews' desk."

"What? I thought you weren't looking."

Paul dropped his hands from the lock, and glared at Tommy. "Yeah, I was looking. I just didn't want them to know it. I'll bet it's about us, too."

Tommy's shoulders slumped. "Ain't this just great. One minute you're Mister Tough Guy. The next you're making predictions like some kinda crystal ball seer." He mumbled, "What'd I get myself into?"

Paul grabbed Tommy's shoulders, and gave him a shake. "Relax, will you? We might go down, but at least we're gonna be fighting every step of the way."

"Oh, Jesus. I guess I can forget the beach. Hell, I'll be lucky to still be on the force by the time you get finished."

Paul heard footsteps on the other side of their lockers. "Here they come," he said.

Lieutenant Matthews came around the corner followed by a detective with a pockmarked face and a natural scowl. To Paul, this monster of a man could pass for an executioner out of the dark ages.

From behind, Tommy whispered, "Please, Sarge. Don't fool with this character."

The detective stepped forward, handed an official looking paper to Paul with one hand, and with the other, handed a like document to Tommy. In a voice as scary as his looks, he said, "Paul Kostovic. Thomas Covello. Those are search warrants for your lockers. Open them up."

Tommy's knees buckled. He might have collapsed if it weren't for Paul, who put a clandestine hand on the young officer's belt and held him erect.

Nobody was going to intimidate Paul, and he said, "Before we open up anything, ain't it customary for you to identify yourself to the person you're issuing the warrant to?"

The detective's eyes turned to slits, and he bore a set of

jagged teeth. "That's right. An old homicide man, ain't you. I'm Detective John Angotti, Internal Affairs Division. You got a problem with that?"

"No," Paul shot back. "What I got a problem with is the newspapers making me out for some kinda criminal. So now it's the IID's turn, huh?"

Tommy started to sag again.

Angotti gave Paul a wry smile. "Listen, Sergeant. Ain't no way around it. Those lockers gotta be searched."

"Fine," Paul said, trying to sound as defiant as his mother would have. "I'd just like to know why."

Matthews said, "That's only reasonable, Detective."

Angotti said, "The crime lab confirms that the slugs removed from Shoestring's body match those from that unlucky Columbian what got himself killed during the diamond robbery. Get it? This means both the Columbian and Shoestring were killed by your service revolver."

He paused, which meant he wanted to see what kind of reaction Paul would make. Well, Paul had tried that stuff plenty of times himself. He stared back, gritting his teeth like his mother just before she went into one of her famous spiels on what it took to be a Kostovic.

As if not surprised, Angotti continued. "So right away some fool politician comes to the conclusion you were pissed off about getting your gun stolen, went and found the culprit, and took a little revenge. Of course, then my phone rings, and it's my job to prove it."

Matthews said, "Paul. I told you this might happen."

Paul, all red in the face, said to Angotti, "You think me and Tommy found Shoestring, took back my gun, shot him dead with it, then run him over for good measure? Jesus, but you people are too much."

Matthews rubbed his jaw, and said, "Look, Paul. Detective Angotti didn't say that's what happened. He said some politician said that's what happened. Come on, let's just get this search over so we can be done with it."

Paul gave Matthews a glare, and turned to Angotti. "All right. But I still don't know what you think you're gonna find." He flung his locker door open.

Angotti answered as he crouched in front of it. "Sarge, going on the assumption you murdered Shoestring, the man who stole the diamonds, and he don't got 'em, then maybe you do."

"That's stupid," Paul said. "I wouldn't be surprised you wanna search my apartment, too."

Angotti addressed Paul with a somber tone. "Got a team of dicks doing just that right now." And with hands deep in Paul's locker, "Your place, too, Officer Covello."

"What?" Tommy said. "Ain't this a joke. My old lady searches my room every day. They sure as hell ain't gonna find anything she ain't already."

To Paul, nothing was amusing about the search of his apartment. Only his mother's words of admonishment kept him from telling them all to go to hell.

Angotti stood up. "Okay, that's done. One more thing and I'll be outta here. Sergeant Kostovic, there's an allegation of brutality at the Cabrini Green Housing project. A young lady says you deliberately hit her in the face. What you have to say about that?"

Paul remembered the girl from the Mission Baptist Church. "Is her name Katie… uh, something or another?"

"Yeah, that's the one."

"She's lying. That girl's a nut case."

"Maybe so," Angotti said, "but she says you bashed her in the head with your patrol car door."

"You mean after we left the projects? Yeah, I hit her. It was an accident and she knows it. I thought she was gonna break the window on our patrol car, and when I tried to get out and stop her she got hit by the door. Ask Lieutenant Matthews and Officer Covello. They were there."

Angotti nodded, as if this were the answer he'd expected. "I already talked to your boss."

"I don't get it," Paul said. "If you already knew I didn't do it, then why'd you even bring it up?"

"Your friends would be expected to back you up. Don't you know that stuff? I mean, you worked homicide, right?"

"Yeah, yeah," Paul said, and leaned against his wall locker, realizing it was a whole different story when you were the suspect. He said, "That broad swore she was gonna get me. I guess she's doing a pretty good job of it, too."

"Don't give up just yet," Angotti said. "I've got her downstairs. We've got a little experiment planned for her. If it works out the way I think... well, you'll be outta the woods."

Paul looked at Angotti, then at Lieutenant Matthews, who said, "As long as you've got this thing hanging around your neck, believe me, there ain't gonna be any rest. Trust us this one time, and I think you can put it behind you once and for all."

Paul took a moment to think. He liked Matthews, and coming from him, Paul was inclined to accept. "Okay, If you say so," he said.

Angotti went face to face with Paul, spewing a strong odor of garlic. "One thing, though. For this to work, you gotta keep your mouth shut. You think you can do that this one time?"

Paul gritted his teeth, wanting Angotti to know he'd go along, but didn't like it.

"Okay," Angotti said, "but I don't think we should all go. It'd only give the lady more people to play off of."

"You're right," Matthews said. "Me and Covello'll wait in my office."

Angotti looked at Paul. "Let's do it." He led the way down to ground level.

Paul followed into the roll call room. Katie was standing by the podium, facing the windows. Her long, jet-black hair was combed straight back, curled at the small of her back. The morning sun shone on her light brown business suit, revealing the outline of a taut waistline. He knew this girl was treacherous, but couldn't help but think she was even more beautiful than the first time he'd seen her.

She turned to them. Paul winced when he saw her eye, all puffed closed.

She pointed an angry finger at him. "That's the pig. Look what you did to me, you—you—"

She started toward him, but Angotti intercepted her. With her one good eye bulging and her face distorted, she said, "I want him arrested, and now."

Angotti said matter-of-factly, "He says it was an accident."

"And you believe him. Just what I expected."

Angotti shrugged off her accusation. "It's not a matter of believing, Miss. Being a law student, and working in the legal aid office, you oughta know that." Paul made a mental note of this new bit of information. "Prove to me this was a deliberate act, and Sergeant Kostovic will be charged with battery like any common criminal."

"Isn't that supposed to be your job?" she said with a sneer.

Angotti went on unaffected. "You're right, it is my job, and that's just what I did, see if it could be proven. I went all over the Cabrini looking for somebody to corroborate your story. Turns out you've got lots'a friends down there. Witnesses were coming outta the woodwork saying you got beat by the police. But when I asked them to be specific all I got was a mishmash of wild tales." He opened a thick manila folder. "Let's see what we got. Okay, here's a Mister Alonzo Diggs. He says he saw four cops beating on you with their batons." Angotti turned the page. "Here's another. Mrs Penny Unger says you got pistol whipped, and that the cop who did it also tried to rape you." He slapped the folder closed. "I've got a dozen more. Not one account for the same location. Not only that, according to them you got beat morning, noon, and night. Best of all, all I hadda do was show them a random photo of any cop. They identified it right away. For Christ sakes, I could lock up half the cops in the Task Force based on your witnesses."

Katie glared at Angotti. "That doesn't mean it didn't happen. Look at my eye, you idiot."

"Nobody's saying it didn't happen. The question is, was it intentional?"

Katie struck a pose. "So, he gets away with it. Same old story, huh?"

Angotti jumped on her words. "Are you saying Sergeant Kostovic is being protected just 'cause he's a cop?"

Katie moved up close on Angotti, the top of her head well below his chin. She snarled, "Any dummy could see that, dummy."

Angotti, eyeing down at her like a judge to an accused murderer. "I'll tell you what. You take a lie detector test, and if you pass, count on it, I won't rest until you get justice."

"Why should I?" She pointed at Paul. "Make him take it. He's the criminal."

Paul felt as if he were an inconsequential object not worthy of being heard, and not able to stop himself, hollered, "Damn right. Give me a lie…"

"I'll handle this," Angotti said, glaring at Paul. Before Paul could answer, Angotti switched to Katie. "First you, lady. Then him. That's the way it works."

Standing her ground, Katie said, "You cops are all alike. I should've known better."

Angotti shook his head at Katie, as if dismissing a whining child. Paul was beginning to be impressed by this IID detective. Oh-oh, that is until he saw Angotti cross his fingers behind his back. Paul flicked to Katie, who looked like she was ready to explode. An agonizing moment passed, and then she shoved out with both arms, pushing the huge detective against a wall locker. The way it rattled, Paul thought it was going to come crashing down. But when he looked, Angotti was upright, and staring back at Katie with a satisfied smile.

Angotti saying, "Exactly what I expected. And exactly what happened back at the Cabrini, right?"

Realization shown on Katie's face. But only for a flash, and turning to Paul, she said, "You'll get yours sooner or later. And I'm the one who's going to see you get it." She snapped her head at Angotti. "And all the theatrics in the world aren't going to save him, either."

Angotti gave her a big smile. "I guess this means you've decided to forgo the lie test."

Paul thought Katie would be ready to kill, but her face had brightened. She walked toward the exit door as if she had won instead of being beaten. Passing in front of Angotti, she stomped the toe of Angotti's shoe. Singing over her shoulder, she said, "Sorry, just an accident. You know how it goes."

Angotti held his foot while jumping up and down on the other. "I shoulda known better than to let my guard down," he said.

Paul propped Angotti up, saying, "You knew she'd go off, didn't you?"

Lieutenant Matthews appeared from the stairwell, where

he must have been listening the whole time, because he said, "Well, not for sure, we didn't. It was a pretty good bet, though."

Paul thought for a second, then, "And you knew I wouldn't be able to keep quiet either?"

Matthews gave Angotti a wink, saying, "That we knew without a doubt."

Even Paul had to smile.

Regaining his balance, Angotti said, "I can't tell you officially, but once my boss sees my report you'll be exonerated."

"That's it then?" Paul said.

"Yeah. She can scream her head off, but after that little episode nobody's gonna listen."

"What about my gun? And the guy in the BMW, the one who killed Shoestring? And the robbery back by the Drake, and Ditty?"

"Not his problem," Matthews said. "The rest is up to homicide."

"Who's working the homicide end of this thing anyway?" Paul said, "Kyle Debolt. You know him?"

Angotti rolled his eyes. "Good luck with Kyle." He walked outside.

Matthews, heading up the stairs, and saying, "I'll send Covello down. His gun's ready at the department armory, and they got a replacement for your lost one. You two go get them, and report back for evening roll call. I got something in the fire."

"What?" Paul said, curious.

"Still working it out in my head," Matthews said. "See you after awhile," He climbed the stairs.

Paul walked outside to wait for Tommy, feeling relieved to have this whole thing behind him. Matthews' plans, and where Paul fitted in, didn't matter. He'd do any menial job Matthews had in store for him, beach detail included. God. Even with Tommy.

Katie was leaving in a Volkswagen Bug, and pulled up at the curb. "I told you I'd get you and I will. Just wait and see," she said.

Don't let her get under you skin, Paul told himself. He turned his back on her.

"Hey," Katie hollered. "I know you're stupid. Maybe you can't hear, too."

Paul, making an effort to be deliberate, turned back around. Controlling his voice, he said, "You know what, Katie... whatever your name is? That was an accident when I hit you with the car door. But you go ahead, believe anything you want. I just don't give a damn anymore."

Katie stepped out of her car. "Yeah, sure. And you weren't responsible for the riot at the Cabrini, either."

"I was trying to make an arrest, simple as that."

"Who do you think you're kidding?" she said. "I was there, remember? You'd have killed those boys if you caught them. And I'm not convinced they did a damn thing, either. Except be black and poor."

Paul gave her a disgusted smirk. "That's right, you were at the Cabrini. But I was on Michigan Avenue when they robbed that diamond salesman. I thought they were gonna kill the guy."

She stuck up her nose, and started back to her car.

Paul reached for her, taking care, but as soon as he touched her arm, fear of another brutality complaint made him let go.

She spun around, but before she could go into another of her tirades, he said, "I'll tell you what. Sooner or later they're gonna arrest the one who's still on the loose. When they do, they'll have to call me in to identify him. When that happens I'll give you a call. You can come talk to him yourself, see I'm telling the truth."

Glaring, she said, "Just keep your filthy hands off me, unless you want your eyes scratched out."

Paul stuffed his hands in his pockets. "There, now you're safe from the big bad wolf."

Which all of a sudden didn't appear to have been the best idea, because from what he knew of this crazy girl, she could attack at any moment. He was trying to think of a way out and still not make a fool out of himself, when her finger appeared in front of his face.

Unprepared, he flinched back two steps.

Katie laughed. "The big bad wolf you aren't. Know what,

I'm going to take you up on your offer, not that I think you'd really call."

Attempting to recover his dignity, Paul looked away, as if to ask a make believe bystander, can you believe this girl? He pulled a pen and notepad from his breast pocket, and handed it over. She scribbled a moment, and gave it back to him. Paul took it, meaning to stuff it back in his pocket. Then it occurred to him that he knew only the first name of this obnoxious girl. He looked at his notepad. Her writing was nothing but a bunch of loops and swirls.

"What is it?" Katie said. "Could it be that besides being a brutal pig, and deaf, you can't read, either?"

Paul snapped, "Nobody could read this scrawl." Seeing Tommy coming out of the station house, he handed him the notepad, and said, "See if you can read that."

"Katie Bartovich," Tommy said without a moment's hesitation. He handed it back to Paul.

Katie burst out laughing.

Which bit Paul deep. But there was something else. Tommy had said her name was Bartovich, and Bartovich was Slavic, Croatian probably, or maybe Russian. He had to know. "Okay, little Miss Comedian," he said. "If you're done with your silly games, maybe you'd like to answer a simple question for a dummy like me?"

"Shoot, dummy. Or is that a poor choice of words? With your IQ, who knows? You might take me literally and pull your gun out."

Ignoring her, Paul said, "Are you a Crow?"

"Crow? What's that?" answered Katie with a broad smile. "Some kind of Indian? Nope. I'm not an Indian, not that it's any of your business."

"Crow, as in Croatian. Yugoslavian, get it?" Paul wondered if maybe Katie had lost her heritage somewhere along the way.

"I knew what your tiny brain was thinking from the very beginning. Yeah, I'm Yugoslavian. Only not Croatian. Serbian is what I am."

Finally Paul had her. "My God!" he said to Tommy. "Right in front of my eyes, a real live Serbian." Then to Katie, "I should've guessed. My Dad said I'd meet up with one of you people someday." He spread his arms wide, and looking south as if speaking to his father some three hundred miles away, said, "Like always you were right, Cace. I only wish I knew what she was when I first saw her. I'd of run like hell."

Katie spun on her heels, saying as she went to her car, "You just watch and see this Serbian go. And don't forget you promised to call when you find Ditty Caldwell."

Paul was startled that Katie knew Ditty by name. He blurted out, "Where you know him from?"

Katie stopped long enough to say, "I work in legal aid, and helped Ditty before. You know, when pigs like you tried pinning some phony case on him." She slid into the driver's seat, putting on a dazzling show with her perfectly rounded hips.

Paul glanced at Tommy, catching him licking his lips. "You like that, huh?" he said.

Tommy cocked his head. "On a scale of one to ten, a solid eight, maybe even a nine."

Chapter 10

THAT SAME AFTERNOON.

Smedley needed a limo for the operation's next phase. He rode the Elevated out to O'Hare Airport. Dozens were parked on the arrival level, all in a row. Waiting for loads to take into the city, he figured.

Smedley knew he had his mark when he saw a scraggly looking driver sneak a half-pint from under his seat and take a long pull. All Smedley needed was one little prop to assure success. A quick run into the airport gift shop to make a special purchase and he was ready.

Now, where was Halfpint and his limo? There on the far end, and he'd just snuck himself another pull. Smedley jumped into the front seat, saying, "You gotta get me downtown, and quick."

The red faced, blurry eyed driver shoved his bottle under the seat. "Sorry," he said, "but I gotta bunch'a stewardesses coming in from LA."

Smedley plopped a fifty into Halfpint's lap. "It'll be worth another fifty if we're parked in front of the Drake Hotel by two. You could make it down there and still get back for your stewardesses in plenty of time."

Halfpint wavered for a second, then shook his head. "Uh-uh. Just can't do it. The company's already got me on probation. One more screw up and I'll be out on my ear."

Smedley turned on the tears. "Man, I'm late for a reunion with some old army buddies." He gave Halfpint the other fifty, and along with it the quart bottle of Southern Comfort he'd just purchased at the airport gift shop.

Halfpint's eyes skipped past the two fifties, landing on the booze like a one-year-old to its pacifier. "Hold on," he said, and threw the gearshift into drive.

They were going fifty within a hundred yards, sixty by the time they'd hit the entrance to the expressway, and cruising at near seventy when Halfpint fished his original bottle out from under the seat. "How's about a little taste?" he said. "I know what it's like to be an old soldier. Served a year in Korea myself."

"Yeah, why not?" Smedley said, thinking the one-way windows on the limo were perfect for his purposes. He checked the expressway traffic. Not that heavy, and all were giving the fast moving limo a wide birth. A little too fast moving, and he said, "Hey, GI, why not slow it down some? Getting there is what's important, not when I get there."

"No problem," Halfpint said, sipping from his bottle.

Smedley pulled out the cop's .38, and watched the speedometer slowly drop. When it hit fifty-five, he squeezed off a round into Halfpint's ear. At once, the limo swerved hard right, and Smedley had to jerk the steering wheel in order to get himself heading straight again.

Now running straight and true, he pushed the deadweight body out of the driver's seat, and slipped in behind the wheel. Man, look at these ninety-proof brains splattered all over the window. And Smedley's clothes, blood all over. Would've been a lot cleaner to uses his Ka-bar, but that wasn't the plan.

He stopped off at the garage he'd rented for his BMW, changing into a clean set of clothes. Another half hour's work with soap and water made the limo suitable for what Smedley had in mind.

With Halfpint stuffed in the trunk, he headed for the Cabrini Green Housing Project, to make one last reconnaissance run before tonight's operation.

Chapter 11

"EVERYBODY UP," Lieutenant Matthews hollered as he walked into the roll call room.

Fourteen Task Force men got to their feet. They lined up side by side. Paul took his place at the far right hand side of the column, wondering where that idiot Tommy was.

Matthews said, "We're going down to the Cabrini tonight, boys. All seven cars. See if we can't dig up that Ditty Caldwell kid."

Paul couldn't be happier, but the Cabrini was a dangerous place. He spied to his left, expecting at least a few sour looks. Just a sideways stare here and there. These Task Force coppers, with their silent confidence, reminded Paul of a bunch of Marines, locking and loading before going out on a search and destroy mission.

"No heroes, you hear me?" Matthews said. "Stay on the perimeter. Check with your informants, see what you can find out." He chomped once on his Parodi. "Any questions?"

Which must have been the signal to go, because all fourteen men filed toward the door.

Matthews, with one parting shot. "And dammit. Be safe!"

Paul was just about to ask where he fit in to all this when Tommy came strolling in, saying, "You forgot me, Lieutenant. I'm getting my job back at the beach, ain't I?"

Matthews looked at Tommy with a face that said 'I give up'. And then to Paul, "Every one of those guys got their own snitches. Anybody can find Dittybop Caldwell, it'll be them."

"The beach," Tommy said. "What about the beach?"

"Shut up for a minute, will ya?" Paul said. "I wanna help down at the Cabrini, boss. And I promise, nothing stupid this time."

"In a second," Matthews said, and he looked at Tommy. "The beach it is, kid. Go jump in my car. Me and the sergeant'll drop you off."

"No shit," Tommy said. He headed for the parking lot.

Matthews, from the driver's seat. "Just a stop here and there, and we'll take you over to the beach, Covello."

"Suits me," Tommy said from the backseat.

Paul stayed quiet, concentrating on what was going on outside. People of all ages roamed the Cabrini Green streets, usually in groups of two or three, never acknowledging the many Task Force cars in their midst. Meanwhile Matthews conducted a running oratory on everything from the Cubs, to Mayor Daley, to Elvis Presley, even alluding to his wife when every other topic was exhausted.

Tommy, every once in a while answering with a, "So the beach, Lieutenant. About time I got down there, ain't it?"

Matthews continued as if Tommy had said nothing. "Me, one of these days I'm gonna find a nice spot in the cool hills of Northern Wisconsin."

"They got bad guys up there, too," Paul said, still surveying the Cabrini.

"Maybe so, but not Cabrini Green type bad guys."

Tommy, going along. "Maybe I'll go even farther north, to Minnesota. There's places in those backwoods where nobody's even heard of a shithole called the Cabrini. Uh, how's about the beach?"

Matthews laughed. "Good luck, 'cause knowing you, you'll try fooling with some Indian type princess. Hell, they'll come after you with hatchets and whatnot, chase what's left all the way back to the Chicago. That is if you're lucky to make it that far."

Matthews made a U-turn. He headed up Halsted Street, stopping for the light next to the North Avenue subway station.

Paul's curiosity finally got to him. "We've been making passes by here for hours, boss. You don't figure Ditty to come around here, do you?"

"Nah, not really," Matthews said. He peered out the window at the streetwalkers who were lined up on the curb. "Lookit them go." He laughed as first one, then another, and the rest abandoned their posts, running for the subway station. Matthews saying, "Like a herd of spooked cows, soon as they spot a cop car."

Still wondering, Paul said, "You know something I don't?"

Which earned another, "Nah, not really." Matthews turned the corner, parking in front of the subway station. "See, right there?" he said, pointing. "Right in the middle. That's Marilyn."

"You mean the white one?" Tommy said, rubbernecking out his window. "Man, what a pig. Who is she?"

"Depends. Marilyn Black, Marilyn White, Marilyn any color of the rainbow. Whichever color she decides to use on that particular day."

Paul looked too, easily picking out the only Caucasian amongst a dozen or more black and Hispanic streetwalkers. Marilyn Whatever was wearing a low cut blouse over minuscule breasts, which drooped loosely toward a pink short-short skirt. On her chicken bone legs, she had black stockings hiked up to the knees, where purple garters took over and ran under her skirt. She was tapping her gaudy red platform shoes on the pavement, and staring back at the patrol car, as if to say, ain't one cop in this town got balls to come after me.

"What's so special about her?" Tommy said.

Matthews looked at Paul with the face of a school boy who had just placed tacks on his teacher's chair. He said, "Know what. I think it's time Tommy got to know Marilyn, being the legend she is." He yelled out the window, "Yo, Marilyn, we got somebody wants to meet you."

Marilyn chewed up a cheekful of what must have been chewing tobacco, because she spat a dark red stream in the direction the patrol car. "You can kiss my pimply red ass, Jack Matthews. You smelly piece'a dog shit."

Seen by Paul, but not Tommy, Matthews waved a ten dollar bill at Marilyn. Which made all the difference, because she clopped her platform heels up to the patrol car, snatched Matthews' money, and stuffed it under her skirt.

From a distance Paul had seen Marilyn as unattractive at best. But now, standing only inches away, she was sickening. Thick layers of paint couldn't hide her sunken eyes and heavily lined cheeks. And when she spit again, Paul was repulsed by her exposed three upper teeth, four lowers, all of which were rotting.

Tommy said, "Looking at that makes me wanna go straight home and jump into the tub with a bar of lye soap."

Marilyn moved to the back door. She leaned through the window at Tommy, saying, "Who's the sweety?"

Tommy gagged. "Woman, you got breath like a stray dog." He slid to the other side of the car.

"Where you going, honey pot?" Marilyn said, slimy juice running down her cheek. "The good lieutenant said you wanna meet me. He lying, or what?"

"Hello," Tommy said, turning away. Then to Matthews, "Come on. You've had your fun. Get me outta here."

Only it was impossible for the Matthews to drive, not while trying to hold back a laughing attack. Paul was in the same state, doubled over the dashboard, trying to force back an explosion.

Which only got worse when Marilyn opened the car door. She slid in next to Tommy. Before he could defend himself, she threw her arms around his neck, and dove on top of his chest.

"Help me, dammit," Tommy yelled.

Which wasn't going to happen. It was too late, anyway, because Marilyn kissed him full on the lips, trying to force her tongue into his mouth. Tommy tore his head away, gasping for clean air. Marilyn came down on his exposed neck, drawing skin into her mouth, sucking with a vengeance. They grappled back and forth, Marilyn hanging on, Tommy trying to kick loose. Marilyn's bite must have been excruciating, because Tommy screamed, "Get her off, before I catch a case of hydrophobia."

Matthews and Paul couldn't help if they wanted to, fully engrossed in their own laughter.

Somehow, Tommy found one of Marilyn's ears, took a strong grip, and yanked with everything he had. Marilyn came loose. Her face hovered above his with a wild, animal-like look in her eyes. She screamed at the top of her lungs, "Rape, rape, somebody save me!"

Paul roared with delight. Matthews banged his head against the steering column.

Tommy scratched for the door, hoping to get out of the car, succeeding in getting a hand on the release, even got it open. Only Marilyn was on him before he could scramble outside, throwing one arm around his waist, and grabbing hold of his belt buckle. While Tommy was trying to pull loose, she slipped her other hand under his pants, taking hold of his crotch. Tommy yelped, and fell out of the car, landing face down on the sidewalk. Marilyn toppled on top of him. She'd lost her bite, but still had a hand down his pants. Tommy tried crawling away, but she clamped down between his legs, and pulled him back.

Tommy yelled, "Help me, dammit. Before she castrates me."

Which sent Paul into another fit. He fell out of his open door, plopping to the pavement alongside Tommy and Marilyn.

Tommy finally ripped his way free, and ran around to the other side of the patrol car.

"Bring that loving child back here," Marilyn yelled as she got to her feet. "I ain't but hardly started."

Matthews emerged from the car waving at Marilyn. "Shut up, you silly broad. The fun's over."

Marilyn faked like she was going to dive across the car at Tommy, giggling like a witch when he flinched. "You ain't seen the last'a me, sweet stuff," she said. "One'a these days I'm gonna capture your ass, and when I do it's gonna be upside down rape. You wait and see." She headed back to the subway station, flicking her hips side to side with each stride.

"God!" Tommy said to himself as much as Paul and Matthews. "I gotta have me a drink, a lotta drinks." He started for the car.

Matthews said, "That's a lesson for you, kid. Maybe the next time you go chasing broads on the beach, you'll think twice."

Tommy leaned against the side of the patrol car. "Could I be wrong? I thought you guys were starting to like me."

Matthews wrapped an arm around Tommy's shoulders, giving him an affectionate hug. "I'm gonna make a Task Force man outta you, come hell or high water."

Tommy shook his head. "This is just great," he said, still wrapped tightly in Matthews arm. "Some day, when I'm a veteran copper, and breaking in some rookie, I'll tell him, listen, you wanna be part of the gang, all you gotta do is go down to North Avenue, call out the whores, have one of them jump you in front of everybody." He raised his voice an octave. "That's all, and life'll be all wine and roses from then on in."

Matthews shrugged. "Nah, I wouldn't try that shit if I was you. Most coppers, even Task Force men, they just ain't got my deep appreciation for the human species. Nope. Not a good idea." He sprang into the driver's seat. "Come on, it's time we called it a day. The kid can buy at Woody's."

Paul started to get into the back seat, but stopped short when he saw Tommy fiddling with something on the pavement. "What'sa matter? You lose something?" Paul said.

"Uh-uh. Look what I found." Tommy held up something shiny and small between two fingers.

Paul suspected a practical joke, and he approached only to arm's length. Then seeing what Tommy had, "Son-of-a—! That looks like... Where'd it come from?"

Matthews, now crouching alongside, produced a wry smile, and said, "I'll go get Marilyn."

Who was standing at the corner, banging on the window of a station wagon with a man at the wheel, a woman at his side, and a load of children in the back. "Come on out here, lover," she said to the driver, "so's I can deliver what Mary Poppins over there ain't never gonna give up."

Matthews lifted the grungy streetwalker off her feet, and carried her like a bag of laundry back to the patrol car. He deposited her in the rear seat, handcuffing her hands behind her back.

Tommy said, "I ain't going to the beach, am I?"

Chapter 12

SMEDLEY THOUGHT perhaps he'd better call off tonight's operation, with all these cop cars patrolling the Cabrini neighborhood. Mostly TF patches on the cops' shoulders, too. The hard working cops. In the Corps, Smedley had learned safety came first. When outnumbered, and the marines had a choice, they backed off, picked another day when the odds were better.

On this day Smedley had a choice. He spun the limo around, intending to head back to the garage. Then he stopped, looking at the commotion over by the subway station. A couple of cops were wrestling with a broad. And on closer observation, the cops were Lieutenant Matthews, Sergeant Kostovic, and that kid, Covello. The broad, a whore, looked like. Yeah, a real slut, too.

These Task Force cops, supposed to be Chicago's best. Looked more like a carnival act, rolling on the street with some whore. And Smedley had thought the odds were against him. He turned back around, confident that one of him outnumbered a dozen of these Task Force cops.

Chapter 13

PAUL HELD HIS HAND OUT, displaying three tiny diamonds. "Where'd you get them, Marilyn?"

Marilyn, handcuffed to Matthews' desk, cackled like a witch, and said, "That lady cop you got to search me. I fought her like hell." She winked at Tommy. "The kid hadda hold me down. I think he enjoyed himself, too."

"I need a good hot bath," Tommy said, studying his fingernails.

Paul, not letting go. "You come up with the right answers, we'll make sure you get a walk for your troubles." He skipped out of harm's way as Marilyn shot a wad of chewing tobacco in his direction.

Marilyn, switched to Matthews, giving a sober stare. "This guy. Can I trust him?"

"You can trust me," Matthews said, lounging against a far wall.

She flashed between Paul and Matthews. Finally saying, "You know damned well where I got them. So quit the bullshit."

Paul, careful to keep his distance. "We gotta hear it from you."

"And I get a walk?"

"Yeah," Paul said. "I'll drop you off by the subway myself."

"I'd like that," Marilyn said. She pointed at Tommy. "Only how's about Sweety Pie doing the dropping?"

"You gonna tell us, or what?" Paul said.

"What you really wanna know is where he's at, right?"

"Where who's at?" Paul said, bearing down.

Which brought delight to Marilyn's eyes. She said, "The Bopper, of course."

Matthews, coming to Paul's side. "Just say it, Marilyn."

Sitting erect, like a third grader about to recite her multiplication tables, Marilyn rang out, "Right there in the Cabrini, on the sixth floor of the Eleven-sixty building. Where'd you think?"

"Come on," Paul said, starting for the door.

Matthews held him back, saying to Marilyn, "How come

Ditty gave you those diamonds?"

Looking defiant, Marilyn said, "You told me I come up with the right answers, I was gonna walk. Only here I am, still shackled like some damned slave."

"You'll walk," Matthews said. "First, though, tell us how you got hold of those diamonds."

Marilyn stared at Matthews as if she were trying to read his mind, and said, "Ditty's running scared, man. You guys are searching high and low for him. The gangbangers, too. Every one of them know he got away with a big score. Wanna rip him off."

Matthews pulled up a chair, and sat down across from Marilyn. "That we already know. Answer the question, how you come to have the diamonds?"

"Gimme a chance, will ya? I was just coming to that." She wiped brown slime from her chin. "Uh, you ain't got some chew, do ya, Matt?"

Paul looked at Tommy, who was staring nonchalantly out the window, unconcerned with any of this. "Hey, Covello," he hollered. "Run across the street, to Woody's. See if he's got some chewing tobacco."

Tommy spun around, looking like he was about to argue. And then his face softened. "Okay, why not. Anything's better than hanging around here."

Matthews, eyeing Tommy. "You stay outta Woody's booze, you hear me?"

Marilyn, hollering to Tommy as he started out, "I like Beachnut, they got it." Laughing when he gave her the finger.

Paul sat on Matthews' desk, leaning across at Marilyn. "The lieutenant asked a question. The diamonds."

Marilyn grinned. "This one's kinda pretty, Matt. Can I have him? You know, just for practice until I get my hands on Sweety Pie?"

"The diamonds," Paul said.

"Okay, already." Marilyn spit a long line of juice into the nearest waste basket. "Ditty and me, we go way back. So's who else he gonna ask when he need someone to do a chow run, stuff like that?"

"I get it," Matthews said. "You do Ditty a favor, he crosses your hands with a reward. And since the only reward he's got is a bunch of diamonds, that's what you get."

Marilyn made another spit. "That's the long and the short of it. So now, do I gonna walk, or what?"

Matthews' cigar flopped from one end of his mouth to the other. He said, "You'll walk, just like I said. Only first we gotta check out your story. You ain't holding back, are you? 'Cause that'd piss me off, you know that."

Marilyn raised her hand. "Scout's honor, Matt."

Paul wasn't so sure. Whores, he never did trust. Pulling Matthews aside, he whispered, "She's got you convinced, huh?"

"Yeah, why not? Sounds like something Ditty might do. And Marilyn. She could'a told a hundred people by now. If the gangbangers get wind of where Ditty's holed up, that he's got a pocket full'a diamonds, they're gonna be on his case in a flash."

Marilyn, listening. "Really, Ditty ain't got all that many diamonds."

Paul turned to her. "What you mean? There hadda be dozens."

Marilyn shook her head. "Uh-uh. He only had a seven or eight from what I could see. 'Less he's holding back on me, which I doubt."

Paul pulled Matthews into the hall. "Remember about Shoestring, the night he was killed? If Ditty did it, how come he hasn't got a load of diamonds?"

Matthews mulled for a second, saying, "Marilyn said he might be holding back."

"No, I don't think so. There's someone else involved, simple as that."

"Maybe," Matthews said. "Only that's not the problem right now. We gotta grab Ditty before the gangbangers get him. They'll pick his bones clean for sure. That happens, won't be a diamond left."

"Well, I gotta agree with you there, but…"

Matthews headed for the door. "Tell you what. I'm gonna head down to the Cabrini. You get on the phone, tell communications to notify all our units to meet me on Division Street, across from the Eleven-sixty building. Soon as you get

Marilyn put away, meet me there."

"With what? All the cars are being used."

"Jesus, I gotta do all your thinking for you? Take your own car and transfer into mine when you get there. And don't worry. I ain't gonna do anything 'til you show."

"You're sure?" Paul said, not wanting to miss Ditty's capture. Matthews looked at Marilyn, and held up his hand. "Scout's honor, huh Mare." He skipped down the staircase.

"All units notified," the dispatcher said.

Paul hung up, thinking about Katie, how he'd told her that he would call when they made headway on the investigation. But it would be stupid to call before they had Caldwell in custody. Still, he'd promised. And what could it hurt? Knowing Matthews, Ditty was probably already surrounded.

"For crying out loud!" he said to no one. "That crazy Bartovich broad's got me doing her bidding, and she ain't even here."

Tommy came up the stairs, a packet of Beachnut in his hand, and said, "You ain't thinking of calling her, are you?"

"I told her I would. What would it look like if I went back on my word?"

Tommy threw up his arms in mock frustration. "As far as your word goes, you could serve heaven on a golden platter, it still wouldn't mean a thing to that broad."

Paul got his notebook out, and leafed back to the page where Katie had scribbled her phone number. As he dialed, he said, "I told her I would. That's all there is to it."

Tommy made a sign of the cross. "Go ahead on. Only don't say I didn't tell you not to."

Paul let the phone ring, again and again. Well, at least he'd tried, and just as he was about to hang up, a click replaced the ringing. Then a loud clank. Paul pressed the receiver tight to his ear, and got the most unwelcome, but familiar, screech for his trouble. He made a mental note. Serbians and Croatians use the same curse words.

"This had better be important," Katie hollered into his ear. "Could this be the high class young lady who goes around making false accusations about police officers?" Paul couldn't resist himself. Besides, he being Croatian and her Serbian, it was his duty.

No distinguishable answer, only a sucking noise which sounded like Marilyn when she had forced her kisses on Tommy's neck. Maybe something was wrong with the connection. "You still there?" Paul said.

"Yes, I'm still here. Where'd you think I was? You're just plain stupid, aren't you?"

But the irritating noise continued.

"What's that sound?" Paul asked.

"If you must know, you made me break my lamp. I cut my hand on it, and I was sucking the blood before it dripped on my bedspread."

"Makes sense," Paul said, "you being the nearest thing to a vampire I've ever met."

There came a pause. Paul wasn't used to this. Could he have finally gotten in the last word on this obnoxious Serbian girl? Doubting it, he said, "Are you still there?" Silence. "Hey! Are you still there?"

"That's all you can say? 'Are you still there? Are you still there?' And you don't have to scream. Oh, that's right, stupid people just naturally yell all the time, don't they?"

"I thought you'd hung up. Or should I say I hoped you'd hung up."

"No, not yet. I was putting a Band-Aid on the grievous injury you've inflicted on me. I'll probably have to go to the emergency room over this. If I do, you'll be hearing about it."

"Give me the name of your hospital. I'll call ahead, make sure they get a straightjacket ready for you."

Paul was still congratulating himself for his latest comeback when more strange noises were heard from the phone. At first he thought Katie was working on her hand again, but when it was repeated he realized she was laughing. Muzzled laughter, but laughter just the same.

"Lord in heaven, she's actually got a sense of humor," he said. "Maybe you're human after all. Serbian-type human, but you can't do anything about that, so I won't blame you."

"I was *not* laughing," she growled. "Enough of this. Just

what is it you want? Because if this is your idea of a joke, we'll just see who's laughing when I get through with you."

"Listen to me, honey," Paul said, remembering how Tommy had irritated her that first day. "I told you I'd call when we arrested Ditty Caldwell. Well, I'm calling. You wanna come down, see I was telling the truth, that he robbed that diamond salesman, that's up to you. We're at the Task Force office."

"You have him there?" she said, sounding concerned.

"Not just yet, but we will before you can get here." Paul gave Tommy a satisfied nod.

Who said, "Listening to you two spar at each other makes me glad I was born Italian, and raised with good common street sense."

Paul had to endure Tommy's, "Street sense," in one ear, and in the other Katie's repeated oaths on what she planned for him if, when she got there, she found one little hair out of place on Ditty's head.

He'd had enough, and shouted into the phone, "Just shut up and listen for a change. I don't have'ta take that kinda abuse from anybody, especially a nutcase like you. I don't know how much longer we're gonna be here, so make up your mind if you're coming or not." He slammed down the receiver, happy to have finally gotten the last word in on her.

"Nice girl. You two make one hell of a match," Tommy said.

"You stay here and watch Marilyn," Paul said. "I'm going down to the Cabrini."

Tommy jumped up, saying, "You can't leave me alone with her."

"Yeah, I can. You two will get along fine, both having such great street sense, and all."

Paul looked at Marilyn, who had a finger crooked at Tommy. Spitting, she said, "Come on over here, hun-nee. Where I can get my hands on you."

Chapter 14

ARRIVING TWO MINUTES BEFORE ELEVEN, Smedley parked on Division Street across from the Cabrini Green projects. He looked up at the sixth floor of the Eleven-sixty building. No doubt Ditty was staring right back at him, and would be down just as ordered. He'd better be.

Enough time out in the open. He pulled deep into the alley. He had to because Task Force cops were everywhere. Although he hadn't seen Matthews and the other two cops since he'd left them grappling with the whore. There were probably at the station house, locking her up. Good, three less cops to worry about, even if it was The Three Stooges.

He walked back to the mouth of the alley to see if Ditty was coming yet. Okay, there he was, peeking out the entranceway of the Eleven-sixty building. Being cautious. Terrified would be a better word, not only of getting picked up by the cops, but of Smedley too.

And that's just the way Smedley wanted him.

He inched back into the alley's depths, watching as Ditty raced across the Cabrini playground, eyes only for the alley. Uh-oh, because here came a cop car, right on Ditty's tail. Ditty seeing nothing, though, and reaching the alley mouth, waded into the darkness, saying, "Where you at?"

Maybe there was still enough time. Smedley hollered, "Come on, hurry."

Ditty ran straight up the alley, and was only a few strides from the limo when the cop car turned into the alley. Ditty stopped dead in his tracks, staring back at the patrol car's headlights like a wandering deer on a lonely country road.

A cop came out of the car, and using his door as a shield, leveled his gun on Ditty. The cop hollering, "Don't make me kill you."

Smedley recognized the voice first, then the cigar, and finally Lieutenant Matthews. Thinking safety first, he thought about running for it, but Matthews looked to be alone. Yeah, he was. Smedley would stay put, see what developed. Maybe an opportunity would present itself.

Ditty stretched his hands above his head, saying, "I give up."

Matthews, with his service revolver cocked and at the ready, moved in behind Ditty, and snatched him by the collar. "Grab some wall," he said, and shoved Ditty against the brick warehouse.

Ditty assumed a submissive position.

Matthews touched his revolver to the side of Ditty's head. "Don't move an inch. Less'n you wanna get dead."

Ditty remained rigid as Matthews made a quick search.

Then came a female voice from the alley mouth. "Don't you hurt that boy."

Smedley looked to see some white broad come running at Ditty and Matthews. Matthews lowered his gun, looking back at the broad. This was Smedley's chance. He took aim on middle of Matthews' back, took a deep breath, held it, and squeezed one off.

The explosion was deafening in the close corners of the alley. While it echoed, Smedley watched as Matthews spun to the hood of his patrol car.

"No, don't shoot," the broad yelled.

Smedley took aim at her chest, but Matthews lurched back to his feet, getting in Smedley's sights, and stumbled toward the broad.

"Run, save yourself," Matthews croaked, blood seeping from his mouth.

Taking aim, Smedley cranked off two more rounds in rapid succession. Matthews' bear-like torso flinched in unison with each blast. Somehow the cop managed to keep his feet, took two more steps, and threw himself on the broad, propelling her backwards. They fell together, the cop's deadweight landing on top of her.

Smedley moved close. He trained the revolver on the cop's back, and was about to finish them both off when another patrol car screeched to a halt on Division Street. "No time," he yelled at Ditty. "Come on, into the limo before it's too late."

Chapter 15

PAUL KNEW SOMETHING WAS DRASTICALLY WRONG when he saw two fire trucks parked on Division Street with their portable flood lights trained on the front wall of the Eleven-sixty building. Two more had the playground lit up, and the alley across the street was teaming with uniformed police officers. Paul counted eight patrol cars, all beaming pulsating blue and red streaks in never ending circles. One of the cars was parked broadside in the middle of the street, blocking traffic.

Paul pulled his pickup alongside.

"Get moving!" the cop hollered, squinting through the glare of Paul's headlights.

Paul stepped onto the street, to show his uniform. "What's going on?" he wondered as much as asked.

"Oh, sorry, Sarge. A Task Force cop's been shot. The shooter's some gangbanger from the Cabrini." He pointed at the Eleven-sixty building. "They're in there now, searching for him."

"Who was the cop that got shot?" Paul said, but knew full well the answer, and jumped back into his pickup, backing away before the policeman could answer.

He drove directly for the nearest hospital with one hand on the steering wheel, the other clutching the confirmation medal chained at his neck, reciting Hail Mary's all the way.

The emergency room parking lot was so jammed with patrol cars Paul had to find a spot on the street. He rushed to the entrance only to find a line of Task Force men watching in glum silence as fire department paramedics carried a rubber bag-filled stretcher out of the emergency room and to a waiting ambulance.

Paul felt lightheaded. He rested on the side of the nearest patrol car. He had rode with Jack Matthews only hours earlier. They'd been through so much together on the streets of Chicago. And now those same streets had taken Matthews, brutally, and without warning.

Paul wanted to believe this was just another of Matthews' sick cop jokes, like when Matthews had sicced Marilyn on

Tommy. That pretty soon the rubber bag was going to fly open and Matthews would jump out laughing and pointing at Paul.

But this was real. Matthews was gone. Gone forever, and Paul felt terribly alone without him. He knew he was about to cry, and turned to leave.

But stopped when one of the Task Force men said, "Let's go splatter us a two legged dog."

And another, "Yeah, we can't let that scumbag get away with this."

"If we don't stand up now, none of us are gonna be safe," said a third man.

Paul stopped short, remembering that abbreviated tour he'd had Vietnam. How on one dark nigh, his platoon had been caught in a crossfire and started taking casualties, Paul included. First the platoon leader, then the First Sergeant had gone down. No hesitation, the next ranking man had assumed his leadership roll, and the rest feel in behind with no question.

"No!" he hollered.

Fourteen Task Force men looked at him in unison. Paul pointed his face to the pavement, taking in a deep breath, knowing tears were streaming down his cheeks. "We lost a friend tonight. I know, you're pissed, so am I. We all wanna go over to that damn Cabrini and rip some hearts out. Only that ain't gonna happen."

A stirring among the men communicated marked outrage.

"I know what you're thinking," Paul said, looking up. "You're Task Force, and can't just stand by. But it's outta our hands. Homicide knows exactly who the shooter is, and they're digging through the Cabrini for that lowlife right now. It's only a matter of time before they make an arrest. Meanwhile we stay the hell outta the way." Paul picked out a man in the front of the crowd, and glared into his eyes. "I'm telling you, get your asses back to the station house, put up your gear, and go on home."

The younger men began to move away, but some of the veterans stood fast. The man who Paul had picked out at the front, saying, "The sergeant's right, boys. Knowing us, if we go in there, pretty soon we're gonna have to fight our way out again. The papers'll be all over us about beating some poor innocent fool's head in. Won't be long the rat who killed the lieutenant will be made out for a martyr."

He walked toward the parking lot, and was soon followed by the rest.

Paul was about to get into his pickup, when he heard, "Hey. I could use a bit of help in here."

Paul looked, and there stood Kyle Debolt at the emergency room entrance. A bit of help? How many times had Paul heard that over the past few years? Well, for once, anyway, Paul was going to leave the idiot flat.

Debolt saying, "I mean it, man. I'm swamped here."

Paul still wanted to go, but couldn't bring himself to, not on this night. Not if there was a chance of grabbing Ditty. Getting that rat alone. Doing to him what needed to be done. That's what was important.

He followed Debolt inside, to a cubical adjacent to the emergency room. Not surprising, Katie was sitting against the wall, her shoulders slumped, and staring down between her knees. Gorgeous, even in a simple short-sleeve blouse and blue jeans.

Debolt took a stance over her with clipboard in hand, and said, "What were you doing there anyway?"

Katie wiped her eyes. "Sergeant Kostovic had told me Ditty Caldwell was about to be arrested, so I went down to the projects. You know the rest."

Debolt looked at Paul. "That true, you told her?"

"I probably shouldn't have, but I'd promised her I'd call if we arrested Ditty. And you know how I feel about cops keeping their word."

He'd keep his word, too. To Matthews.

"Unbelievable," Debolt said. Then to Katie, "That's it then. It was Ditty Caldwell what did the shooting?"

Katie's body convulsed. Between sobs, she said, "I told you it was him. He shot the lieutenant down like he was... was nothing."

"And you'll testify to that in court?"

Katie managed a, "Yes."

"I don't know," Debolt said, dropping his hands to his sides.

"You don't remind me of somebody who'd wanna be a witness against a cop killer."

Still with her head down, Katie said, "I said I'd be there, and I will."

Debolt looked at Paul, saying, "How are we supposed to know that?"

Paul had had enough of Debolt for one night. For one life. Anyway, this wasn't getting him any closer to Ditty. He went to Katie's side, and said, "Dammit, Kyle. She told you, didn't she? What more you want from her?"

Katie's snapped her head up at Paul. Here he was, coming to the dingy broad's defense, and still she had it in for him. He waited, expecting the screeching to start. It didn't come. She just stared into his eyes like a stranger seeing him for the first time. Her hand brushed up his side, coming to rest on his arms. Her fingers encircled his wrist, grasping him tight. She rose to her feet, clinging to him. Resting her head on his chest.

Confusing. Mind boggling, this girl.

"Wait a minute, will ya?" Debolt said, looking shocked even for him.

"Don't worry, I'll see she's in court," Paul said. He walked Katie out of the hospital.

Katie was like a rag doll, the way she let him put her inside the pickup. When he got into the driver's seat, he expected her to tell him where she lived, but she remained silent, almost comatose, as if in a far off place. Paul didn't know what to say, or how, so he just started driving. Yeah, this was best. Sooner or later she'd come out of it.

Katie began to cry, quietly, and she slid over, leaning her head on Paul's shoulder. He hesitated at first, then dropped an arm on her shoulder, and patted her elbow.

She responded by snuggling tight on his side, and whispered, "This kind of thing's only supposed to happen in history books, like D Day, or something."

"I know," Paul said, and he was drawn back to the sight of the body bag being carried to the ambulance. "I can't believe he's gone."

"He saved my life, did you know that? He jumped in front of me just as Ditty shot. I have to go to his wife, tell her what a hero he is… was. You have to take me to her."

Neither one of them able to utter Matthews' name.

Paul pulled to the curb. "Katie," he said, using the softest tone possible and still be heard. "First of all, I don't have the slightest idea where he lived. Come on, there'll be a wake, a funeral. You'll have plenty opportunity to pay your respects."

Katie began sobbing, and attempted to wipe her eyes, which were wet again, before she removed her hand.

Paul didn't know what else to say, so he said, "Where do you live? I'll take you home."

"I do not want to go home," Katie said, emphasizing each word. Something Paul was getting used to whenever she was upset.

"Okay, okay, whatever you want." He sensed this willful girl was about to explode, and didn't want to be the point of her anger. Not again. Not *ever* again if he could help it.

Katie sniffled at him, her voice wavering between words. "It's just that I don't want to be alone. I keep thinking about, about… It was so awful." She looked up at Paul through puffy eyes. "Why is that so hard to understand?"

Paul squeezed her shoulder, and said, "I understand. Just sit back, close your eyes. We'll take a ride."

He drove in no particular direction, just kept going. If it had been anybody else, he would have tried to sooth their pain with idle talk. But he was well schooled with Katie's temper and didn't want to take any chances, maybe set her off.

Thankfully, she remained silent. After awhile she scooted down, laying her head on his lap. Her hand landed on his knee, gripping it. Paul stroked her lovely, long black hair, and was relieved when, as he continued, her grip on his knee slackened.

And then she started, taking long breaths between words. "Lieutenant Math…" She whimpered. "He laid on top of me. He took the bullets meant for me. 'Just play dead,' he told me. God almighty, he had to know he was dying."

She broke into tears again. Paul too, he couldn't help himself. He drove on, both of them blubbering. He stroked her hair, feeling a sense of comradeship with her. Or was it pity? No, not pity. H felt something for her. What he just didn't know.

She quieted then. And finally she slept.

As Paul drove through the cool night, Matthews' face appeared before him. No more nights for that man and his stinky cigar, cool or otherwise. Paul shook his head at this big ugly city that was now his home. It had taken one of the good guys and left behind his killer. Just wasn't fair, none of it.

Keeping up with the sparse traffic, he reflected over the whole set of events which led up to this day. The diamond heist, Shoestring getting killed, the arrest of the whore, the recovery of the diamonds, the discovery of Ditty's hideout. Everything seemed so very inconsequential compared to the murder of Jack Matthews. Paul had had enough. As soon as this was over, he'd turn in his star and point his pickup for home. His mother? He'd just have to deal with her when the time came.

The huge digital clock on top of the Edgewater Beach Hotel emerged over the next rise. Paul hadn't realized how late it had gotten. Another realization hit him. He was exhausted.

He turned around, and drove back toward downtown, telling himself he'd better find a place to lay his head before he ran them into the lake. He looked down at Katie, who was tight against his lap, still quite asleep. Her body emitted a curious warmth, a feeling he'd never felt from any other girl, no matter how close they had gotten to him. Above it all there was this intriguing something about her. Intriguing? Before it was comradeship. Maybe pity. Infuriating was closer to it, when she got going. He'd better never forget that. Like now, her expecting him to keep this up for how long? Forever, knowing her. That was it. He was going to his place, get some shuteye. If she didn't like it, that was just tough.

Back through the Loop he drove, through the tunnel that led under the Central Post Office, onto the spaghetti bowl exchange, and onto the Dan Ryan Expressway. Off on the Eighteenth Street exit, then a few blocks west to his apartment in St. Jerome's Parish. Thankfully, he found a parking space directly in front of his building.

Now Katie, what about her? Maybe he'd better wake her after all. Uh-uh. Knowing her, good chance she'd raise all kinds of grief when she found out he hadn't brought her home. But he couldn't just leave her in the pickup, not in this neighborhood, not any neighborhood in this city.

To hell with it. He scooped her into his arms. When she stirred, he froze, and then she curled against him, like a baby to its mother. Only for how long? He headed up to his apartment, taking each new riser with the greatest of care. Inside, he placed her on his bed, and inch by inch removed his arms from under her feather-like weight, watching her eyes for a sign of recognition when finally he pulled free.

Nothing came.

He placed an extra blanket over her, and stood back, looking around. Where was he to sleep? Really, even if he had a place to lay his head, would he be able to rest? Probably not. Not with Dittybop Caldwell running free. He'd go back to the Cabrini, exhausted or not. With Debolt heading up the investigation, he'd better get there quick, too. Who knew what that clown was going to do next?

At the door he looked back at Katie, nestled deep under the bedspread. No doubt when she woke and discovered where she was at she'd be ready to kill. Well, she wouldn't have him for a target, not this time, because he didn't know when he'd get back here again.

Chapter 16

SMEDLEY, DRIVING THE LIMO through Chicago's late night traffic, said, "Who was the broad?"

"Uh, her? Just some pain in the ass do-gooder," Ditty said. He sunk deeper into his seat as another patrol car went screaming past.

"We got away clean," Smedley said. "So stop your worrying." He turned the limo towards the Drake Hotel. "Back to the broad. Who was she? And don't lie to me, either, 'cause I saw the way she looked at you."

A sarcastic smile came to Ditty's face. "I guess you were too busy offing that cop to hear her screaming, or you'd know why she was looking at me."

"Saving your worthless hide is what I was doing. So what was it she said?"

"What you think she was saying? 'Don't shoot,' that's what. She must'a thought it was me with the gun."

Smedley pictured the dark alley. He'd been back in the shadows when he'd shot the lieutenant. The girl couldn't have seen him. Flashing a smile, he said, "Guess you're right. How's it feel, being a cop killer?"

Ditty popped his head up. "First it was Shoestring, now a cop. Every time you shoot somebody, it's me gets blamed for it."

"Goes with the territory, kid. About the girl. What's her name, and what was she doing there?"

"Jesus!" Ditty said, "All you can think about is that ding-a-ling broad. I'm telling you, she ain't nobody. And anyway, she didn't see you. So don't be worrying about it."

Smedley turned his eyes ice cold, knowing how Ditty would react.

"Okay, okay. Her name's Katie, Katie… hell, I don't know. She works at the Cabrini Legal Aid Office." Ditty pulled a card out of his pants pocket. "Here," he said. "There's her name and address. Call and see for yourself."

Smedley put the card in his breast pocket without so much as a glance. "You called her, didn't you? Yeah, you called her all right. I'll bet you were gonna turn state's witness, have her get the cops after me." Smedley nodded at the limo's windshield, agreeing with his hypothesis.

Ditty slumped back down. "All right," he said. "I was scared, so I called the broad. But no way was I gonna give you up. I wouldn't do that, not to anybody."

Smedley turned the corner. The Drake Hotel's forty-some stories loomed in front of him. "Bullshit!" he said. "If I was in your place, I sure would." He shot Ditty his best evil smile. "Too late now though, ain't it? And anyhow, it don't make no difference. Soon as this one last job's done our little partnership will be over?"

"I've been wondering about that," Ditty said. "Just what you got in mind for me?"

Smedley didn't answer. He was thinking about the broad from the alley and how she might affect his plan. The plan, that was what was important. He'd get tonight over, then depending how it went, he'd find out if the broad was a threat to him. If so, she'd have to go.

He parked at the side entrance to the hotel as a teenage girl was getting out of the passenger side of a Lincoln Continental. Dressed in a prom dress, she stepped up to Ditty's tinted glass window, and checked her makeup. A boy in a white tuxedo, with a pink carnation mounted in its lapel got out of the Continental's driver's seat. He stood over the girl's shoulder.

"You gotta love these limos," Smedley said. "Perfect for robbing and stealing with their one way windows."

"Yeah, just great," Ditty said, looking like he wanted to make a run for it.

Smedley wasn't going to let that happen. Not a chance.

"Hurry up, Betty. Everybody's waiting," the boy said.

"Just a sec," Betty told her boyfriend as she brushed her eyelashes. "Nice couple, huh?" Smedley said.

"Yeah, nice," Ditty said. "So what're we doing here?"

"We're gonna rob us some more diamonds, what else?"

"I figured as much. So where do I come in?"

Saying it deadpan. This kid was ready to run, no doubt about it.

Which forced Smedley to activate the next stage of his plan.

He said, "That's just it. You don't come in. In fact this is where you go out."

He flicked his arm, striking a crushing jab to Ditty's adam's apple. Ditty recoiled forward holding his neck, and gagging for air. Smedley delivered a rabbit punch to the back of Ditty's neck, then another, pounding Ditty's head between his legs.

Ditty, back up and gagging, yanked at the door latch, but no matter how hard he pulled it would not open.

"No use, kid," Smedley said, certain that he was in command. "That's another reason I go for these limos, the way you can control everything right here from the driver's seat."

He struck again, this time with a hammer-like elbow to Ditty's face, and felt bones give way as Ditty collapsed against Betty's window. She and her boyfriend inches away, arm in arm, nipping lips. Unknowing.

Smedley said, "See, Betty, how my partner tried double crossing me? I mean, what could I do? For sure, he was planning on taking the loot and skipping out on me."

She gave the boy a hug, and they walked away arm in arm.

"See how folks can be, Ditty boy?" Smedley said. "Just don't give a damn." He pressed a finger to Ditty's neck, feeling for a pulse. Weak and erratic. Smedley estimated that he had at least an hour before Ditty would be coming out of it. "I wasn't lying," he said to the limp body. "I do need you. Well your body, not necessarily you."

He pushed the button that controlled the glass partition dividing the limo's front seat and the passenger compartment. When it came fully open he heaved Ditty over the seat, letting him crumble to the rear floorboards.

"Okay, here we go," he said, and stepped outside.

Betty and her boyfriend were snuggling when he went past. He caught Betty's eye, and gave her a wink. Giggling, she winked back as he headed for the hotel. Straightening the tie he'd removed from Halfpint's body, he stopped at the entrance to the hotel's lounge. He scanned the bar area. There Randolph Laidlaw was, on the same stool as last night. His own private perch.

"Mister Laidlaw," Smedley called, using a submissive tone.

Laidlaw spun on his stool, skidding to a stop facing Smedley. "Don't you move," he hollered, and lurched from the bar, bouncing off two tables as he stumbled across the floor. Arriving in front of Smedley, he braced himself against the wall, and blurted out, "What'd you run for last night?" Smelling the booze on Laidlaw's breath, Smedley couldn't believe his luck. Just too perfect. He held out Henry's diamond wallet in clenched hands, gulped, and made a terrified face.

Laidlaw pried open Smedley's hands, exposing "HS" stenciled on the cover of the wallet. Laidlaw smiled. The fool thought he had Smedley exactly where he wanted him. Smedley recoiled, just to give Laidlaw an added measure of confidence.

"Where'd you get Henry's diamond wallet," Laidlaw said.

Smedley ripped the wallet away, and shoved it into his coat pocket. He said, "Look, I'm sure you're a nice man, Mister Laidlaw. But it's Mister Shakleford I gotta talk to. So if you don't mind…"

"I talked to Henry right after you ran out of here last night," Laidlaw said. "He's authorized me to talk for him."

Smedley knew Laidlaw was lying, but had to keep up his act. Last night the submissive Chinaman routine had worked so very well, so he slumped forward, saying, "About my reward?"

"Yeah, sure," Laidlaw said, as he panned up and down the hallway. "But we can't talk here. Too many ears."

"I don't know…" Smedley bolted out of the lounge, down the hall, hurrying through the arcade of shops and boutiques, back out the side entrance to the street. He stopped at the limo's driver's door, his hands at the door like he was using a key. All while he used his peripheral vision to confirm that Laidlaw was coming.

More than coming. He was standing just inside the hotel's entrance, fingering the same bulge beneath his shirt that Smedley had seen last night. Uh-oh, maybe too long Laidlaw was standing. Had Smedley enticed the dope enough to come out of the safety of the hotel? Smedley wasn't sure. He had to do something quick or take a chance on losing Laidlaw altogether.

"Hey!" he yelled at Betty and the crowd of teenage prom-goers. "Whoever Betty is, I'm leaving without you if I don't see you pretty soon."

Betty gave him a confused stare, but Laidlaw didn't see it. He pushed through the revolving doorway, and ran up to the curb. "Like I told you before," he said. "I called Henry and explained about last night, that you were asking for him."

Smedley waved Laidlaw off. "Forget it. I'll do my business with Mister Shakleford."

"Hey, I'm trying to make a deal here," Laidlaw said. "Henry told me if you've got his diamonds, well, I was authorized to give you a reward."

Smedley counted with each breath, one, two, three, four, and at five, gave Laidlaw the best hope-filled face he could muster. "Reward?" he said. "What kinda reward?"

Laidlaw's anxiety disappeared, and was replaced with his natural self absorbed ego. "Well, that all depends. You know, on what you've got."

This time Smedley counted to ten, then reached into his coat pockets, and pulled out Henry's diamond wallets, two in each hand. "This is what I got," he said, making his voice waver.

"Are you nuts? Put that stuff away." Laidlaw rubbernecked at the crowd of teenagers.

"Why?" Smedley said, acting innocent. "It ain't like I done anything wrong. All I wanna do is return these diamonds, maybe collect a little reward for my trouble. You did say I had a reward coming, right?"

Laidlaw lay an arm around Smedley's shoulder, saying, "Listen, why not come up to my hotel room? I'll check the merchandise. Depending what's there, I'll give you your reward."

Smedley stepped back a pace, feinting suspicion. "What you take me for?" he said, and hurried to the driver's side of the limo. Looking back at Laidlaw, he said, "Let's just forget the whole thing." He stepped into the limo, slamming the door behind him.

Hidden behind the one-way windows, he watched in total confidence as Laidlaw yanked open the passenger's door, and leaned in.

"What are you so paranoid about?" Laidlaw said. "You don't think I'm gonna rob you or something, do you?"

Smedley switched on the ignition. Looking steadfast through the windshield, he said, "Close the door and go away." He shoved the gear shift into drive.

"Wait! Wait!" Laidlaw hollered. He brushed his hand on the bulge under his shirt, hesitated, and slid onto the seat next to Smedley. Drawing the door closed behind him, he pulled a roll of cash from his pants pocket. "Look," he said. "I got your reward right here."

Brimming with satisfaction, Smedley eased the limo away from the curb. He made a quick U-turn, drove across the intersection, and flipped up the nearest alley, parking in a dark corner with Laidlaw's side of the limo flush to a brick wall. Snapping off the ignition, he said, "Never were in the service, were you, Randy?"

"Huh," Laidlaw said, forcing a nervous laugh.

Smedley pulled the cop's .38 from under the seat. He pointed the muzzle at Laidlaw's nose, and said, "Dammit, answer me when I'm talking to you." Just for fun, he gave Laidlaw a violent jab in the face with the barrel.

Laidlaw cupped his flattened nose in his hands, and played peekaboo through his fingers at the gun's muzzle.

Smedley gave him the same evil eyes that he'd used on Ditty. "I guess you know you just made the biggest mistake of your life," he said.

Words quaking, Laidlaw said, "Whatever you want, take it. I'm not going to give you any trouble."

Smedley placed the .38 under Laidlaw's chin, pushed him back against the side window, and cocked the hammer back. "I want you to answer my question, is what I want. Was you ever in the service?"

Laidlaw, groveling, "Uh—I had some ROTC in college. That's about it."

"You, an officer? Not a chance. Well, maybe a shitty one. You kinda remind me of this Second Louie we once had in the Ninth Marines. He went chasing into the bush by himself, after a couple'a gooks. I don't know, maybe the dummy figured he'd make himself a hero. Those gooks set up an ambush. Blew him away, they did." Smedley shrugged. "Turned out that Louie was right. He was a hero, only a dead hero. Now in your case, you can be forgiven, seeing as I did such a sweet job of bullshitting you outta the hotel."

Laidlaw pulled his shirt out of his pants, exposing his money belt. "Go ahead, take it. There's plenty there. Just don't hurt me anymore." And when Smedley stared back at him, Laidlaw said, "I can get you more, if that's what it takes."

Smedley looked back at the mouth of the alley, which was vacant. He had time, and turning back to Laidlaw, said, "More?"

A glimmer of hope shown on Laidlaw's face. He said, "I know this other diamond salesman from New York. He's ten times bigger than me. I can set him up for you. It'd be easy, and when you're done, I'd even buy the stuff off you. Give you a good deal, too."

"Tut, tut, selling your friends out," Smedley said. "First Henry and now you. All you diamond hustlers must be alike."

He squeezed the trigger, exploding a .38 caliber round through the brash diamond salesman's throat.

Smedley would have liked to listen to Laidlaw's offer, but knew it would just give him ideas, ideas that would prolong the operation. Not an option. With time a factor, he got the limo going, and headed back in the same direction he and Ditty had just come. Off to his right the night sky over the projects was lit up with flashing blue and red lights. The cops, looking for Ditty. Good, because now there was less chance of being interrupted while he was finishing his night's work.

He turned up a predesignated side street, drove in two blocks, past a line of warehouses, parking in a secluded field that bordered the North Branch of the Chicago River. He ran the driver's door window down, turned off the ignition, looked and listened. No one around, the only sound a soft undertone supplied by an army of crickets. He'd expected as much, because the night before he had scouted this same spot.

He went to the back door. With one last look around, he dragged Ditty's still unconscious body out of the rear compartment, and stuffed it into the driver's seat. He pulled the money belt from around Laidlaw's body, and one after another opened its compartments. Man, he'd hit the mother lode, because each was filled with diamonds of every shape and color. He emptied the diamonds into his own pants pockets, then threw the money belt at Ditty's feet. He placed the .38 in Laidlaw's hand, curling Laidlaw's limp index finger onto the trigger. Taking care, he twisted the barrel around so that it was pointed towards Ditty's side of the car. Then making sure it was pointing in the direction from which Laidlaw lay, he pulled the trigger. Ditty's body jerked as the bullet skimmed past his side, embedding itself in the driver's door.

Smedley set the gun down between Laidlaw's legs, and stepped back to take in the scene. Laidlaw was sprawled in the passenger's seat, with Ditty behind the steering wheel.

"I told you I needed you," he said to Ditty. "I just didn't tell you what for."

He leaned into the car, and twisted the ignition key, firing the limo to life, then shoved the gear shift into drive, and stepped back. The oversized vehicle rolled forward, picking up speed as it rode over the wooden pylon bank. With one big whoosh, it splashed into the river. For a moment it bobbed in the murky water, but soon sunk into the depths.

Smedley took a few extra seconds to watch the whirlpool subside, then turned and walked to his waiting BMW. He drove into the night satisfied that everything had gone just as planned. It would be awhile before the cops found the limo. When they did it would look as though Ditty had made a bungled attempt at robbing Laidlaw, and that Laidlaw had tried to grab the gun from Ditty's hand, wounding the kid, and in the process, getting shot himself. They'd think that during the fracas the limo rolled into the river, trapping Ditty inside, drowning him.

Smedley's only worry was the girl from the alley. He pulled out the card Ditty had said was hers. Now, with his adrenaline beginning to recede, he wondered if he should check this girl out, see just how much Ditty had told her.

Yes, of course he should. He'd worked this operation out to the last detail, and had made it work perfectly. No broad was going to foul it up, especially when he was so very close to the end.

Chapter 17

Paul checked his watch for the third time in the last ten minutes. Just going on four in the morning. And here he was sitting in the Cabrini Green playground, helplessly watching Debolt and a small platoon of uniform cops scurrying in and out of the Eleven-sixty building. Obviously Ditty hadn't been found yet. Knowing Debolt, Paul wanted to be here if they did. Even with Katie as an eyewitness, Debolt was just the type to do something stupid, make it easy for some slick attorney to get Ditty off on a bullshit technicality.

If Debolt failed to find Ditty, Paul planned to pick the idiot's tiny brain, see in what direction he was going. Probably nowhere.

And about Ditty. So many things didn't add up. First off, Paul would never have made Ditty for a cop killer. But Katie was right there and saw him pull the trigger. An irrefutable eyewitness in anybody's book.

Made Paul want to rage, Lieutenant Matthews snuffed out like that. When Paul got his hands on Ditty, well, it wasn't going to be pretty.

Hold on. He had just been thinking about the probability of Debolt screwing up. Now, here he was ready to beat the hell out of Ditty, take a chance on losing the entire case on some brutality beef. Why, Paul didn't know, but his mother popped into his head with one of the sayings she was so famous for. "Don't get mad, get even."

Like always, mom was right. Paul had better get his head straight if he was going to revenge the lieutenant.

The police radio in the patrol car sitting alongside Paul buzzed static, and the radio dispatcher said, "Come in, One-eight-seven-oh."

Nothing.

Paul had to laugh. Eighteen-seventy, Joe Holloway and Volly Dickman's call sign. Those two bums, probably in the hole someplace, sleeping like babies.

Again the dispatcher called, and finally Volly's raspy answer, "This is Eighteen-seventy. Sorry, Squad. We had us a little tussle with a couple'a whores. Couldn't get away 'til now."

A cop came up on the air. "That old fart's lying. They were getting laid in the back of that paddy wagon again."

Somebody else said, "Yeah, and believe it or not, those two actually pay for it."

After the hooting and hollering died down, the dispatcher came back on. "Eighteen-seventy, go to Schiller and the river. You got a floater."

"Ten-four, on the way, Squad," Volly said.

The dispatcher again. "Any Homicide unit available to assist Eighteen-seventy?"

No answer.

Paul took the microphone from the patrol car. "This is Task Force Sergeant Kostovic, Squad. They're all busy at the Cabrini. With the search."

"Ten-four," the dispatcher said. "Sarge, I got nobody else. Could you take a ride over there and supervise?"

Paul looked at the Eleven-sixty building, where nothing positive seemed to be happening. If it did, he'd hear it on Volly and Joe's radio. "Sure, Squad. On the way."

Paul arrived to find Volly standing outside the paddy wagon's passenger door, hollering at Joe Holloway who remained inside, comatose, and snoring like a dozen foghorns. Giving up on screeches Volly switched to shoves and punches. After a particularly swift elbow to the back of the head, Joe sprung awake. With both hands braced against the dashboard, his eyes bulging, he said, "Voll. What happened? They shooting over at the Cabrini again?"

"We got a job, you sack'a shit," Volly said.

"What kinda job, you gotta holler like your mammy calling you for bar-b-q?"

"Kiss my shiny black ass." Volly walked to the edge of the river. Hands on his wide hips, he said, "Oh, for Chrissakes."

Joe followed behind, stretching. "What'd I do now?" he said.

"Not you, you idiot. Look, in the water."

Paul got out of his pickup, and stepped up alongside Volly

and Joe. There, just a few feet from water's edge, was a body floating face down, bobbing along in the gentle current.

Joe gave Volly a jab in the ribs. "Tell him there's no swimming allowed around here, partner."

"Go ahead, make stupid," Volly said straight-faced. "Only remember, it's us that's gotta drag Mister Aquanaut outta the soup."

Joe shrugged. "What's the big deal? You act like this is the first floater you've ever run across."

"Think, Joe," Volly said. "By the time we get through, it'll pretty near be lunch time before we get off."

"Oh, man. No way I'm gonna make it that long without my Budweiser."

Volly picked up a handful of stones, and lobbed one at the body. He missed on the first few tries, then got the range. Soon he was pelting the body with regularity. Joe picked up his own stones, and joined in. In no time the water was splashing, and the floater started drifting.

Paul said, "Dammit, let's get this over with so I can get back to the Cabrini."

"Hold your horses," Volly said. "I got me an idea." He ran to the paddy wagon, and grabbing the noose they used to catch wild dogs, hurried back.

"What you gonna do with that thing?" Joe said.

"You'll see." Volly poked the floater with the noose's wooden handle, pushing away from the shore.

"Good job," Joe said, throwing up his arms. "Now you made it just that much harder to get hold..." Joe's voice trailed off, and laughing, he said, "You're no good, you know that?"

Paul just shook his head.

Volly gave the body one more good shove. It drifted outward into the river. "Perfect," he said, and went to the paddy wagon, saying proudly into the radio, "Eighteen-seventy, Squad. You was right about that floater, only it's way out in the middle of the river. We tried like hell, but no chance reaching it. Better call the Coast Guard."

Paul would have protested, but wanted to get back to the Cabrini. Anyway, who cared about one more floater in the Chicago River?

The dispatcher came back on, saying, "Ten-four, One-eight-seven-oh. Stand by."

Volly produced a surprised look. "Stand by? For what? The Coast Guard ain't gonna need us, and it's almost time to go home."

"You never know, Seventy. If nothing else, you can direct them to where the body's at."

Volly cursed under his breath. "Damn! We're right back in the same shitbag we started from."

Then from Joe, who had wandered into a thicket of weeds. "Hey, Volly. Get yourself over here, see what I found."

"Now what?" Volly said. Frustration showing, he looked up at the flickering early morning stars. "Lord, why is it me what's gotta do everything around here?" He hollered at his partner, "I spoze now you want me to hold your donger for you, so's you can take a piss."

"Nu-uh. This is serious shit. You too, Pauly. Come and see."

Volly stormed at Joe, hollering along the way, "Damn it, you're the white guy. Me, I'm the black dude. Don't you pay attention when you go to the movies? You're spoze to be the smart one, do all the thinking. I just carry on, do a little tap dance, some singing. In the end get my head shot off." Volly pushed some branches aside, and came to where Joe was standing.

As Paul joined Volly, the wagon man said in a huff, "Okay, what?"

Joe took two steps to the side, and pointed into the bushes. There on the ground, with his head between his knees, sat Ditty Caldwell.

Joe said, "Ain't that the dude what spoze to've killed Lieutenant Matthews?"

Paul rushed to Ditty's side, checking for a pulse.

From his rear, Volly said, "Joe, you cluck, you. Here I been doing my damnedest to get us off this job. And now, thanks to you, we gonna be on it 'til who knows when."

"No, you won't," Paul said. "I'll take over from here."

A stupefied expression appeared on Joe's face. "Screw it," he said. "Let's dump the asshole in the river. Seeing as the Coast Guard's coming to get one floater, we might as well make it two."

Ditty snapped his head up at Joe, giving him a horrified look.

Paul told him, "Don't worry, kid. I ain't gonna let nobody throw you back in the water."

Ditty made a nervous nod of the head, but kept a vigilant eye on Joe.

"Damn, Joe," Volly said. "You got the kid scared shitless. Go ahead, tell him he don't have'ta worry."

Joe would not answer. He just stood there staring at Ditty, looking aggravated.

"I think I been knifed," Ditty said. He showed Paul a gash on his side.

Paul took his flashlight from his gun belt, and trained it on Ditty's side. "That's a gunshot wound, and from up close, too. You'll be okay, though. It's just a scratch." And thinking out loud, "Who the hell shot you?"

Ditty looked thoughtful, but would not answer.

Paul figured as long as Joe was there he wasn't going to get anything of out of Ditty. "Joe, go call for an ambulance."

Joe mumbled something under his breath about Budweiser, and headed for the paddy wagon.

Paul waited until Joe was out of earshot, and restarted on Ditty. "What happened here?"

Ditty shook his head.

Paul tried again. "There's a dude out in the river floating face down, and he ain't never gonna tell how he got there. What you know about that?"

Still nothing from Ditty.

Joe returned, saying, "They're on the way."

Which wasn't going to help Ditty loosen up. Paul decided to give up for now. He'd continue once they got Ditty into the station house.

It only took a few minutes before the ambulance arrived. Volly threw a set of handcuffs on Ditty, and he and Joe got him up and into the ambulance.

Paul told the paramedics, "Take him to the Henrotin. Joe, you ride with them. Me and Volly will stay here with the body."

"Wait a minute," Volly said. "I mean, me'n Joe, we're partners. Where Joe goes, so do I."

"You're staying," Paul said. He couldn't trust those two idiots together.

And then a Coast Guard cutter came chugging up the river. Paul watched in admiration as they located the floater with no help from him, and were already in the process of fishing it out. A net was dropped into the water. When it was hoisted out, the floater came with it.

"Me'n Joe, we gotta get us one'a those nets," Volly said. "Seems like ever time we try yanking some damn floater outta the drink it ends up squishing into two, maybe three pieces."

The Coast Guard cutter swung around, and drifted to within a few feet of where Volly was standing. "You do good work, boys," Volly yelled. "Take it on down to the morgue, will ya?"

Which sounded good to Paul. This way he could get over to the hospital and get to work on Ditty. The floater, he could check out any time.

A first class petty officer hollered from the conning tower. "Don't try none of that bullshit on us, copper. This guy's all yours." He craned the net so that the floater was hanging just above Volly's head.

Volly had to make a quick move or the body would have landed on his head. Looking up at the petty officer, he shouted, "Hey, you can handle a simple-ass floater just as good as I can."

The petty officer lowered the net to just below Volly's eye level. "Take a good look," he said, smiling.

Paul pushed past Volly, and steadied the net. The body was laying face up, exposing a neat round hole in the bottom of its chin.

"See," the petty officer said to Volly. "What you got here is a homicide, pure and simple. Or as you so eloquently put, simple-ass homicide." He lowered the body the rest of the way to the ground.

Volly hollered at the petty officer even as he maneuvered the boat back into the river, "Hey, come on back here. This ain't no murder. It's a plain old suicide."

The petty officer, as he got the cutter turned down stream. "Sure, first the poor slob shoots himself in the head. Then he jumps in the river just for extra measure. See ya, pal."

Volly kicked the floater in the knee. "You dog, you," he told its unseeing eyes. "I hope you know you've ruined the shit outta my day."

"Shut up a minute," Paul said. He made a cursory check of the body, getting an overall mental picture. It was a man in his mid-forties, dressed in an expensive suit. Had a large diamond ring on the pinky finger of his right hand, a gold bracelet on one wrist, and a Rolex on the other. All of which indicated he had not been a robbery victim. Paul bent low, and inspected the gunshot wound under the chin. The bullet's trajectory was upwards, into the head. Therefore he must have been shot from close range. That or the victim was looking straight up at the time. Not very likely.

Okay, so what else? He rifled through the floater's pockets, looking for identification. Finding nothing in the suit coat, he switched to the pants pockets. All empty except for a waterlogged business card. Its printing was illegible, but when Paul held it up to the early morning light, he made out a large diamond-like design centered across its top.

Jesus! The diamond salesman.

Paul took a good look at the floater's face. He didn't recognize it, but the body had been in the water for hours, maybe, and Paul had only seen Henry Shakleford that one time, just after the robbery. It had to be him. What the hell was going on?

He pulled out the rest of the floater's pockets, hoping to learn something more. Nothing, except a gold plated money clip that contained a wide roll of paper money. Paul counted out over five hundred dollars.

He looked up at Volly, whose body was sagging. Paul stuffed the cash into his breast pocket, and said, "I know what you're thinking, old man. You just let big bucks fall through your fingers, right?"

Volly pressed his fingers to his barrel chest. "Not me, never," he said.

"Sure, Voll. Look, I gotta go see what Ditty's got to say for himself. I'll get somebody to bring your partner back. As soon as he gets here, I want you to take the floater over to the morgue, got it?"

Volly smiled. "That's it? No reports? No waiting for homicide dicks to show up?"

"Yeah, that's it. You can call it a day soon as the morgue signs for the body."

"Great, then me'n Joe, we'll have plenty'a time to go out—" Volly stopped short, then started again "—go home and get some rest."

Paul laughed. "Yeah, go on home, Voll, get yourself some sleep." He headed toward his pickup.

Hurrying to catch up, Volly hollered, "Pauly, wait a minute. You gotta do me a tiny favor."

Paul stopped. "What now?"

Volly sported a sheepish grin. "Uh, that five hundred you got off the floater, uh…"

"Yeah, what about it? Don't tell me you want me to divvy it up with you and Joe?"

"No, no. I know you better than that, Pauly. It's just that, well, you know me'n Joe, and all…"

"Talk, man. Time's a wasting."

"Okay, okay. Listen, you don't have'ta tell Joe about the cash, do you? You know how it is."

Paul laughed. "Sure, Voll. Don't you worry. Joe'll never know, not from me anyhow. Could be he'd murder your ass if I did. And I wouldn't want two good cops like you and Joe busting up 'cause of me. It'd eat on my conscience."

Chapter 18

PAUL DIDN'T WANT TO TALK TO DITTY without having a grasp of what had taken place by the river, so on the way to the hospital he took time out to think.

Okay, the diamond salesman was dead. Only why? Go with what you know and start from the beginning. Ditty and Shoestring had robbed the diamond salesman, that was a fact. But from day one the robbery hadn't added up. Ditty and Shoestring were low class street thieves, would not even consider a diamond heist, not by themselves anyway. Had to be somebody else, somebody with a little class, somebody who knew about diamonds. Even more so, knew diamond salesmen and how they operate. A few Cabrini thieves came to mind but just as quickly were discounted. They wouldn't have any more idea what to do with diamonds than Ditty would. Paul hated to admit it, but maybe Debolt had been right when he said Ditty and Shoestring had simply picked out the first Cadillac they saw and smashed its window. Bingo, they hit the jackpot.

Paul mulled this over in his head, trying out the many possibilities. Conceivable. Afterwards, when Ditty and Shoestring get back to the Cabrini and check their take from the robbery, they go apeshit. Then they come down to earth and realize diamonds aren't something they can unload at the local pawn shop like a television or a stereo. So they get the bright idea the only way they're ever going to make some cash out of the deal is to sell the goods back to the salesman they just robbed. Yeah, Ditty was a gangbanger long before he partnered up with Shoes, and knows his way around the extortionist game. He just might try it. And that would explain what Shoestring was doing when he got killed that night. Ditty sent him for a meet with the salesman, or better yet, some thug the salesman hired to do his dirty work. The deal goes wrong, probably because Ditty and Shoestring held back some or all of the diamonds. Bang, bang, Shoestring gets his ass plugged. This also explained how Ditty had diamonds to give to Marilyn.

Paul didn't quite know if he accepted this notion, not totally, but it made a lot more sense than Debolt's theory, that Ditty killed Shoestring over the diamonds.

So anyway Ditty holes up in the Cabrini. That part Paul knew for sure. Marilyn had verified it, and where else would he go? Ditty couldn't stay there forever, though, not without some heavy cash. So he schedules another meet with the salesman to deliver the goods, this time by himself. That's when Lieutenant Matthews sees him coming out of the Cabrini. Matthews corners Ditty in the alley, and with nothing to lose, Ditty turns on Matthews, gets lucky, and kills him.

Dumb luck? Maybe, but not smart, leaving Katie alive. Something about what happened in that alley didn't quite wash, but again, hadn't the Katie said she saw Ditty do it? Why would she lie? It had to have been him, that's all there was to it.

Okay, so then Ditty makes the meet with the salesman, only something goes wrong. Maybe the salesman tries to cheat Ditty. There's a tussle. The salesman gets shot. Ditty too, and when the salesman falls into the river, he drags Ditty in with him. Paul wasn't sure if this was exactly how it had happened. First of all, how did they get to the river, and why? He was fairly sure he was close, though. Given time, he'd work it out.

He parked at the emergency door entrance to the Henrotin Hospital. Okay, that's the angle he'd use on Ditty. If something else came up he'd just have to adjust as he went along.

With newfound confidence, he started for the emergency room, but just then something flashed out of the corner of his eye. On the sidewalk, about a half block down, somebody was pushing a mobile stretcher, the kind commonly used in hospitals to transport bedridden patients. Whoever it was and the mobile stretcher were going in the opposite direction, and in a hurry.

The computer in Paul's brain kicked in, calling up a database crammed with years of experience on the streets of Chicago. Meshed in its memory bank was a program that sorted out what was fact and what was not. Fact, mobile stretchers were often used to transport patients outdoors to waiting ambulances. But ambulances were parked directly outside the emergency door, not down the street a few blocks.

No compute.

Paul was about to turn off the computer, use common street sense and leg power to make the final analysis when Joe Holloway came running through the hospital's swinging door, and crashed over Paul. Finding himself flat on the pavement, Paul felt like an unsuspecting quarterback who had been blind sided by a gorilla-sized linebacker.

Joe scratched his way to his feet, stomped on Paul's face with what had to be a size thirteen, triple-D shoe, and chased after the man with the mobile stretcher.

Putting together the rest of the facts didn't require a computer, human type or otherwise. Paul stumbled up, and got going in the right direction.

Joe, up ahead, and screaming at the top of his lungs, "Come on, Pauly. It's that Ditty kid. He got away!"

No shit! Paul raced after them.

With those long, skinny legs, Joe was actually starting to narrow the gap. Within a few feet, he took a flying leap, and landed on Ditty's back. Joe's momentum carried then both onto the stretcher. Joe was flailing his long arms and legs, trying to keep from falling off and hold on to Ditty at the same time.

Paul could hardly believe it, because they rode on for some fifty yards, Ditty screaming at the top of his lungs, Joe too. That is until the stretcher veered off and smashed into the side of somebody's brand new Lincoln Continental. Ditty and Joe were catapulted onto the Continental's hood, landing together in a tangled mass.

Before Paul could get there, Ditty scooted off. Hitting the ground at full tilt, he disappeared around the corner.

Paul knew he had no chance of catching Ditty, and started back for the patrol car, to put out an all call. Only what for? This neighborhood was the equivalent to Ditty's backyard. The kid had a hundred hideouts. No way anybody would be able to find him. Another reason. The important one to Paul— if other cops got their hands on Ditty, Debolt would have to be involved. He wanted Ditty for himself.

Still breathing hard, he hurried up to Joe, who was just then rolling off the Continental's hood.

Joe showed Paul a skinned elbow, saying, "How much injured-on-duty time you think I can get outta this?"

"You let him get away," Paul said, wheezing.

Joe, as if he'd just remembered. "How'd he do that, anyhow?"

Paul, still breathless. "How am I supposed to know. What I do know is you, which tells me maybe you weren't watching him too close."

Joe, losing interest again. "Know what? I think maybe I broke something. You're my witness, Pauly. You know, for the medical board."

Paul heard crying coming from inside the Continental. When he looked, a teenage boy was struggling to pull up his pants in the rear seat. With him was a young girl, who was scrambling to drag a party dress over exposed hips. The boy was rubbing his hand on his pant leg, as if to erase some unseen stain.

"You two okay?" Paul said.

"I am," the boy said. "How about you, Betty?"

The girl ducked her head behind the seat. "I will be as soon as you get me out of here."

The boy climbed into the front seat.

"Your car, it's scratched up pretty good. Don't you wanna report made on the damages?"

"Tomorrow will be just fine," the boy said, and he drove off, still wiping his hand on his pants.

Joe, smiling. "Nice kids, huh? My third wife's name was Betty. A Scotch drinker. Too expensive. I hadda dump her."

"Forget that, dammit." Paul went face to face with Joe. "And save that injured shit for the brass, you idiot. Just tell me, how in the hell Ditty got away? I mean, he was shot for crying out loud."

"Aw, it turned out to be just a nick."

"Still, you had him handcuffed." And then Paul remembered who he was dealing with. "Or did you take them off?"

"Not a chance. What you take me for, anyway?" Joe pointed at the stretcher, where one half of Volly's handcuffs was locked to its broken frame.

Paul fingered the chain to the missing half, finding that it had rusted through.

Joe said matter-of-factly, "I ain't never seen handcuffs rust through like that. How bout you?"

Paul had not, but since they belonged to Volly it almost made sense. "Okay, so you had Ditty cuffed. That don't mean you didn't have to stand guard on him."

Joe said, "I'll be damned if I know what happened," scratching the back of his neck. "One second we was talking, you know, about Lieutenant Matthews, and the next thing I know…"

"Wait a minute. You telling me Ditty admitted he did the shooting?"

"Nah. Not exactly, he didn't."

"Come on, Joe. Just exactly what did he say?"

Joe wiped a bloody elbow on his ruined police shirt. "I don't know. I heard they got an eyewitness says it was him, so what's the difference?"

Paul held Joe's shoulders as a father might his wayward son. "Forget what you heard and concentrate," he said.

Joe's brow twitched low, obscuring his bloodshot eyes. "All right, let's see. At first Ditty wouldn't say nothing. Then all of a sudden I couldn't shut him up. I wasn't much listening, though, so I'm not real clear on it. He was going on about how it was somebody else killed Matthews." Joe's eyes reappeared. "Yeah, right. Like I was supposed to believe him."

"He denied it then."

"Yeah, blamed it on somebody called—let me think— Smedley, I think it was. Yeah, I couldn't forget a name like that. It was Smedley, I'm sure of it."

Paul stepped away, trying to file this new information into his computer. Ditty saying he hadn't kill the lieutenant didn't mean a lot. Wrongdoers usually denied their involvement in crimes, even when caught red-handed. But Ditty had gone a step further, naming who he said was the real shooter. Paul used a criteria when he had worked Homicide: If the accused was vague, he was probably making up lies. But if he got specific, named names, he was probably telling the truth.

He turned back to Joe. "Did Ditty say anything else about this Smedley guy, like what he looked like?"

Joe rubbed his elbow. "Not really. Only that he had a Ka-bar knife." His brow went low again. "The hell is a Ka-bar knife, anyhow?"

"Forget that. Give, will ya?"

"Yeah, uh, lemme see. Ditty was surprised Smedley didn't use the knife on Lieutenant Matthews instead of a gun, the alley being so dark and all."

Paul didn't think this bit of information was of any importance. "Anything else?" he said, trying to drag something worthwhile out of Joe.

"He didn't get a chance. That's when I went and got myself some coffee, you know, by the nurses' station. When I come back, the punk's halfway out the door."

"Then that's all you know?"

"Yeah. Ain't it a bitch, Ditty running off and all?"

Paul shook his head. "It's a bitch all right. The brass is gonna be pissed. What you gonna tell them?"

Joe's face went blank. "I don't know. What if we didn't tell them anything?"

"Think, Joe. The hospital. They keep records on their patients."

"Oh, yeah, right." Joe chewed on his lip. "Wait! They were super busy at the emergency room. I never did get around to signing Ditty in."

Paul, thinking this might just work. "Okay, then. Let's leave it like there never was a Ditty by the river. Uh, Debolt doesn't gotta know, either."

Joe's eyes got pensive. "One thing worries me."

Paul knew exactly what Joe meant. "Volly, right?"

"Yeah. I ain't so sure he'll go for it. He's pretty sharp, you know."

Paul couldn't help but laugh. "You can tell Volly, Joe. I'll tell you what. If he gives you too much trouble, just ask him about a certain money clip, see if he don't all of a sudden shut his face."

Joe's face grew contorted, as if he were trying to absorb what Paul was trying to tell him. "Oh, you mean..." Then with a half grin, "We're cool then?"

"We're cool. Can you find a way to meet up with Volly, because I'm heading home?"

"Not a problem. You go ahead."

On the way Paul tried to put his mind on this new development, Smedley. But he couldn't. Not exhausted like this. And besides, he had Katie to think about, she asleep in his bed. No way did he want to be there when she woke up. Only where else was he to go?

When he arrived in front of his building, he still didn't have an answer, and was much too tired to really care.

Chapter 19

"COME ON, get out of there, Paval," yelled an unwelcome Croatian voice.

Paul came alive with a start, slamming his knee against the steering wheel of his pickup. No pain yet, but he knew it was coming. Yes, there it was, delayed by a split second, but torturous all the same, and he bent to hold his leg, suffering through the moment.

Somebody was laughing. Paul knew that laugh, and jerked his head in its direction. "Cace?" he said, more out of surprise than question.

Switching to English, Paul's father said, "Boy, it's a good idea to sleep in your own bed at night. If for some reason you can't, you oughta look around, check things out so when you get up there's less chance of getting hurt."

Paul remembered the night before. Oh, my God, Katie. All he needed was his Croatian father finding a Serbian girl in his apartment, and in his bed no less.

Joseph Kostovic opened the pickup's door, and taking Paul by the arm, coaxed him onto the street. "Come on, Mom's up stairs waiting."

"Mom's up stairs?" Life as Paul knew it was over.

"Yeah, and she's got breakfast going."

Paul breathed a sigh of relief. If Katie was still there, his mother would hardly be making breakfast. War would be more like it. He said, "How come you didn't tell me you were coming?" Then thinking. "And when'd you guys get here, anyway?"

His father spoke as they climbed the stairs. "It was a spur of the moment thing. Your mother was up late and heard on the radio about that policeman getting killed. Of course she tried calling you, but she couldn't get an answer. After that there wasn't any stopping her. We got into town about four in the morning, and let ourselves in with the key you'd given us from the last time we were here."

Paul surmised the rest. Katie must have awakened shortly after Paul had returned to the Cabrini. She had gone home just before mom and dad showed up. When mom and dad found the place empty, they went to bed. And mom, being mom, got up with the chickens, even if the chickens were three hundred miles away. She checked the street, and there Paul was sleeping in the pickup. He'd have some explaining to do over that, but at least it wouldn't include Katie.

He stepped inside his apartment, and looked into the, fresh, Slavic face of his mother. She walked into his arms, supplying a hug like only she could: nestling her chin into his chest, and squeezing her free-flowing, print housedress against him.

Then from behind Paul, "Isn't this a sight to behold? There's nothing like the love between a mother and her son."

Paul snapped around. There stood Katie, giving him a light wave of the hand. He felt his jaw droop, knowing this girl, radiant even with only a few hour's sleep, was about to be the instrument of his death. And at the hands of his mother.

Katie's eyes sparkled. She put a hand over her mouth, choking back a laugh. Paul wanted to murder her right then and there, only his mother still had him in a bear hug.

Paul's father said, "Imagine us when we walked in this morning and found Katie in your bed. At first we didn't know what to think."

Paul was glad his mother was in his arms. If not, he probably would have collapsed.

Katie, grinning from ear to ear. "I told Catherine and Joseph what happened, how when I needed somebody to stay with me, you volunteered." She shot Paul a clandestine wink. "And when you had to go back to work, you gave me your apartment to sleep in."

Paul's mother said, "And then, when you were through at work, to sleep in your pickup so Katie would not be disturbed. That's a good boy."

Paul looked at his mother's smiling face, then to his father. They believed it. He was saved.

He stood like a statue, afraid to move as his mother walked to the tiny stove. Picking up a spatula, she ladled breakfast onto a large serving plate. Paul's view was blocked, but he knew it was brains and eggs. He'd recognize that awful smell anywhere. Under the circumstances he was not about to protest. No, because he just wanted to get through this morning. Alive!

Katie put coffee and toast on the small, two-chair table that Paul used for his meals. His mother was right behind with the main course. It was a bit tight; Paul's mother and Katie got chairs, Paul had to sit on the edge of his bed, his father pulled up a footstool.

His mother bowed her head, and made the sign-of-the-cross. Which Paul knew was inevitable, being a Kostovic family ritual for every meal no matter the time or place. He signed himself, and peeked up at Katie, hoping upon hope she would throw away that foolish stubbornness of hers and do the right thing, sign also, make believe she was Roman Catholic along with the rest of the lie.

Katie did, but with her left hand, using only three fingers as practiced in orthodox tradition.

Paul chanced a glance at his mother, who was looking at Katie with an inquisitive stare.

It was over, and so was he.

"Katie," his mother said in the kindest of tones. "If you would, show us how the Serbians say grace."

Paul grabbed the rickety table, or he might have fallen off the bed. As it was, he knocked over the coffee, spilling it into the brains and eggs. Everybody scattered to avoid the scalding liquid.

"What's the matter with you?" said a perplexed looking Catherine Kostovic. "Katie'll think you're a clumsy ox."

"She had to find out sooner or later," Paul's father said, brushing coffee stains from his Oshkosh-By-Goshes.

Katie threw an arm around Paul's mother. "Don't you get it, Catherine? The buffoon thinks because I'm Serbian you're going to try and kill him."

His mother snapped a vicious stare at Paul. "So that's it." She grabbed a ladle from the kitchen sink. Waving it like the axe Paul was used to seeing her using on chickens, she turned back around.

Paul cringed, waiting for the first blow. His mother rushed past him, and shoved the ladle in the face of her husband. "See what you've gone and done. All those years telling your kids,

117

Serbians this, Serbians that. No wonder the boy thinks the way he does."

Joseph put Paul between himself and the waving ladle, cowering.

Having a new target, Catherine turned her wrath on Paul. Using Croatian, she said, "It's partly my fault, I suppose. I never stopped your father's stupid blabber about the Serbians. He knows just as well as me they're honest, hardworking people, no different than us." She looked at her husband. "Are you gonna tell him, or should I?"

Still keeping his distance, Joseph said, "Maybe you should. If I get it wrong, you'll be waving that ladle at me all over again."

She looked at Katie. "See, he makes me do everything," and turned to Paul. "Okay then, listen to me so you'll know once and for all. Back in the old country, right across the river from our village, there was a Serbian settlement. Me and your father, we were only teenagers then, but we remember, don't we, Joseph?" Obedient nodding from Paul's father. "They had their ways, we had ours, but we got along okay. All right, maybe they had some hotheads, but so did we." She eyed her husband. "Didn't we?"

"The boy doesn't need to hear everything," Paul's father mumbled, his chin on his chest.

Catherine set her eyes on Paul. "Oh, yes he does. You ever hear us talk about the *Ustasi*, Paul?"

Paul tried to find a meaning for *Ustasi* that might fit in his limited Croatian vocabulary. The closest he could come up with was, *Spudesa*, which meant wake up, or get up.

And Katie said, "The *Ustasi* were Croatian guerrillas who fought against the Serbians."

"That's right," Paul's mother said, looking impressed with Katie's knowledge. "They were pigs. Not like the *Dombran*, the regular Croatian army. One night they came to our village, looking for men to fight in their army. They dragged us all out on the street, and were ready to take our men when help came from across the river. The Serbians, they attacked, and with nothing but picks and shovels." Tears streamed from her eyes. "I can't say it, Joseph."

Who took his wife in his arms, and looked at Paul. "I was one of those boys, so was your uncle Anton. Your mother had two cousins there, too. Afterwards, when the Ustasi were driven off, us that were still standing took to the mountains. We stayed up there 'til the end of the war, when the American soldiers came. If it wasn't for those Serbian villagers, good chance I wouldn't be here today."

Paul forgot his own predicament, and said, "I've never heard you talk about this before. How come?"

Joseph pecked Catherine on the cheek. Clearing his throat, he said, "A lotta Serbians boys got killed that night, some of us, too. Your mother lost one of her cousins. All by the hand of our own kind. Not something a man likes to talk about."

Catherine gave her husband one last hug, moved over to Paul, and patted him on the arm. "So you see, whatever you've heard, Croatian, Serbian, no big difference to us." She leaned up to Paul's ear, making like she was whispering, but spoke loud enough to be heard by all. "And this Katie girl, she's a good one. I better not hear you let her get away."

Paul looked at Katie.

And there she was, gleaming back at him with a full and knowing smile.

Look at her gloat, knowing she had him under her thumb again. Paul wanted to tell his mother how he despised this girl. He thought he did, anyway. Or maybe not. Jesus, he didn't know what to think when it came to her.

And there she was again, giving Paul's mother one of her pretty smiles, the kind Paul knew her to use when things were going her way. He also knew that no matter how she appeared on the outside, down deep a plan was being hatched in that evil brain of hers. He hoped he would avoid being in the way when she put it in motion.

The phone rang. Thankful for the distraction, Paul picked up the receiver. "Hello," he said.

"Sarge?" It was Tommy, and from his tired voice, Paul guessed he had been up all night.

Which, knowing Tommy, didn't make any sense, and Paul said, "Yeah, what's up?"

"I'm at the morgue. I think you'd better get down here."

"What're you doing there?"

"You coming, or what?"

"I haven't had but a couple hours sleep."

"I know, but... I think you oughta see this."

Then Paul remember that Volly and Joe had taken the dead diamond salesman to the morgue. What had those two goofs done this time? "Okay, I'm on the way," he said, and hung up.

Deep in thought, he started for the door, then remembered his manners. "Baba, I'm sorry. Don't you worry, though. I'll get this over with fast as I can." He checked his father. "We'll still have most of the day to spend together. The three of us."

He looked at Katie, to make sure she knew what "three" meant. And got that bright smile in return. She just didn't know when to back off.

His mother squeezed his hand. "We understand. You go ahead. It'll give us time to get to know Katie better."

Oh, man. His mother wasn't backing off any more than Katie was. Paul didn't like this even a little bit. He was about to suggest that he take Katie home when she went to his mother, saying, "Anyway, I need something to keep my mind off..." Her eyes glistened. "...what happened."

Paul's mother touched Katie's shoulder, saying, "You sure you're okay?"

Managing another sweet smile, Katie said, "Yeah, I'm fine. I'll show you and Joe the sights."

Good God! By the time Paul got back she'd have mom and dad converted to Serbians.

His mother grabbed a clean uniform shirt from the closet, and threw it at Paul. She pushed him toward the bathroom, saying, "Remember to change your underwear, too." And returned to an animated conversation with Katie.

Minutes later Paul was shoved out the door, his mother telling him to be sure to meet them back there that evening, only not before Katie finished showing them the town. He made the walk down to his pickup wondering which he should worry about more, Tommy's summons, or his poor defenseless parents left alone in the clutches of Katie Bartovich.

Chapter 20

SMEDLEY WATCHED as Henry searched the Drake Hotel's front desk area, then hurried back by the bank of pay telephone booths. Returning, he threw his hands on his hips, and scanned the crowded lobby. What an idiot. Probably couldn't find his own ass without a compass. As if to prove Smedley right, Henry shuffled over to the long, wide-flowing staircase which led to the street. Smedley was tempted to help old Henry out. No, let the buffoon suffer. Would be good for him. Smedley, too. Now Henry was on the other side of the lobby, behind the elaborate, stone-carved fountain. Looked like he was about to burst out crying. And this guy was a diamond salesman! Just amazing.

Then Henry rubbernecked to the sitting area.

Where Smedley had strategically placed himself, and making sure he had a big grin on his face, waved for Henry to come over.

Henry's eyes dropped to the chrome attaché case next to Smedley's knee. Exactly what Smedley had expected Henry to do, and he rested a protective hand on the case, just to let Henry know it still belonged to Smedley.

Henry pulled a handkerchief from his breast pocket, wiped it over his forehead, and strode across the expansive, oriental rug. Was an exaggerated walk, as if he were trying to appear confident.

Yeah, right, Henry confident.

Smedley suppressed a laugh, and with the attaché case in hand, sauntered toward Henry, meeting him at the center of the lobby. Smedley offered his hand and a patented smile as proof that all was well.

Henry, forcing a smile of his own. "I see you've got what's important." Nodding at the attaché case. "Everything must've gone according to plan, huh?"

"You bet. Exactly like I told you. Believe it or not, it was easy."

Only Smedley didn't think any part of this was easy. This was business, the deadliest kind of business, and he treated it as such. Ever watchful, he had proceeded stage by stage, ready to disengage at the first sign of danger. On the outside he showed a man at ease. Inside he was peaked, all senses putting forth one-hundred percent effort. The smile was designed to put his target off guard, but that was only one small part of his overall plan. He'd put weeks into this operation. He'd murdered, maimed, and taken more than one chance with his own life. That was okay, though, because his calculations had paid off, and were about to reap rich dividends. That is if these final moments went according to blueprint.

And Henry, even though he appeared the fool, still wasn't to be taken lightly.

Smedley absorbed every part of Henry's demeanor, filtering it through his inborn warning system. Experience had taught him that a person with a hidden agenda will always give himself away. One only had to know what to look for. Might be a slight change in the tone of voice, maybe a twitch of the hand, or a flicker in the eye, but surely it would come.

Henry was jabbering about Randolph Laidlaw. Smedley hadn't had to get physical, had he? Henry didn't want to see anybody hurt.

Smedley showed the appearance of a man totally engrossed in Henry's conversation. But he was listening only obliquely, taking in just enough so he could answer intelligently, if need be. Actually, he was making one last observation of their surroundings. Was anybody paying him and Henry any unusual amount of attention? He noted the face of every person who had come off the elevator with Henry, kept them under particular close surveillance. He looked for bulges under their coats. Were they wearing old, out of style ties? Their shoes, were their toes and heels worn thin, and were they black, unshined black?

Women couldn't be discounted. A lot of cops were female nowadays. Best way to pick out a lady cop was by their physical appearance. Generally, they let their bodies go even faster than their male counterparts. And their clothes, Smedley had never seen a lady cop wear anything but rags when on duty.

Okay, it looked like a go, and he said, "I told you, old buddy, I don't believe in the physical stuff. If it came to that, I'd have dropped the whole thing, pulled out a long time ago."

Henry held up his hands in an expression on apology. "Don't get me wrong," he said. "It's not like I don't trust you. I was only asking, is all. A guy like me can't help but worry."

"Well, if you're gonna look at it that way, I really can't say Mister Laidlaw's all that good. After all, the man just got taken for a half-mil." Smedley tapped the attaché case with his finger, and grinned broadly, even bigger than usual.

"Good. I'm relieved Randy isn't hurt. I don't think I could live with that."

Smedley patted Henry on the shoulder, and let his hand linger. One affectionate touch carried more weight than a paragraph of phony words. The ploy served a second purpose, to monitor Henry's breathing. It was up, but not that up. That was to be expected. Had Henry's heart been pounding, Smedley would have known he was being set up for the cops. He would abandon the operation, and invoke a long thought-out auxiliary plan of escape. Once safe, he'd simply cut his losses and disappear, never to be seen again.

Smedley slid his hand onto Henry's back, and guided him toward the bank of telephone booths. "What you say, Henry? Time for that all-important phone call, ain't it?"

"Ready and willing," Henry said. "Only there's been a little change in plans."

"What change?" Smedley said, and he narrowed his eyes. Changes weren't good.

"I want the diamonds put in the hotel safe before I call New York."

Smedley eased off. "Don't trust me, huh? Okay, why not? All I want is my money."

"Only not just yet," Henry said.

Suspicious, Smedley said, "Now what?"

Henry sported a wry smile. "Aren't we forgetting something?"

"Forgetting what?" answered a truly confused Smedley, his mind racing. Had he read Henry wrong? Was he being set up after all? He spun around, half expecting to see a squad of cops rushing toward him. His hand automatically slid under his suit coat. Ready to strike out at the first menacing figure, he fingered sweaty fingers on his Ka-bar knife.

"Wow!" Henry said. "And I thought I was the scared one."

Smedley whipped his head back around, and gave Henry a murderous stare. "This is no time for games," he growled.

"Take it easy, will you? It's the diamonds. I think I'm entitled to have a look before we close the deal. I mean wouldn't you?"

With eyes glaring, Smedley pushed the attaché case into Henry's hands. "Here, and take a good look," he said. Gritting his teeth, he scanned the crowd again.

"That's just what I intend to do," Henry said. He found a corner chair. Snapping the clasp on the attaché case, he pulled it open. Inside were six neatly placed bags, each the approximate size of an adult male's fist. All were of a smooth velvet material, royal blue in color. "No plain diamond wallets for Randy," he said.

Beginning to regain control, Smedley said, "Open one or two, friend. See for yourself I'm not trying to cheat you."

Henry looked at Smedley with a confident eye, as if to say, you're in my world now. "Don't mind if I do," he said, and taking one of the bags, he picked the knot on the leather strap which was tethered around its top. Pulling it open, he poured a small measure of its contents into the palm of his hand.

"Looks like the real thing to me," Smedley said.

Henry rolled the diamonds around in his hand, and smiled up at Smedley. "Right here, in this little pile, there's got to be close to thirty-thousand dollars worth, and I'm talking strictly wholesale."

Smedley whistled. "Sounds like we hit the mother lode," he said.

"Uh-huh. But that's no concern of yours, is it? The deal is you get two-hundred and fifty thou, I get the ice."

"I don't know," Smedley said. "Sounds like all the odds are on your side. Maybe I'll just take the diamonds and peddle them to somebody else."

"I don't think so," Henry said, his newfound confidence overflowing. "Gems, even diamonds, aren't that easy to get rid of, not for somebody outside the business. You wouldn't get more that a nickel on the dollar. With me, at least you're getting half their worth."

"Okay, Henry. I guess you got me. Let's do it your way." Henry's confidence was replaced with a suspicious stare, as if he were weighing his options. Finally saying, "You don't have any objections to the diamonds going in the hotel safe?"

"Only fair," Smedley said. Afraid Henry might change his mind, he took Henry's arm, directing him toward the front desk. "Come on. The sooner I get my bread, the sooner you're on your way home with the diamonds."

Which seemed to relax Henry. He placed the attaché case on the marble-topped counter, saying to no one in particular, "I'd like to speak to somebody in authority."

A middle-aged man, short, with prematurely white hair, looked up from a pile of paper work. "I'm Mister Connington, the reservations manager. What is it, sir?" He looked at a tall, rangy redhead with a trainee badge pinned to her lapel. "See how it's done, Miss Ackerman?"

"Yes, sir," she said, standing at attention.

"Yes, very professional," Henry said. "Would it be all right if I checked this into the safe for the afternoon?" He taped a finger on the attaché case.

"You're a guest here, sir?"

"Yes, room seven-fourteen." Henry produced his room key for identification, and smiled at Smedley.

"Of course, sir. Miss Conners will help you. Susan, this man needs access to the safe. Take care of it."

He pushed the attaché case in front of her, and went back to his work.

"Gladly, sir," Susan said, and she gave Henry a toothy smile. "If you'll wait here please, I'll be just a second." She took two steps, and was stopped by a glaring Mister Connington. Turning back to Henry, she said, "Uh—and thank you, sir."

She disappeared with the attaché case into an office behind the front desk. Moments later she returned, and handed a receipt to Henry. "Just show this to whoever's here when you need your property. They'll be happy to assist you."

She was about to turn to the next customer when she received a rude elbow in the ribs from the reservations manager. "Oh, yes," she said, rubbing her side, "and thank you for choosing the Drake, sir."

The reservations manager gave Susan a pompous nod, never giving Henry a second glance.

Henry placed the receipt in his wallet, and walked around the corner to the pay telephone booths. Taking charge, he motioned Smedley to join him. "I'm going up to my room now, to call my bank. You wait here. I'll call you as soon as I'm through transferring the cash."

"Why not call from right here? I mean, you don't think I'm stupid enough to try something out in the open, do you?"

"It's not that. Just that I'd feel safer. Uh, in my own room, if you know what I mean."

"What about the bank? Remember, I need your signature to get the cash out."

"I've thought of that too," Henry said. He took a slip of paper from his coat pocket. "I came into town a day early, and went straight to the bank. I told them you'd be coming for some cash, and gave them a pre-signed withdrawal slip. That's a copy." He looked at Smedley as if to say, don't you trust me?

Smedley checked at the bank slip, and said, "And I'm supposed to take your word that you'll make the call, that right?"

"I'm not going to cross you," Henry said. "I'd never be able to sleep knowing you were out there someplace."

Smedley had let Henry play big shot long enough. Now it was time to show him who was boss. He moved in close, his chin all but touching on Henry's nose. "That you're right about," he hissed, making sure his spittle splattered into Henry's face with each word uttered. "Remember, I know everything there is to know about you. Where you live, your wife's name. Those two daughters of yours, too. They live in their own apartment just off campus, at Penn State. The place you popped for, Henry. Also, you got a son. Must be a good kid. Already married, and from what I understand the little lady's something to behold. They got two rug rats. I know exactly where they live and where he works, even where the kids go to school." Smedley paused long enough to let his meaning sink in. "I can go on, but I think you get the point, don't you, old buddy?"

As Smedley spoke Henry sagged against the phone booth, an obedient nod here and there, looking as if this was all that he could muster.

"Good," Smedley said. "So go ahead on. Make the call. I'll be waiting."

"I want you to know one more thing before I go," Henry said, his confidence all but gone now.

"There's more? Okay, get it off your chest, and then get the hell outta here."

Henry gulped. "Just in case you've got ideas about robbing me after I get the diamonds from the hotel safe. I intend to have an armored car meet me at the front desk and take me directly to the airport."

Smedley, showing a weary face. "Very impressive. I don't give a damn if you get Superman to fly you all the way to New York. Now please, will you go on?"

Henry started, then faltered, managing to say, "Okay, I'm going. But so help me, if I see you following, I'll scream for the cops."

Smedley plopped into the nearest phone booth. "Just go, will you? I'm getting tired of this shit."

Chapter 21

PAUL HAD NEVER gotten used to the morgue. Especially the sub-basement, where the stench of formaldehyde alone was enough to make him sick to the stomach. Apparently Tommy didn't like it either. He was waiting just outside the main body room, holding his nose.

Tommy, sounding like Mickey Mouse, "I'm pretty sure there's been a mistake."

"What mistake?" Paul said, surprised Tommy would care.

"Come on, I'll show you," and Tommy started for the door.

"Wait a second," Paul said. "I mean, what is it with you all of a sudden? 'Cause this I would classify under the heading of police work."

Tommy, fighting back tears. "The Lieutenant, getting killed. I want that Ditty kid dead, Sarge."

"You're serious?"

"Yeah, I'm serious. Why wouldn't I be?"

Paul, still unbelieving. "Is that really you in there, or maybe your twin brother?"

"Ain't no joke, Sarge."

Paul noted Tommy's uniform, open down the front, and pulled out of his trousers. "Where've you been, anyway?"

"Helping with the search. You know, at the Cabrini, with that lamebrain Debolt. Let me tell you, Ditty's home free as long as Debolt's running the investigation."

"No kidding?" Paul said, still having a difficult time believing this was Tommy talking.

"Yeah, after awhile I decided to go on home. That's when I heard on the radio that you were sending a body to the morgue. Figuring you'd be here sooner or later, I came on down."

"You're serious then, about catching Ditty?"

Tommy nodded. "And while I was waiting, I took a look at what you fished out of the river."

"Yeah, so?"

"Come on, I'll show you." Tommy led the way into the main body room, which had always reminded Paul of a vacant

128

swimming pool; long, deep, and bare.

Tommy stepped through a maze of canoe shaped, metal trays that were lined up in rows on the cement floor. Each one containing the remains of a human body. All of which were naked, except for identification tags on their big toes.

Tommy pointed at one particular body. "Recognize this guy?" he said.

"Yeah," Paul said. "Henry Shakleford, the diamond salesman."

"Nope."

"Whatta you mean, 'nope?'"

"It ain't him, is what I mean."

"Well look again, because it sure as hell is."

"Uh-uh. I don't know who you got here, but it sure ain't who you think it is."

Fatigue overtaking him, Paul hollered, "Don't give me that shit, dammit! You know it's him just as well as I do."

Tommy bent over the body, and gave it a good long look. "I'm telling you, this ain't Henry Shakleford. Not the one that got robbed, anyhow. And remember, I was lucid that day. Well, as much as you were, anyhow, smashing your head into the side of that Caddy."

Paul couldn't argue with Tommy about that. And maybe this made more sense than it looked like it did. He stared for a moment, and then, "Let me alone for a second."

Head down, he forced the morning's events on his tired brain cells. Ordinarily he used the time tested process of listing all the facts, putting them side by side, then coming to a logical conclusion. But in his present condition the simplest deliberation was muddled and forgotten before it could be digested.

He'd better go back home and get some rest, start in again tomorrow. No, no, something deep inside argued. He had a fresh case here. If he let it go, good chance there'd be nothing left but dead ends by the time he got back to it, especially once Debolt got there.

He had to think, think hard, and he needed to be alone. Looking about, he spotted an empty corner, and threading his way through the bodies, squatted down on the bare cement floor. He pulled out his notepad, and opened to a blank page.

129

On top he scribbled, *salesman*. And then alongside he put, *Dittybop Caldwell*. Underneath he wrote, *floater*, and underneath that, *accomplice?*

"Okay, okay," he said out loud, happy that at least he was able to remember the main characters in this investigation. Investigation? More like comedy show, as far as he was concerned. Except the lieutenant had been killed. Nothing funny about that. Okay, so what next? He added more names and places until satisfied every bit of the known data was listed in front of his eyes. Now, holding the notepad between his legs, he stared at his entries, playing with them in his brain, testing every possible scenario. It was slow coming, but one sobering piece of wisdom began to materialize. He'd thought the floater was the diamond salesman, Henry Shakleford. And thinking that, he'd surmised that Shakleford and Ditty were in cahoots. The one part Paul had not quite understood was how Shakleford ended up shot dead, Ditty wounded, and the both of them in the river. Only now he knew the floater was not Shakleford. So who was it then? From the soggy card he'd found in the floater's pocket, it had to have been some kinda diamond salesman. And if it was, then maybe Ditty's deal was with him, not Shakleford. Could it be that Ditty found another diamond salesman to make his deal with? Not likely. Too complicated for somebody like Ditty. Too complicated for himself, too, dammit.

Trying another technique, he started at the top of the page, mulling over each entry, checking it off when nothing particular came to mind. Until he got to *accomplice*. Yes, accomplice. This went back to his original theory, that somebody other than Ditty had set up the entire job. Was the floater the accomplice? No, the floater was a diamond salesman, and diamond salesmen didn't go around setting up elaborate robbery schemes with Cabrini Green street thieves.

Wait! Ditty had told Joe Holloway that somebody named Smedley had shot the lieutenant. This Smedley, whoever he was, had to be the accomplice. Paul had to find Smedley, but how? He leaned back against the wall, trying to think. Nothing was coming. He was stymied and he knew it.

"Sarge?"

Paul looked up. It was Tommy, and he looked bewildered. Why shouldn't he be? Paul sure was.

Tommy saying, "The body, how come you thought it was the diamond salesman?"

Paul caught his upper lip between his teeth, and tried to digest the rookie's question. One of the questions Paul had been trying to figure. Maybe the better question was, if it isn't Shakleford, then where in hell is Shakleford?

Paul looked into Tommy's befuddled eyes, saying, "Astounding. Tommy Covello thinking like a cop."

"You okay?" the rookie said with a confused stare.

"Yeah, I'm okay. Why wouldn't I be?" Paul jumped to his feet, adrenaline erasing any evidence of the exhaustion that had, only moments before, consumed every muscle in his body. But adrenaline lasted only so long. He'd better act now, while his brain was still functioning.

"A phone, I need a phone," he muttered, and looked at the morgue office. Heading for it, he skipped over rather than going around the bodies spread out along the way. Banging through the door, he found the room vacant except for one lone secretary. At least fifty pounds overweight, she was lounging behind a huge desk with the office telephone cradled between the top of her shoulder and her ear. Seemingly, she was hard at work.

Who she was or what she was doing was of no concern to Paul, not at this moment. "Police business," he said, and grabbed the phone out of her hand.

Tommy arrived as Paul dialed the information operator. Paul looked up at him. "That salesman. He was staying at the Drake, right?"

"Yeah, only he's back in New York by now. I'm pretty sure, anyway."

Someone picked up, and Paul said, "Give me the Front desk." While he waited, Paul said to Tommy, "You've got a patrol car, right."

"Yeah. Why?"

"Gimme the keys."

"Here, take them. What's going on?"

A loud click came from the phone. "Front Desk," came a woman's formal voice.

"Good. Check your registration for a Henry Shakleford."

"Yes, sir. One second." The phone went quiet.

Paul looked at Tommy. "I'm laying odds our salesman friend's back in Chicago."

The formal voice came back on. "You're looking for Mister Henry Shakleford?"

"Yes."

"He's currently registered, sir."

"Great. Gimme his room."

"I just tried, sir. He doesn't answer."

"Are you sure?"

"Yes, sir. I'm sure," the formal voice said with a bit of indignation.

"Well, okay, but if you see him, hold on to him for me. I'm on the way over there right now."

"And you are who, sir."

"Who'm I? That's right, I didn't say, did I? I'm Sergeant Kostovic of the Chicago Police. This is a murder investigation, and it's important I talk to Mister Shakleford, so whatever you do, don't let him go."

Chapter 22

SMEDLEY WAITED by the front desk, watching as the indicator above Henry's elevator flashed on and off— 3, to 4, to 5.

He could just imagine Henry feeling safe in that tiny cubical as he rose up through the hotel. Probably enjoying the moment, thinking about his babe back in New York, and what fine gift he was going to bestow on her as soon as he got home. Smedley laughed. And what she'd bestow on Henry in return.

The elevator stopped on the seventh floor, where Henry said was his room. A long pause, and then up again.

Smedley checked his watch, specifically the second hand, and counted off as it stuttered around the dial. He had promised himself he would wait exactly five minutes. But, God, the first minute seemed to have taken an hour. To hell with this. He went to the elevator, and pushed the call button. Another agonizing minute passed as the indicator rolled downwards. When the doors finally sprung open, he rushed inside, and stubbed his thumb into the up button. The elevator jerked to life, lights on the panel flashing as it took him upwards, past the seventh floor, gaining speed, faster, 8-9-11-13. Then slowing, humming to a stop on the fifteenth floor.

The door slid open.

Smedley stepped out, checking up and down the hallway. Vacant. Good. With his key at the ready, he went to the room he had strategically taken yesterday evening. Going inside, he eased the door closed behind him. Leaning a shoulder against it, he set the deadbolt lock, and fit the safety chain in place.

And felt the tension drain from his body.

Now to the side door, with an ear pressed tightly. Listening. Quiet.

Had he waited too long? He hoped not. Gripping the key in both hands, he twisted fraction by fraction until the deadbolt clicked open. Okay, so far so good, and he pulled the door ajar, making not a sound. Of course, because he had applied a thick layer of grease to the door's hinges, and had made at least a half dozen dry runs just to make sure. Marine training.

The cops would be in a world of trouble if every thief were schooled in it.

From the other side, a familiar voice. "David Whittingham, please."

Making Smedley smile.

A moment and, "David, that you?—Yeah, Henry Shakleford.—Good, then you're ready to send the money to First Chicago."

Smedley eased through the door. Crouching into a hand-to-hand combat stance, he pulled his Ka-bar from its scabbard, wetting its razor-like blade on his tongue.

Henry, head down, still on the phone. "Okay, here's my PIN number." He recited, "S-A-L-L-Y-B-A-B-Y. Got it? Great. Then that's all there is to it, right? Okay David, and thanks."

Smedley held his breath, and inched closer.

Henry, on the phone again, dialing. Waiting. And saying, "Hey, babe—yeah, who else? And, Sally, wait until you see what I got for you—no, you're just going to have to wait. Not long, though—this afternoon, about three. You be ready, because we're going out to celebrate." He laughed. "On second thought, we'll stay in. All day! Yeah. Until then, huh?" He hung up.

Even from behind, Smedley could see Henry's jowls spread with a satisfied smile.

"One more, and off I go," Henry said as if congratulating himself, and dialed again. "Give me the front desk, operator. Yes, front desk? Page Mister Smedley Butler for me, please. He'll be right there in the lobby."

"Don't bother," Smedley said.

Henry dropped the receiver as if he'd been hit by lighting. Twirling around, he looked wide-eyed into Smedley's smiling face.

"Greetings," Smedley said, flipping his Ka-bar from hand to hand. "How?" Henry said, his eyes running to the still locked hallway door, and then back at Smedley, growing wide.

"How indeed." Smedley said, enjoying the moment.

Henry slid out of the chair, stumbling backwards, trying to put distance between himself and Smedley. But before he could get far, Smedley shoved him down on the bed, and held the Ka-bar to his quaking chin.

Glaring, Smedley pointed at the side-door. "See that. It's access to the next room. All these old hotels got them. You know, in case somebody needs extra space. Yesterday morning, you called to reserve your two separate rooms. Using your company name on the second room, that was slick, you devil you. Only I know you backwards and forwards, don't I? I called the registration desk, told them I was a friend, and needed rooms next to yours, the keys for the doors in between, too. These hotel people, they mean to please. So before you ever got to Chicago, I was ready. Only I still wasn't sure which room you were gonna use. Then, when you checked the diamonds into the hotel safe, you told the front desk you were in seven-fourteen. 'Specially for me, wasn't it it?" Smedley laughed. "After that, I guess I knew where you'd really be, didn't I?"

Henry pulled out the receipt for the diamonds, holding it in trembling hands. "Go ahead, take it. Only please don't hurt me."

"Thanks. Just put it on the bed. I'll get to it when our business is finished."

"Business? What business?"

"You'll see soon enough. Just do like I say, and put the receipt on the bed."

Henry, keeping his hand as far away from the Ka-bar as possible, placed the receipt down. And he said, "If you're thinking I've got something else worth stealing, you're wrong."

"Nope, it's not that. You've supplied me with as much as I'll need for a long while." He placed the Ka-bar back in its scabbard, and snatched Henry off the bed.

Henry struggled, trying to get his feet under him, but Smedley held him just off the floor. Smedley was surprised at his own strength. It was as if he were some super human being, and Henry a rag doll. And now, moving away from the bed, all the while watching Henry's terrified eyes searching, searching for where Smedley was taking him. And fixing on the balcony.

Henry crying, "you can't! No!" Then ever louder, "Nooo!" Scrapping his feet, trying to hold back.

Smedley said, "You're disgusting. Be a man, just once in

135

your life." He yanked Henry high over his head.

"Oh, God," Henry cried. As they approached ever-closer to the balcony, he flailed out with his arms, somehow seizing the French door which separated the balcony from the room.

"No, you don't," Smedley said. He jerked so that Henry became suspended between himself and the door.

A tug-of-war raged, and after a ripping yank, Henry lost his grip with one hand. Still managing to hold on with the other, he cried, "You don't have to do this. I'll never tell."

"Too late for that stuff."

Wanting to get this over with, Smedley let go of Henry's feet. Henry thumped to the floor, still holding tight to the French door with one hand. Smedley flashed his Ka-bar, and Henry, with a puzzled face, stared at the bright red flow spurting from where his fingers should have been.

"Sorry about that," Smedley said. "But it ain't gonna make any difference where you're going."

Chapter 23

"YOU COULD AT LEAST tell me what the hell's going on," Tommy said as Paul raced the patrol car through the Chicago Loop's busy traffic.

Turning up the next alley, Paul said, "We'd better get there quick, or our diamond salesman just might end up like whoever that was back in the morgue." He drove the wrong way up a one-way street, cutting off traffic on Michigan Avenue, screeching to a halt in front of the Drake Hotel's main entrance.

"Come on," he hollered, and ran past a startled doorman, into the lobby. Against the far wall stood the front desk. Paul rushed up, and picked out an official looking man in a royal blue uniform coat. "RESERVATION MANAGER" embroidered on his sunken chest.

Paul said, "I'm the cop that just called about Henry Shakleford. You seen him?"

Looking up, as if board with such a silly question, the reservation manager said, "To my knowledge Mister Shakleford checked out some time ago."

A young lady with "TRAINEE" clipped to her lapel was standing alongside. "That was me you were talking to, Sergeant." And to the reservation manager. "No, Mister Connington, sir. Mister Shakleford is still here. I know, because his attaché case is still in the safe."

Connington produced a, don't you correct me, stare. He looked like he was about to follow it up with choice words for the trainee when Tommy came running up. With mouth agape, he tugged on Paul's sleeve, pointing toward the street.

"What?" Paul said, as Tommy pulled him away from the front desk.

Tommy made an unintelligible gurgle, finally forcing out, "A couple'a feet one way or the other and I'd got crushed."

"Crushed? By what?"

"You'll see," and Tommy pulled Paul through the swinging door entranceway, shoving through a milling crowd, to a United Parcel truck which was parked at the curb, one pace in front of their patrol car. "There," he said, leaning on Paul for support, and looking at the truck's driver.

Who was sitting erect, hands firmly on the steering column, screaming one long bellow that could pass for a foghorn on a seagoing vessel. And then her scream began to lose clarity, wavering, before going silent all together. Even though, her eyes remained constant. Staring as if she was watching a horror movie.

Paul followed her stare, coming upon a human arm, which was draped down over her windshield. "Uh-oh," he muttered, and with Tommy glued to his side, walked around to the front of the truck, receiving a panoramic view of a mutilated body, spread-eagled on the truck's flattop roof.

Paul said, "Take a good look. You know, to make sure it's who we think it is. While you do, I'll see if I can clear this crowd away."

Tommy, still listing against Paul. "What you mean, 'who we think it is?'"

Paul propped Tommy up, saying, "Forget it. I'll look." He shoved him toward the patrol car, "Go call for backup."

Chapter 24

SMEDLEY CAME OUT of the hotel entrance to see cops everywhere. A milling crowd was circled around a United Parcel truck. With them was the reservation manager and his trainee. Excellent. This was just the diversion Smedley had hoped for. He went back inside, to the Bell Captain's desk.

"Excuse me," he said, making himself sound like high society. "I need my valuables from the hotel safe, and I don't see anybody at the front desk."

"Sorry, sir," the bell captain said, glancing at the entranceway. "They're, uh, busy."

Smedley had difficulty holding back laughing. "I'm in kind of a hurry," he said. "Maybe you can help." He produced the receipt for the attaché case.

The bell captain checked the receipt. "Dominic Capri at your service, Mister Shakleford. I do need a second piece of identification, though. For confirmation. Sorry, but that's procedure."

"I fully understand. After all, it's only to protect people like myself." He handed over Henry's Gold Card.

Capri made a brief inspection of the credit card, and returned it to Smedley. "One second," he said, and headed across the lobby floor, to the front desk. Moments later he returned with the attaché case.

"Just sign your receipt and you'll be on your way, sir."

Smedley signed, and handed the bell captain a five dollar tip. "That's for your prompt undertaking."

"Glad to help, Mister Shakleford." The bell captain returned to his station.

Things were going great, so great Smedley figured he'd see how the cops were coping with Henry and all. When he got outside, one of the cops came away from the United Parcel truck, saying, "It's the diamond salesman all right."

A shockwave reverberated up Smedley's spine. How'd they know so quickly? Sucking air, he maneuvered around the crowd to get a better look. And when he recognized the cop to be—damn—Kostovic! A second shockwave hit him.

Lightheaded, he wobbled out of the crowd. Resting against a nearby mailbox, he looked to see if he had been noticed. The cops, much too busy to spot one man out of a hundred spectators. And the crowd, every head pointed at the real-life sideshow. Made Smedley feel like passing the hat, because after all, wasn't he responsible for the entertainment? Like sheep, these people.

Thankfully.

Beginning to recuperate, he made himself think. These cops, they couldn't have just happened along. Somehow he had tripped up, left a clue somewhere. He had to get closer, see what he could find out, even if it meant taking a terrible chance. Back through the crowd he went, nudging an old lady here, elbowing a business suit there, until he found a fairly secure spot behind some six-footer in the front row.

There, just beyond, stood the scared-rabbit cop who had taken pot shots at Ditty and Shoestring during the robbery. Both of them were here. Before Smedley knew what he was doing, he blurted, "Son-of-a-bitch!"

Prompting the cop to spin around, and look Smedley straight in the face.

Fighting panic, Smedley pushed back through the rows of onlookers. And flashing over his shoulder—nobody coming—hurried up the sidewalk and around the corner. Four doors down, he ducked into a small fashion boutique, and took up surveillance from inside the display window.

What a careless fool he'd been, letting somebody, especially a cop, look him straight in the face. He made a quick decision. If a bunch of cops came around the corner he'd make a run for it out the back of the boutique. He touched his Ka-bar knife. If the young cop came alone, that cop would be made dead, and quick.

Chapter 25

"STOP YOUR LOLLYGAGGING. This ain't Oak Street Beach. Ain't one broad in that crowd cares one way or the other about some nobody copper."

"But, Sarge. That man…"

"I need you now, dammit. Debolt just radioed he's on the way. We gotta get some work done before he gets here and goes into his clown act."

"Sarge…"

"Just shut up. I gotta think," Paul stepped off by himself. He hoped Debolt would take his time, because there was so much to do. He wanted to check out Henry Shakleford's room, and not with Debolt along to muddle everything up. He also needed to take a good long look at the attaché case Shakleford had left in the hotel safe.

Which first? The attaché case was locked up. It could wait.

To Tommy, he said, "I gotta get some stuff done inside. Can I trust you to take care of things while I'm gone?"

"Yeah, sure. But Sarge…"

"Not now." Paul turned to the reservations manager. "Now's as good'a time as any for you to show me Shakleford's room."

Connington already had the key for room 714, and took Paul directly up on the elevator. Upon being let in, Paul stopped in the doorway. The room appeared unused, the windows, closed tight. "You sure this is Shakleford's room?" Paul said.

Looking indignant, Connington said, "Yes, I'm sure. I don't make mistakes like that."

Connington's feelings were of no consequence to Paul, now or ever. He said, "Don't you get it? The windows. They're closed."

Connington looked. "So?"

"Forget it." Paul opened the closet, finding it empty. He checked the dresser drawers. They also were empty. Sitting on the edge of the bed, he said, "It don't even look like Shakleford's been here. Jesus! Every time I think I've got this case figured something new pops up."

Connington raised his hands palms up. "Look, I've got work to do. So if you don't mind…"

"Just a minute," Paul said. He dropped his head in his hands, trying to think. Last night had started out so promising. The whore had told them where to find Ditty. Then the lieutenant got killed. Paul wished Matthews were here now. Yeah, the lieutenant would know what to do, and he said, "Damn! Why can't I—" He picked out Connington inching toward the door. "Where you think you're going?" he said.

Connington went rigid. "I'm right here, Sergeant, at your service." His falsetto voice squeaking.

Keeping Connington's image in the corner of his eye, Paul went by the windows. Somebody had killed Henry Shakleford, but who? Ditty was the logical suspect, only he was on the run. The last thing on Ditty's mind would be murder. Anyway, how would Ditty know Shakleford was back in town? More and more Paul was convinced somebody else was involved. Had to be this Smedley guy Ditty had told Joe Holloway about.

Just had to be.

Maybe it was Smedley who shoved Shakleford out the window. Only not the windows in this room. So what room then?

Paul played with the telephone cord, twisting it one way, then the other as he tried to come up with a feasible explanation. It looked like Shakleford had been making a deal with Smedley. In that case, wouldn't he do everything he could to protect himself? If Paul were Shakleford, what would he do?

First of all he'd—Of course. Paul picked up the phone, and dialed the front desk. Susan came on the line. "This is Sergeant Kostovic. Check your register for Mister Shakleford. See if he might've taken another room besides seven-fourteen."

"Yes, sir, Sergeant. Just a second." Paul waited, and then Susan said, "No, sir. Only one room for Mister Shakleford. Seven-fourteen."

"Do this for me. Read off the reservations that came in yesterday."

"Oh, my God," Connington said, fidgeting with his watch. "That could take forever. Over a hundred registrations come into this hotel every day."

Paul waved for Connington to be quiet, and listened as Susan read from the registration book. "Adams, Burkowitz, Charles, Cook, Devers, Downing—"

Paul was beginning to think he was wasting his time.

"—Ethridge, Frost, Gibbons, Henry..."

"Wait!" Paul hollered. "Go back to Henry and read me the complete registration."

He heard a shuffling of paper, and then Susan said, "Henry Limited. New York, New..."

"That's it," Paul said. "What room?"

"Fifteen-eleven."

"Get the key and meet me there." Feeling his adrenaline flowing again, Paul pushed Connington into the hallway.

Paul did an anxious tap dance while they waited for the elevator, and when it finally came, with Susan inside, shoved Connington in. All but jumped in himself. When they arrived on fifteen, he pushed into the hallway before the elevator was barely open. Susan found 1511, and turned the key.

Paul eased her aside. Careful to protect possible fingerprints, he pushed the door open with his elbow. Taking one step inside, he scrutinizing the room. The windows were closed, but unlike 714 this room had a balcony. The bed had not been slept in, but it was disheveled, as if somebody had been lying on it without pulling back the covers. One pillow had been pulled out, and was on the floor. The chair by the phone was turned sideways, facing away from the desk. A suit coat had been thrown in a corner.

Paul put his eyes to the floor, watching for anything out of the ordinary, maybe crumpled paper, a spent match. Step by step he crossed the room. Nothing that he could see. Reaching the balcony, he looked down on the hotel's main entrance.

The UPS truck was directly below.

This was the place, he knew it.

And then a loud shriek came from behind. When Paul turned to look, Susan was standing in the middle of the room. Her horrified eyes were frozen on the French doors which opened into the balcony. Paul followed her stare, spotting three severed fingers sticking to one of the door knobs.

At once he remembered what Ditty had told Joe Holloway,

that Smedley enjoyed using a Ka-bar knife. "Okay, everybody outside," he said, and helped Connington walk Susan into the corridor.

"You gonna be all right?" he asked her.

Susan, beginning to perk up. "Yes. I think so. As long as I don't have to go back in there."

"Good girl." Paul slammed room 1511's door closed. To Connington, he said, "We're gonna have to seal this room off until the crime lab gets here."

"Not a problem," Connington said. He handed Paul the key. "Now can I leave?"

"We're all leaving," Paul said, thinking Debolt had to show pretty soon. "I wanna check how things are doing out front. After that we'll see about that attaché case in your safe." He pushed the call button for the elevator.

Chapter 26

WHEN PAUL GOT OUTSIDE, Tommy was guarding the crime scene like a junkyard watchdog. He had the sidewalk completely blocked off, and had traffic stopped in both directions. Horns were wailing, drivers were screaming, but Tommy remained steadfast. The kid was turning out okay.

All right, time to go back inside and check that attaché case. But then a paddy wagon pulled up. Volly Dickman and Joe Holloway got out grumbling. Joe saying, "Damn, Pauly. Why you always gotta go to playing big shot detective about the time we spoze to be going off shift?"

Volly went by the UPS truck. Surveying bloody guts seeping down its windshield. "You owe us. Double!" he said.

"Let's get it done," Joe said. He climbed onto the truck's front bumper, and grabbed Henry Shakleford's dangling leg, dragging the body over the side. Volly was waiting, and caught the arms. Together, they lugged Shakleford's body to the paddy wagon, and pitched it inside. As they pulled away, Volly yelled, "Pauly, you can tell that lummox Debolt for us, he's gonna have to go to the morgue he wants to look at this stiff."

The morgue. A good place for Debolt as far as Paul was concerned.

Tommy, standing alongside. "Did you see that? Don't they care about destroying evidence?"

"What evidence?" Paul said. "The guy got pushed out a window. Simple as that."

Tommy gawked. "I guess I know that, but—well—don't the crime lab have to look at the body, stuff like that?"

"Here, the morgue, what's the difference?" Paul pictured Henry's severed fingers in room 1511. "Don't you worry," he said, "they'll have plenty to keep themselves occupied upstairs, body or no body." He turned to Connington. "Let's go see what Shakleford put in your safe."

They started back into the hotel, but then a detective car came flying around the corner with its siren wailing. It screeched to a halt next to the UPS truck. Kyle Debolt got out, waved at Paul, and went directly to the UPS driver.

Paul leaned against Tommy, silently cursing himself for not having the good sense to check the hotel safe before Debolt showed.

Bracing himself, Tommy said, "You know, I'm as tired as you are. Let's give it up for now and report to the detective, let him take over. I mean, how bad can he screw up with all this help around?"

Paul, report to Debolt? Just about the funniest thing he'd ever heard. He said, "I'm telling you, once you decided to start acting like a cop, you went all the way, didn't you?"

Tommy smiled. "Yeah, I guess. Still, though…"

"Tell me. From what you've seen so far, is Debolt the kinda detective who's gonna listen to anything we got to say?"

Tommy looked at Debolt, who had his notepad out and was standing over the UPS driver. "We could try," he said. Sounding like he himself didn't believe Debolt would listen.

The way Paul saw it, Debolt was more hindrance than help. He sure as hell wasn't going to find anything Paul hadn't already found.

Then Connington stepped up, and said, "Should I tell the detective about what Mister Shakleford put in the safe?"

Paul looked from Connington to Debolt. Two of a kind, these two. No, nobody was as dumb as Debolt. Look at him, still interviewing the UPS driver. As if she knew a damned thing. Paul said, "He looks like he's pretty much occupied right now. We'll take a look, though. If it turns out to be anything important, I'll make sure he knows about it."

Connington marched back into the hotel, and took Paul into his office. A steel box sat in the far corner. Connington knelt in front of it. Reading from a three-by-five card, he spun the combination, first one direction, then another. He clicked open the handle, bent low, and looked inside.

"What the…?" Connington looked up at Paul, his face pale white. "Uh, it's not there."

Not funny at all, but Paul laughed just the same. "I'm not the least bit surprised," he said. "Nothing has gone right, not since Ditty and Shoes robbed Shakleford."

Connington, looking infuriated, pushed past Tommy, and rushed out the door. Paul followed. He came into the lobby in time to see Connington in a clandestine conversation at the bell captain's desk. Connington was asking the questions, what looked like the bell captain was doing the explaining. Voices began to raise, arms started waving.

Paul stepped between the two combatants, giving Connington a look that could kill.

Connington put his hands on his hips, and with his head pointed at the oriental rug, said, "I'm sorry, Sergeant. According to my bell captain, a man came into the hotel while we were outside. Regrettably, whoever the man was, he now has Mister Shakleford's valuables." Connington made a disdainful face for the bell captain's benefit. "Our procedure is to get authenticating identification before turning over items held for safekeeping. I'm afraid that policy was not adhered to." He looked at Paul as if he expected to be admonished.

And showed surprise when Paul said, "It's my own damn fault. I should've checked the safe before going up to Shakleford's room."

Connington, breathing easier. "Be assured," he said, "the Drake Hotel is a reputable establishment. We'll be happy to pay Mister Shakleford—uh—Mister Shakleford's benefactors, the monetary equivalent to his loss."

"Ain't that heartwarming," Paul said, "considering the fact that any lawyer worth his salt is sure as hell gonna make you pay up anyhow. And get ready for a shock, 'cause I figure you're gonna be taking a beating. I wouldn't be surprised to the tune of a hundred thousand or more."

Connington pointed an accusatory finger at the bell captain. "I'll have your job for this," he said.

"Wait just a minute," the bell captain said. "Sergeant, my name is Dominic Capri. I've been captain around here for a lotta years, and I know my job. The man had a receipt. He also had proper identification to back it up. How was I supposed to know he was an imposter?"

Connington hollered, "That's right, you're the bell captain. Today, you are. But not tomorrow."

"Whoa," Paul said. "This ain't getting us anywhere. Whatever was in that safe is gone. Let's see what we can do to get it back." He looked at Capri, who sounded like he had a lot more common sense than Connington. Paul saying, "What'd this guy look like, the guy with Mister Shakleford's receipt?"

Capri gave Connington a good, long eyeballing, and turned back to Paul. "I don't know. He was a big guy, over six feet. Built pretty good, too, especially for a man his age. I make him about thirty-five, could be a little older. He was wearing a business suit—black, yeah, it was black. Very nice, too." Capri looked at Connington, saying with conviction, "There wasn't a thing about this guy to suggest he was anything other than what he said he was."

"That's if you're telling us the truth," Connington said.

Paul had been right about Capri. He had some grit, because he grabbed the receipt out of Connington's hand, and offered it up as evidence. "The guy showed me a credit card in the name of Henry Shakleford. I wrote down its number on the receipt. I always do just to protect myself against finger-pointers like you. Also, I had him sign on the bottom. Look for yourself, it's identical to the one on the original copy when the case was put into safekeeping."

They formed a huddle in order to see the signature. Tommy, too, and he bumped shoulders with Paul.

Unable to help himself, Paul said, "Still acting like a real live copper, huh?" He took a moment to draw his conclusions. Whoever the imposter was, he must have practiced Shakleford's signature. Which meant he'd planned to get the attaché case out of the hotel safe from the beginning.

Slick.

This also explained why Shakleford was thrown to his death instead of being killed quietly. The imposter had to create a diversion to draw the front desk staff outside so he could safely use Shakleford's identification.

Not only slick. Smart. Very smart. Also daring.

Paul needed to know more about this cold-blooded killer, and said to the bell captain, "See if you can describe this guy a little better: color of hair, complexion, how he talked, anything you can remember."

Capri rubbed the back of his neck. "Hair, I don't know. Blond, I think. It was cut short so I couldn't really tell."

"You say it was short. Are you sure, or could the guy've

been bald?"

Capri took his bell captain's cap off, displaying a bowling ball for a head. "No, he wasn't bald. I would've noticed that. This guy had a full head of hair, thick, only cut super short. You remember the baldy-sour haircuts us kids used to get in the summer? That's what it looked like."

Paul nodded. He began to build a picture of the killer in his head. "Okay, anything else?"

"I don't know if this means anything, but the shoes the guy was wearing, their shine, it was like glass. I mean like nothing I ever saw before."

Paul pulled out his notepad and began inserting Capri's descriptions.

Then Susan said, "When we were upstairs, in 1511, I don't know if you noticed, but the access door to the next room was left open. It shouldn't have been."

Paul stared a hole in Susan's pretty nose. "No, the balcony had all my attention. I guess now we know how the killer got into that room. Next question…"

"I'm with you," Susan said. She went to the front desk, and flipped through the register. "Here it is. The room next door. Fifteen-thirteen. Its registration: S. Butler."

"And the room next door to seven-fourteen?" Paul said.

"Way ahead of you, Sergeant." Susan placed her finger on a second entry. "Room seven-sixteen. Also S. Butler."

Paul spun the book his way, and looked at the registration. "S. Butler," he muttered. "S for Smedley… Smedley Butler."

"Wow!" he said, and turned to the bell captain. "About the shoes, were they patent leather, or was it a natural shine?"

"I've been around hotels all my life, since I was fourteen. I've seen shoes shined by the best of them. These were not patent leather."

Feeling confident, Paul said, "And I'll bet they were plain toed, right?"

Capri's thick eyebrows flipped high. "Yeah, how'd you know?"

"Never mind. Don't really make any difference. One thing more, though. The shoes, were they brown or black?"

Capri looked at Paul as if he were a mind reader. "Brown, a

149

milky kinda brown. Why you ask a question like that?"

Paul mumbled, "Old Corps, I shoulda known." And to Connington, "I'll make sure the detective knows about what happened here. We'll be in touch if need be, but I don't think so. We've covered just about everything."

Capri offered his hand to Paul. "Glad to've helped," he said. "This Butler guy, he was a phony. I hope you get him."

"Phony?" Paul said. "Before you said there wasn't anything to suggest he wasn't who he said he was."

"Well, phony, yeah. Only not about who he was. More like what he was. One of those characters who're always smiling at you. A bogus kinda smile, too. You know, like a used car salesman. Pretty soon you can't stand it anymore, wanna give him a bust in the snoot."

Paul thought about Kyle Debolt, and patted Capri on the shoulder. "I think I know exactly what you mean," he said.

Tommy said, "Sarge. Before, there was this guy..."

"Not now, rookie," Paul said, and hurried for the street.

Where Debolt was just finishing with the UPS driver. Paul, doing his best to avoid his old partner, went directly to the patrol car.

Tommy was late coming out. He jumped into the passenger seat, saying, "I got me that redhead's number from the front desk." Then saw Paul's look. "Hey, sometimes a guy just can't help it."

"I figured," Paul said, "only it better not cost us."

As he was about to pull away, "Hey, Paul," and Debolt lumbered up. "How come you didn't hang around, help out with the crime scene?"

Paul looked at Tommy. "I'm gonna get you for this." Then to Debolt. "Sorry, Kyle, I was busy inside. Go up to room fifteen-eleven, you'll see what I mean."

"That's where Shakleford come from?"

"Yeah, and he didn't jump."

"I can see that. No doubt it was Ditty Caldwell what done it. You know, so Shakleford couldn't testify against him on the robbery case."

Paul sported a big grin. "You figure it was Ditty? Makes sense, I guess."

"There you go. Remember, he's already been identified in the diamond robbery. And last night he killed some other guy, the floater from the Chicago River."

"Volly and Joe told you, huh?" Paul should have known he couldn't trust those two.

"That's right." Debolt's face turned inquisitive. "Who you think the floater's gonna turn out to be, anyway?"

Paul had a pretty good idea, but was not ready to tell Debolt. Not yet. "Your guess is as good as mine, Kyle. I suppose we'll have to wait 'til the fingerprints come back from the lab."

Debolt leaned away from the car with a satisfied look on his face. "Yeah," he said, "and meanwhile I'll get another warrant out on Caldwell. Won't be long I'll have him."

"You're a good man," Paul said, and drove off.

A block down, Paul glanced at Tommy, who had a long face on. "Okay, so I lied," he said. "Confession's still every Saturday night, ain't it?"

"Bring a pillow, 'cause from what I've seen, you'll be there 'til Sunday morning."

"Which reminds me. I'm beat. Let's call it a day."

"Okay, but, uh, where do we go from here?"

"As far as this investigation is concerned, you're done. I'd say it's back to the beach detail for you."

Silence from Tommy, so Paul said, "I thought you'd be happy about going back to the beach."

Still nothing from Tommy, who was staring out the side window.

"What'sa matter with you, kid?"

Tommy, turned to Paul, glaring. "You didn't tell Debolt about the attaché case getting stolen outta the hotel safe. How come?"

Paul stopped at a traffic light. He gave Tommy a fierce stare, and said, "I'm the sergeant here. You're the rookie. So I'll do the thinking, and without any of your help."

Tommy, with a stubborn grimace. "You shoulda told him."

The light turned green, and a horn blasted behind them. Snapping his head away from Tommy, Paul got the patrol car going. They went a few blocks in silence. Paul had to say something. "Okay, it's like this," he said. "Debolt's bound to check with the hotel staff sooner or later. When he does,

151

they'll tell him everything he needs to know."

"Everything? I don't think so. 'Cause they don't know everything, do they? How come you're holding back, Sarge?"

"That'll be enough outta you," Paul said, tired of this rookie's attitude.

"Oh, no, you ain't getting away that easy. I was standing right next to you when the redhead got S. Butler from the registration book. You were mumbling, but I heard you just the same. 'Smedley,' you said. Smedley as in S. Butler I'm guessing. Who's Smedley Butler?"

Paul pulled into the Task Force parking lot, and turned off the ignition. It was time to tell this Covello kid where to get off, but before he could start, Tommy said, "I know you're hot at me. Thing is, I saw this Smedley guy."

Paul looked at Tommy, who had a straight face showing. "You say I've been holding back. Looks like you've been doing a pretty good job of holding back your own self."

"Hey, I tried telling you a half dozen times. You just wouldn't listen."

"Just spill it," Paul said, still finding if difficult to get used to Tommy being serious about police work.

"Like I said, I think I saw Smedley."

"'Think?' You didn't say think a minute ago."

"I know, but…"

Just as Paul thought. The kid didn't know what he'd seen. That is if he had seen anything at all. "Just tell me. Who and what was it you saw?"

Tommy, aggravated. "Boy, you're smooth, ain't ya. And you talk about Debolt."

"You gonna tell me, or do I gotta rip it outta you?"

Tommy bristled as if he were ready to accept Paul's challenge, then took a deep breath, and said, "Before, when we were out by the UPS truck, he was in the crowd."

"Who was in the crowd?" Paul knew his voice was rising. Too bad. Time for Tommy to get a dose of reality.

Tommy, right back. "This one guy. Our eyes met for just a second or so. He was smiling at me. Was just like the bell captain said. 'Once you see that smile you never forget it.' That's why I think he might've been Smedley. Or Butler. Or—

hell, I don't know, maybe Smedley Butler."

Paul waved his arm out the window. "Why not run out and arrest every dude you see with a smile. According to you they're all killers?"

"Only there's more," Tommy said undaunted. "As soon as this guy knew I was looking at him, he run off."

"He ran from you?" Paul said. He'd been ready to discount Tommy's story as inconsequential. Not anymore.

"Yeah, and I wanted us to go after him, but you pulled me away. Remember? That's when you told me to get to work. I looked back, trying to spot the guy, but he'd just plain disappeared."

Paul sat back, wondering if Tommy could be right. Wrongdoers were known to hang around crime scenes long after the fact. Some because they were compulsive, just couldn't bring themselves to leave. The smart ones, in order to find out just how much the cops knew.

Could be. Yeah. Just could be.

Tommy said, "You gonna tell me who this Smedley Butler is, or what?"

Paul looked at Tommy, but was too busy trying to sort out this new information to answer. He didn't know *who* Smedley Butler was, but he sure had a good idea *what* Smedley Butler was. Only what Smedley Butler was could include thousands of men. He had to think of a way to narrow the field. If Tommy was right, and really had seen the man's face, that might make the difference.

"Okay," he said, "I guess I'm gonna have to keep you around for awhile. But don't tell anybody what we talked about, you hear me?"

"Wait just a damned minute," Tommy said, showing outrage. "Don't be including me in your set of lies. I ain't gonna have it."

Paul didn't like having to explain himself to a green rookie, but under the circumstances he didn't feel he had a choice. "Listen," he said, "you've seen Debolt in action. He's a screw up from the word go. If I tell him about Smedley there's no telling what he's gonna do. Remember, Lieutenant Matthews is dead, a guy who did a whole lot for you." Making a stern face. "You want his killer to go free because of some stupid homicide dick?"

Tommy looked thoughtful. "I don't get it," he said. "I thought Ditty killed the lieutenant. You talk like you think this Smedley did it."

Paul said nothing, just kept up his stare.

"Come on," Tommy said. "It's one thing not telling Debolt stuff he's gonna find out anyway. But… I'm telling you, this don't make any sense at all."

Paul felt as though he was about to collapse from exhaustion. He had to get this over with once and for all. "I'm through arguing with you," he said. "You go ahead, tell Debolt all you know if that's what you want. But if you do, I'll send you back to the beach so fast your head'll spin. You keep your mouth shut, I'll keep you on until we find the bad guy."

Tommy stared off into space.

"Make up your mind," Paul said. "You sticking or not?"

"Okay, I'm sticking, but from now on you gotta let me know what's going on."

"You got it, kid. Equal partners." Paul stuck his hand out.

Tommy took it, saying, "Good, then you can tell me who Smedley is."

Paul stepped out of the car. "We got us a friend to put in the ground, boy. Soon as that's done, you'll know everything I know."

Chapter 27

SMEDLEY STEPPED INTO a corner drug store, watching through the street- side window that fool homicide detective playing hero for the crowd around the UPS truck. These cops. So damned easy to beat.

A saleslady came up, saying, "Is there anything in particular I might be able to help with?"

Smedley showed a pleasant smile. "No, thanks, ma'am. I'm just about to leave."

Anyway, nothing more to learn here. He moved onto the sidewalk. Strolling along, he stopped at one window here, another there, seeing everything, consuming nothing as he tried to understand how the Task Force cops had got on to him. Every aspect of the operation had to be given a thorough going over. First, he'd chosen Henry because he was the perfect target, then Ditty and Shoestring because they were so easy to manipulate. In the end, all three had been discarded, along with the rest. All of them, nothing but pawns to be thrown aside when the strategic moment presented itself. Not once had Smedley revealed anything of importance about himself. Well, once he had. On that first day, when he'd played doctor after the robbery. All the cops had seen his face. But would they remember him? Not likely, as busy as they were. Most of them hadn't really done more than glance at him, except for Lieutenant Matthews, that is. He'd even given Matthews his name for the report. Not smart, except Matthews was dead, and who else was going remember a tiny thing like that? Nobody. The cops showing at the hotel. Must have been just dumb luck. He was home free. Yeah, forget it.

He hefted the attaché case from one hand to the other, feeling a deep sense of satisfaction knowing the wealth contained within it. The operation was complete. He had accumulated over $300,000.00 in cash, and more than $600,000.00 in diamonds. Nearly a million, and not one witness left to identify him. Of course there was the bell captain. That was okay. He had a special surprise all planned out for that guy.

He stopped short, staring at his feet. "Okay," he mumbled, "you've covered all the bases, everything coming out perfectly. But those Task Force cops, coming to the hotel…"

He had to know why, even if it turned out to be dumb luck.

A new plan festered in his head as he stepped onto a Chicago Transit Authority bus bound for the bank.

Chapter 28

PAUL STOOD AT ATTENTION, every muscle rigid, except his eyes, which followed Lieutenant Matthews' casket as it was being lowered into the ground. Alongside, Tommy was bent over, weeping. Paul came out of his stance to lay an arm over Tommy's shoulder, wishing he himself could cry. But he couldn't. Tears were going to have to wait until Jack Matthews was revenged.

Paul felt a something touch his opposite hand, and looked around to find Katie at his back. He squeezed her hand, and she responded by resting her head on his shoulder. Then, as quickly as she had come, she melted back into the crowd, reappearing on the facing side. Her eyes fixed on his, telling him, it's all right, let yourself go. Like she was psychic or something.

But Paul couldn't. Not on this day. Not on any day, until— until— Damn, this girl had him so confused he couldn't think straight anymore.

By day's end Paul was spent. After dropping Tommy off in Little Italy, he drove straight for his apartment where he hoped to spend a quiet evening alone. Maybe he'd be able to sort this thing out between him and Katie. Then and only then could he put his mind on finding Jack Matthews' killer.

But no, because Katie was sitting on the front stoop when he pulled up. Rushing to meet him, she stepped into his arms. "Come on," she said. "Let's take another one of our rides. It'll do you some good."

"I don't know," Paul said, trying to come up with an excuse. "The last time we tried that, I had a lotta explaining to do to my Mom and Dad."

A tiny laugh came from Katie. "I got you through it, didn't I? Besides, I saw them off right after the funeral. They've got to be miles away by now."

This girl, so very alluring. "Okay," he said, "but first I gotta take a shower. I must stink like a pig after standing out in the hot sun all day."

Katie wrinkled up her nose. "You've got that right, country

boy. But I've spent enough time in that cubbyhole apartment of yours. We'll go over to my place. At least I've got air-conditioning."

"You do?" Paul said, tempted.

"Yes, and you can clean up there." She held up a brown paper bag. "I cleaned and pressed one of your police shirts, plus picked out some of your ragged underwear from that pile of junk you call a wardrobe."

"You've been going through my things? How'd you get into my apartment?"

"Are you kidding? While you've been out chasing bad guys, I've been in and out of this building dozens of times with your parents over the past few days." She went to the driver's door of his pickup, and with one leg on the running board, her skirt hiked high, said, "Give me the keys. I'm going to show you how a city girl can drive."

Paul knew it wasn't an accident, she giving him a look at those curvy legs. He started to wonder if he was ready for an evening with the likes of Katie Bartovich, and stammered, "I don't know, maybe I'll just stay here."

"Just give me the keys, Pauly," Katie barked.

She had never called him Pauly before. What was it with this girl? He stood motionless, his hand in his pocket, on his keys. Managing to say, "No way. That truck is my baby. I'm the only one that drives it." He pointed at her Volkswagen Bug parked a car's length ahead of the pickup. "Anyway, you're gonna need your car, aren't you?"

Katie slid into the pickup. "We can get it later. Now stop your whining and give me the keys."

What was the use? She'd just get her way in the end. He sat down in the passenger seat, and handed her the keys. Again those legs, exposed halfway up her thighs. Paul couldn't keep his eyes off of them.

"Here we go," she said.

Paul, thinking out loud. "You do know how to drive a stick, right?"

Katie jammed the key into the ignition. Giving it a wrench-like twist, she rammed the gearshift into first, and shoved the accelerator to the floor. Twenty-five feet down the street, she popped second gear. The pickup kicked back, burning rubber, and bore down on the traffic signal which had just turned from green to yellow.

She hollered over the whine of the transmission, "Yellow means hurry up, because red comes next," and swerved like Mario Andretti at the Indy 500, breezing past a truck which had just entered the intersection.

Paul was too busy hanging on to complain.

Katie parked in front of a converted warehouse on the Near North Side. Not far from the Cabrini Green Housing Project. She took Paul onto an industrial sized elevator, which had a steel gate and wooden plank floor. It rumbled and strained the five floors up to her loft. Katie hefted up the gate, and unlocked an inner door, shoving it open. Cool, refreshing air-conditioning hit Paul in the face. This he could take, even it had to be in the company of a screwball like Katie.

"Well, come on, before we air-condition the entire elevator shaft," Katie said. She stepped into her loft.

Paul obeyed, pulling the inner door closed behind him.

After shutting the blinds on the street-side windows, Katie plopped onto the bed, showing those legs again. Swinging them like a schoolgirl. Yeah, a schoolgirl from the hips down, but the way she was eyeing Paul, a total seductress up top.

Her saying, "You came for a shower. So go ahead."

Paul looked around the extraordinarily large one room apartment. Besides the bed, which was centered under an alley-side bay window, a room divider was in the far corner, an oaken wardrobe was placed against one wall, a desk and a bookcase on another wall. But no bathroom.

"Where is it?" he said, spinning on his heals.

Katie pointed at the room divider. "You'll find everything you need behind that thing."

Paul walked behind the room divider, and found a shower stall mounted on the wall between a small porcelain sink and commode. "No door?" he said, testing the flimsy room divider.

"I promise I won't look," Katie said.

159

Paul heard her giggling. He went up on his toes, peeking over the divider. "I don't know about this," he said.

Facing him, and doing her schoolgirl act with those legs of hers, Katie said, "'I don't know about this. I don't know about that.' That's all I ever get out of you anymore. Just shut your face and get in the shower. Nobody's going to rape you."

This girl just loved to play games. Well Paul was not gonna be her toy. He undressed, all the while checking for cracks in the room divider. He got down to his shorts, and stepped into the shower stall. One more look just to be sure. There she was, still on the bed, looking right at the divider. At him. As if the divider was transparent. But it wasn't. Damn, why couldn't he relax around this girl? Screw this, and in one quick jerk, he pulled his shorts down, and kicked them away.

Slowly the shower's invigorating spray eased his inhibitions. He was soaped head to toe, and humming a happy tune, when he thought he felt the shower stall shift ever so slightly. He was about to investigate when something warm and soft brushed against his back. Startled, he turned to look, but his face was covered with soap and he couldn't see. He groped with his hands, landing them upon—upon, "Jeeessus!"

Unable to stop himself, he popped his eyes open, getting one quick glimpse of Katie's mischievous smile before the sting from the soap forced his eyes closed again.

Except his hands, they were still on Katie's—and he jerked them away, banging his elbows on the side of the shower stall. "Yeow!" he cried, and the sting in his eyes returned.

Alternating between scratching his burning eyes, and rubbing his elbows, Paul was unprepared when Katie slid between his arms, pressing her body against his.

He said, "I don't know about…"

"I do," Katie whispered, wrapping her arms around his neck. Making like a monkey, she shinnied up his body, finally anchoring her legs around his hips. Saying, "No more of your, 'I don't know about this,' stuff," she rubbed her nose on his, following up with a lingering kiss full on his lips.

What seemed like hours later, Paul forced his eyes open.

He found Katie staring back at him. And then, ever so slowly, she dropped her head, nestling on his chest like a child sleeping in its mother's arms.

Something told Paul to run. Something else made him stay. Plain old animal instinct, he imagined. He slid a hand under her chin, pulling her face up to his. Their mouths came together, this time fervently so. Paul let himself go as they buried themselves into each other, tongues searching, teeth nipping.

A moment and Paul relaxed his legs, letting himself slide to the shower floor, bringing Katie with him. She dropped into his lap, her legs still wrapped around his hips. Paul let his hand venture down, and with fingers tingling, cupped her breast.

She smiled up at him, saying matter-of-factly, "I love you, you know."

He knew. Oh, how he knew. That was the problem.

Paul lay awake, watching the sun's first rays filter through the bay window. Katie was snuggled next to him, fast asleep, her head cuddled on his shoulder, an arm on his chest, a leg curled up on his belly. Those legs again. Oh, those legs.

How long he and Katie had been like this Paul didn't know, but for the entire time he'd been trying to figure out how last night had come to happen. He hadn't done anything to encourage Katie. Or had he? No, no way. Hell, ever since that first day he'd been busy trying to avoid her. And hadn't she hated him from the beginning? She'd even turned him in to the Internal Affairs Division, told them he was nothing but an animal.

Paul remembered last night. She was the animal.

And now, here she was in his arms. Or closer to the truth, he in her arms. Made him terrified equally with that first day in the jungles of Vietnam, when first he'd come under fire. Only in Vietnam he couldn't run. Not and leave his fellow Marines behind. Here, it was only him and his every instinct that not only told him to run, but to keep on running.

A dozen times during the past hour he'd come to this same conclusion, yet he was still here. Something was holding him back. What, he didn't know. He hadn't made any promises. For crying out loud, there hadn't been time for any such thing once Katie had jumped into the shower with him.

He'd never had a chance.

And God help him, he didn't want one.

He stroked her long, jet black hair, starting at its roots, combing his fingers over her shoulders, all the way down her back, taking special pleasure in running his hand through its tangles, softly playing with the tiny knots. When he reached the last strands, his hand continued down the small of her back, over the firm mounds of her buttocks. Then onto her legs, fondling the silky, smooth skin on the back on her knees.

"That tickles," came Katie's sleepy voice.

Paul felt like a six-year-old caught with his hand in the cookie jar, and jerked his hand away, leaving it hanging in midair just above Katie's perfectly rounded hips.

She made a satisfied smile, and wrapping her arms around his leg, whispered, "Don't stop. Just be careful not to tickle."

Paul was intimidated all over again and he knew it.

Katie knew too, he was sure of it, because she took his hand in hers, holding it to her cheek, saying, "Country boy, when the lights go out, you make like an animal. And then, when the sun comes up, you turn into a prude. What am I going to do with you?"

Paul had better change the subject before he made a complete fool of himself. "I'm gonna clean up. This is a working day, you know." He looked across the room, to the paper bag in which his clothes were contained.

Only he couldn't get it, not naked like he was. He knew he was being silly. For God's sake, all night they'd shared each other's bodies. But this was different. Somehow, it was. Why? He only wished he knew.

He saw Katie peeking up from behind his hand. She said, "Well, are you going, or what?" Sputtering a laugh.

Bare-assed or not, he'd be damned before the likes of

Katie Bartovich was going to make a fool out of Paul Kostovic. He ripped himself free, heading for his clothes. But before he could make two steps, Katie tackled him around the hips, tumbling him to the floor. She scrambled onto his chest, and straddled his sides with her legs. "I'm sorry, I'm sorry," she said. "I couldn't help it. It's just you make it so easy."

Paul pictured Katie hovering over him like this each day the rest of his life. He could get mad, scream, holler, rant and rave, nothing would make the slightest difference, not where this crazy girl was concerned. On impulse, he spread his arms wide, saying, "Okay, I surrender."

She hugged him, purring like a kitten.

And he said, "As much fun as this is, I gotta get to work."

Katie sat up, brushing his chin with the tips of her breasts. "You mean the Chicago Police Department comes before me?"

Oh, man. This girl, whatever her emotion, be it happy or sad, hate or love, she wore them all on the tip of that cute pug nose of hers. Most would call her girl-next-door kind of pretty. Not Paul. Uh-uh. Gorgeous through and through. No wonder he couldn't help but be taken by her.

He was about to carry her back to the bed when the clock above her desk chimed seven times. "No more," he said, and raised her off of his chest, depositing her on the floor. Forgetting his nakedness, he grabbed the bag with his clothes. "God knows I'd love to spend the whole day right here, but I've got some leads to follow up."

"What leads?" Katie said, looking disappointed. She tried to get back on him.

Paul pulled away, and hurried behind the room divider. "I know now Dittybop Caldwell didn't kill Lieutenant Matthews."

Katie came around the side of the room divider, tying a terrycloth bathrobe at her hips. With a serious expression on, she said, "You're wrong. Ditty killed the lieutenant. I was there, remember?"

Paul pulled up his pants, and started on his uniform shirt. "I know you were but things have happened that convince me otherwise." He sat down to pull on his shoes. "Think about it, could somebody else have been in that alley with you and Ditty?"

Katie looked thoughtful. "Just your saying it was somebody else makes me wonder. But—no, it was Ditty, I'm sure of it."

Paul pulled her into his lap. "You say you're sure, but all of a sudden you don't sound like it. How come?"

"You've got me thinking, but it was Ditty, that's it. Don't forget, one day I'm going to be called to testify at his trial. I'm a lawyer, well almost a lawyer, and I know what happens when a witness wavers even just a little bit. Their credibility is lost, that's what." She sat upright, looking into his eyes. "Lieutenant Matthews died saving my life. I owe it to him to make his killer pay."

"Me, too," Paul said, remembering his commitment. "Okay, if you say so. It's just I gotta check a few things out. Make sure." He eased her from his lap, and taking her hand, walked to the elevator.

As he pushed the call button, Katie said, "There's something I've got to tell you. I talked to Ditty."

Genuinely surprised, Paul said, "You did? When?"

"Well, it was twice, really. He called. The first time was the night before he killed Lieutenant Matthews. I tried to tell him to give himself up. He hung up on me. The next time was the night before the funeral." She contorted her face, showing that Katie Bartovich fury Paul himself had had the misfortune to experience. "That time I told him he could go to hell."

Paul gave her a look. "You mean he's got your home number?"

She looked back at him, the fury replaced by hostility. "Yes, he does. That's my job, you know, to help people like Ditty."

"Okay, so that's your job. Only why didn't you tell me before?" Paul knew he sounded like Kyle Debolt during one of his stupid interrogations. So what? She should have known better.

"I was going to, only you and me, we got occupied."

Giving him a schoolgirl smile. Seeing she had him captivated, she followed up the smile by kicking her robe up, showing her legs. "I like you liking that," she said.

Oh, God. Somehow Paul had to keep his head. Flushed in the face, he said, "That's not the point, and you know it." But even as Paul spoke he realized arguing with Katie was an act in futility. "Okay," he said, just wanting to get on with it. "What'd Ditty say, I mean before you told him he could go to hell?"

"I don't remember, exactly. It was in the middle of the night. Mostly, he wanted me to help him."

"You think he'll call back?"

"Maybe. He sounded pretty desperate."

Paul nodded. "Okay, if he does, call the station house right away." He looked at his watch. "I gotta go, and now."

Katie grabbed him by the ears, and buried her face in his neck, giving him a spine-tingling kiss. In a way it was vicious. Also erotic, enough for Paul to want to stay. Pulling away, he said, "You're one gorgeous piece of flesh. And that's why I gotta get outta here."

She skipped off behind the room divider, singing, "Go on, country boy. That was just a little something so you won't forget to come back."

Chapter 29

RUNNING INTO THE Task Force parking lot, Tommy said, "So now do I get told what's going on?"

Paul gave him a short glance, and as if speaking to an invisible bystander, said, "I told the kid this was gonna be an important day." He answering himself by saying, "So what's he do? Show up a half hour late, that's what."

Then back and forth: "Damn! What's this job coming to? Don't nobody give a shit anymore? I guess not."

He got into the passenger seat of the nearest patrol car.

Tommy went around to the driver's side. "Don't we have to make roll call?"

Paul went back to his solitary conversation. "I squared it so I'm on my own for the next couple'a days. Well, me'n this rookie. Lucky me. What I'd give for a real cop for a partner. So what do I end up with?" He thumbed at Tommy. "Mister Shitbird, that's who."

"Screw this," Tommy said. "Every time I open my mouth, I get my teeth jammed down my throat."

"Just get the damned car going, would you?"

Tommy let out an exasperated huff. "Okay, only I don't know where to go?"

"No, kidding. That ain't the only thing you don't know. Matter a fact there's very little you do know. Maybe what you don't know won't hurt you. Ha! Better yet, won't hurt me."

Tommy tried to speak up, but Paul waved him off. "Just leave me be. I'm thinking."

"You're thinking? The other day you said we were gonna be equal partners. I shoulda known." He sniffed at the air like a dog in heat. "Is that you? Yeah, that's you. You smell like a damned broad." A second thinking, and, "Katie, right?"

"That, you don't need to know about," Paul shot back.

But too late, because Tommy said, "Oh, look, the sarge's all flustered?"

Paul, wanting to change the subject. "You wanna know so much, here's a little tidbit. Ditty's been calling Katie."

Tommy stomped on the accelerator, and they lurched into

166

the street. "I figure there's only one place you wanna go. The Cabrini, right?"

When Paul failed to answer, Tommy, looking thoughtful. "I guess he's running scared, huh? Calling her and all."

"Yeah, I suppose," Paul said, and as they approached the Cabrini, "Turn right here and go all the way to the end."

Tommy made the turn, saying, "Why we going this way? I mean, it's a warehouse district." He navigated down the potholed street, adding, "You think maybe Ditty's hiding around here somewheres?"

"Down that way," Paul said, pointing to where the street dead-ended on the Chicago River.

Tommy said, "Like I expected an answer." He looked up ahead. "Hey, what's with the tow truck?"

Paul was more interested in the limo hooked to the tow truck's winch. That, he had not expected.

Tommy again. "And who's the nig—uh, you know, the tow driver?"

Paul glanced at the tow truck driver, dressed in a pair of greasy coveralls, with a railroad engineer's hat pushed back on his head. This guy Paul was not interested in. The other two, both white, who were leaning on a detective car, they he needed to talk to.

"And who're those guys?" Tommy said.

"Them? That's Stash Grabowski and Herman Goebel. They're coppers. Who'd you think they were?"

"Wow! Finally I get an answer. They don't look like any copper I ever saw before."

Paul had to admit Tommy was right, what with the way Stash and Herman were dressed: old clothes: tattered short sleeve shirts, faded blue jeans, work boots. He said, "That's because they're auto dicks, and auto dicks can't help it. It's okay, though. They're gonna do us some good... I hope."

"Wait a minute. I thought you didn't have any use for detectives."

"Me? Not having any use for detectives?" Then Paul remembered Debolt. "Oh, I get it. No, just one detective in particular. These boys you can rely on." Paul smiled. "And Herman. He likes Debolt even less than I do."

Stash Grabowski walked over, pushing an army issue hat back on his head, the kind with doggy ear flaps. Grabowski saying, "Hey, Pauly. You were right on, having us search the river bottom. Our tow truck man found this limo the first time he threw a hook in the water. It took us awhile, but we finally got it outta there."

Paul said, "A lucky guess, is all. Only I thought we we're gonna find us a certain white Cadillac." He and Stash joined the other auto detective by the waterlogged limo.

Tommy followed, saying, "Looks like this is gonna be another one of those wait and see if the great Sergeant Kostovic decides to include the new guy things."

Paul said, "Stop your cry-babying for a minute. Maybe you'll learn something."

The tow driver was talking with the other auto detective. "Okay, Herm," he said. "I found your damn car for you. So we're even, right?"

"Uh-uh," Herman said. "We ain't never gonna be even, Rubin, and that's the way I like it. When you think about it, we're kinda like partners."

"Yeah, sure," Rubin said. "All said and done I just as soon never laid my eyes on your ugly mug."

Paul got ready to get out of the way. No way was any cop going to let anybody talk to him like that.

But Herman didn't seem to mind. He wrapped an arm around Rubin's shoulders. "I know you love me," he said, "or why else would you treat me so sweet?"

Rubin shoved Herman's arm away. "Stop the bullshit," he said. "Just tell me when I can get outta here. My time's precious."

"Yeah, your time's precious all right. All you're gonna do is go on back to that junkyard of yours, get the Lumpkin brothers together and play whist all damn day. Taking turns slapping hole cards on that three-legged table that's supposed to have four. It's a wonder it's still standing. Then, when it gets to nighttime, you all go on out and rob yourselves some cars so's you can start in cheating each other all over come sunup."

Rubin must have heard this story before because he'd

turned his back about the time Herman got to the part about playing whist. Before Herman had finished, he was in his tow truck with the door slammed behind him.

Meanwhile Stash was inside the limo, rummaging through the glove compartment. That completed, he gave the interior a thorough search. When he finally came out, his clothes were wet and soiled, which didn't seem to bother him.

Paul flashed at Tommy, who looked like he was beginning to understand why auto detectives were a whole different breed of policemen.

"Look what I found," Stash said. He handed Paul a .38 revolver.

"That's exactly what I was looking for," Paul said. He turned to Tommy. "Come and see, kid. It's my long lost gun."

Tommy, looking the revolver over. "How can you tell? They all look alike to me." He looked up. "You mean you've got its serial number memorized?"

"Nope, but don't you worry, it's mine all right." Paul shoved the gun under his belt, and checked the limo's driver's door. "One shot through and through, just like I figured." He wondered out loud, "The limo, is there a stolen report on it?"

Herman said, "Yep. And a missing report on its driver, too." With a mischievous gleam in his eyes, he pulled a chain from his gun belt, which contained at least forty keys of all sizes and shapes. He thumbed through them, saying, "Chevy, Ford, Buick, Olds, Caddy—ah, here it is." He slipped the chosen key into the limo's trunk lock, and jiggled it side to side.

Rubin laughed out loud. "Lookit the old man make'n like he know how to rob cars."

Herman, biting his tongue, continued to jiggle. A pop, and the trunk sprung open. Herman looked at his key as if it had done magic, and said, "Can you believe it? I've tried that hundreds of times, but this is the first time it ever worked." Then he held his nose, saying, "Man, what a stench."

Paul moved alongside Herman, looking at a decomposing body curled up in the trunk. "This body, you knew it was gonna be in here?"

Herman shrugged. "A limo stolen. It's driver reported missing. Wasn't hard to figure."

Paul scrutinized the body. "This guy's head's half blown off."

Tommy, keeping his distance, said, "Looks like our friend Smedley's chalked up another one, huh, Sarge?"

"Looks like," Paul said as he wiped his hands on his uniform pants. "Of course Debolt's gonna blame it on Ditty."

"Smedley? Smedley Who?" Stash said.

Paul shrugged. "I only wish I knew. It's a phony name the killer's using. Listen, I know you guys got connections with motor vehicle headquarters down in Springfield. Maybe you could see what they got on a Smedley Butler. Try S. Butler, too."

"Nothing to it," Stash said. "We'll use the phones back at the office. You can get hold of us there."

"Good. I gotta make a couple'a calls myself. Give me a half hour head start, then call Debolt. I'm sure he'll be only too happy to take the body off your hands."

Chapter 30

"WHERE TO NOW?" Tommy said.

"All depends." Paul got in the driver's seat.

"I shoulda known I wasn't gonna get an answer," Tommy said, and he got in the passenger side.

Paul stopped at the first roadside telephone, and dialed a number from his notepad. One ring, and a gravely voice said, "Headquarters Company."

"Gunny, that you?"

"Yeah, you coming, or what?"

"Yeah, only I got a little delayed. No problem, though. Should be there most *skoshy*."

"You know how to get way out here to the boondocks?"

"Yeah, I think. That reminds me. Those boys at the front gate. They gonna let a civilian type like me past?"

"I told them you'd be coming. Just flash your star."

"Won't have to. I'm in uniform," Paul said. "See you soon." He hung up.

As Paul got back into the car, Tommy said, "What's this 'Most skoshy,' stuff."

"Did I say that? Funny how you revert back to your old ways when—well, it don't really make no difference."

"You gonna tell me or not?"

Paul stared into space, remembering times long ago. "*Skoshy*. That's gook for fast-quick-soon-little. Means a whole lotta things, I guess."

Tommy saying, "Skoshy—gook, all Greek to me. Wait, I get it. Some kinda code you and your telephone pal are only privy to. That's what I need, when it comes to the great Sergeant Kostovic. A code breaker."

Paul, still remembering long ago, and saying nothing.

Tommy went on. "Yeah, just like I figured. Well, looks like I'm gonna find out soon enough. The way you're driving we'll be wherever we're going… most *skoshy*." He made a satisfied kind of laugh.

Twenty minutes later Paul spotted a medium sized airport and knew he was on the right track. Yes, he was sure of it, because directly in front of them stood a huge sign which read,

GLENVIEW NAVAL AIR STATION

He pulled up to the gatehouse, and the guard said, "Been expecting you, Officer. Headquarters Company is all the way down on the end, past the airstrip. You can't miss it."

As Paul drove on, Tommy said, "I've heard of places like this. Never been to one, though." He looked about. "Look, everything's so perfect. The buildings, exactly alike, even down to the trim on the windows."

Paul listened only obliquely. The gunny, he had to keep his mind on how he was going to approach the gunny.

More from Tommy. The kid running off at the mouth, now. "Man, I ain't never seen so many jeeps. And talk about looking alike. How's anybody know which one is theirs?"

Paul, still in his own thoughts. This wasn't going to be easy. The gunny's first instinct would be to protect his fellow marine.

"Hey, look at these guys, marching just like on TV," Tommy said. "And all dressed up in nice neat uniforms. Man, I'll bet it's easy making broads in those things."

Paul glanced out the side window, past the marchers, to a second group of ten or twelve men who were running by in a shuffling kind of quickstep. On every fourth pace they stamped the pavement, creating a slapping thump.

Tommy, watching. "Uh-oh. Here come the bad asses, huh, Sarge?"

If Tommy only knew, and Paul took notice of their identical green T-shirts and red shorts. Each with the same haircut; a tuft of hair on top, the sides cut so short Paul could see their scalps. The leader ran slightly to the rear, and was hollering, "One-twoop-threep," a split second pause, and then, "Fow," synchronized with their slapping feet.

Unable to hold back, Paul hollered out the window, "Take that hill, you maggots!"

In unison, the running men raised their right fists high, and with heads still pointed straight to the front, hollered back, "All the way, all the way!"

"Who are those guys?" Tommy said, craning his neck at the back window.

Paul laughed. "Let's put it this way. If it wasn't for people like them we all would've had to learn Japanese along about thirty years ago."

"Here we go again," Tommy said. "Okay, I'll bite. What's that supposed to mean?"

"I'm about to show you," Paul said as they came to the end of the street. He parked alongside the lone building on the block, saying, "They always stick us away from everybody else. It's like we're the black sheep of the family." Smiling. "Maybe so."

"We?" Tommy said.

"Okay, us. Meaning them and me. Not you." Paul laughed out loud. "Especially you."

"You? Why...?"

"Just shut up. You'll see."

Looking bewildered, Tommy said, "How come this building's so much nicer than the others? I mean, it's the same and all. Only the grass, manicured like a putting green. And look at those guys, all in green dungarees. Their boots. The shiniest I've ever seen." He thought for a moment, and said, "What's a bunch'a soldiers doing on a naval base?"

Paul couldn't help but flinch, and said, "Boy, we're going inside in a minute. When we do, don't you dare call anybody soldier. These people won't think you're so damn funny."

"I'm telling you. You've got me lost."

"Jesus, kid. You ain't joking, are you?"

"No joke. I swear it."

Paul, intending to make himself perfectly clear. "For your information those guys are marines, not soldiers. There's a big difference, especially to them. Tell you what, just let me do the talking."

"Yeah. Like there's ever been a day around you when I was given an opportunity to say a word."

"Just remember." Leaving Tommy to his thought, Paul strode

to the front of the building, passing a sign with big red letters, reading:

MARINE BARRACKS

Paul had to admit Tommy was right about one thing. These places were all alike. He walked in the entranceway, instinctively knowing it would open into a wide hallway with floors buffed to a high gloss. And yes, offices on one side, an oversized rectangular shaped room on the other. In the room were two rows of steel framed, double-deck racks.

Coming up from the read, Tommy said, "Lookit how those bunk beds are lined up in perfect columns. It's like somebody took a string, stretched it out, and lined them up on it."

Paul went up to the first bunk. "Watch this," he said. He took out a quarter, held it up for Tommy to see, then dropped it on the lower mattress. It floated down like any quarter, but when it struck the blanket it sprang back up to his hand like an acrobat on a trampoline.

"What you think of that?" he said.

Tommy, sporting an 'I could care less face', "All day long you've been leading me around by the nose. First with the auto dicks, and if that wasn't enough, now we end up on a naval base… or something, I don't know what. Anyway, never do I get told squat. Whenever I ask the simplest question, you give me gibberish. Now I get a demonstration on how quarters bounce on Marine Corps beds. And you ask me what I think. I'll tell you what I think. I think I'm dealing with a raving maniac. That's what I think."

A foghorn-like voice bellowed from behind Tommy. "Boy, You better shut your damned mouth, or do I have'ta come over there and rip you a new asshole?"

Tommy spun around, looking irate, yet confused, at a marine sergeant, who was only about five and a half feet tall. Tommy walked past the sergeant, searching up and down the hallway. He looked back at the sergeant. "Who said that? I know a little shit like you'd have to be crazy to pick a fight with somebody like me, let alone make predictions about ripping new assholes."

The marine sergeant stepped close to Tommy, saying, "And get that damned cover off. You're in my house now. Not your mamma's back porch."

Tommy, looking at Paul. "Who is this guy? And what's this cover I'm supposed to take off?"

Paul removed Tommy's police hat. Stuffing it into Tommy's arms, he said, "I can't take you anywhere, can I?" He went to his old friend, grasping his arms, holding on for a long moment.

With a shake of his head, Paul said, "BJ, your ass is just as black as the day I first saw it."

The marine sergeant threw his arms around Paul, and Paul around the marine sergeant, hugging totally unashamed. After a long while, they walked into one of the offices on the other side of the hallway.

Reappearing at the door, Paul said, "Come on, Tommy. I ain't gonna let him murder you."

Tommy came to the doorway, quiet for a change. The kid doing his best to try to understand.

The office was smaller than the one Paul remembered to be his old gunny's back in the 9th Marines. But it had the same kind of ornamentation. Superbly neat and clean, with a medium sized desk facing the door. A plaque centered on its surface, and on each of its outer edges, Marine Corps globe and anchor emblems.

Printed between them was:

MASTER GUNNERY SERGEANT BJ MCCOY

A poster affixed on the wall, behind and just over Sergeant McCoy's head, read:

THE MAN WHO DIES FOR HIS COUNTRY IS A HERO
DON'T BE A HERO

On the sidewall, another read:

NO EXCUSES

175

BJ took a seat behind the desk. Paul sat down in one of the chairs in front of it. He looked back at Tommy, who was staring at BJ with what appeared to be newfound respect. Paul looked too. The ebony-skinned marine was sitting erect, thick arms folded in front of him. He held his head high, his back straight, and had a flat belly along with a firm chest that any professional weightlifter would be proud to display. Didn't look at all like the forty-odd years BJ had to be.

Paul looked back at Tommy, knowing the brash rookie had come to the conclusion that he had been absolutely wrong to think little of BJ McCoy.

BJ said, "You got yourself a damn impertinent shit for a sidekick, don't you, Pauly?"

Paul cleared his throat. "You're right, BJ. The kid can be a turd."

Tommy looked like he wanted to strangle Paul, and in reconciliation Paul motioned to the chair alongside his own. "Sit down, kid. This is what you've been waiting to hear."

Tommy wasted no time getting to the chair.

Paul went through the preliminaries, explaining about the robbery of Henry Shakleford, and how his service revolver had been lost in the shuffle, ending up being used to kill an innocent bystander. "The kid here, he's been with me all the way, trying to track the killer down." Paul glanced at Tommy. "He's pretty much worthless, but I gotta hand it to him. At least he's got some balls."

Tommy said, "I'm glad I'm sitting down. If I'd been standing, I'd probably fall on my face."

Paul laughed. BJ did not, and Paul went on to tell about Shoestring getting murdered, along with a string of other killings, and that Paul's gun was used in some of them.

BJ looked at Tommy.

"No," Paul said, "It wasn't the kid. Internal Affairs ran us both through the grinder. I did my own checking, too. He came out clean."

Speaking to Paul, and all the while continuing to stare Tommy down, BJ said, "Where's the Corps come into this shit?"

"How'd you know the Corps was involved?" Paul said, surprised.

"Just go ahead, tell me. If need be, I'll let you know."

Paul nodded thoughtfully. He talked about Ditty, how he was involved in the diamond robbery, and later found at the scene of one of the killings. "And there's this dumbshit detective who's got Ditty fingered for the mastermind of the whole thing."

BJ kept the same poker face.

"You ain't making this any easier," Paul said.

"And you ain't got to the punch line yet, have you? Come on, spill it."

Paul sat up in his chair, keeping a sober face at his old marine gunny sergeant. "Okay, if that's the way you want it. After awhile a second suspect started popping up. He was methodical, let nothing get in his way. At first I didn't have a clue who he was. Then he started showing himself." Paul nodded at Tommy. "Him included. Everybody described him the same way: mean looking, lean and hard, with a white side-wall haircut."

BJ leaned back, crossing his chest with his arms.

Paul said, "I know what you're thinking, that it don't mean nothing. Except he told Ditty his name was Smedley."

BJ's hands clinched into tight fists.

"Yeah," Paul said. "Then yesterday he used S. Butler to register at a hotel. Get it? S for Smedley, and then Butler. Put them together and you get Smedley Butler. The guy served the Corps, BJ. What more evidence you need than that?"

"Who's this Smedley Butler guy?" Tommy said.

Paul kept his eyes on BJ, who had not moved, eyes or body.

Tommy said, "Sarge, maybe you need to make yourself clearer. I wish you would, because Smedley Butler means nothing to me."

Ignoring Tommy, Paul gave BJ a little of his own medicine: the same silent treatment. BJ stared back, eyes steady. Paul felt as if they were a couple of rabid dogs. Waiting to see which one would jump first.

Tommy again. "You two gonna tell me who's this Smedley Butler character, or what? And how come, just by his name, you know he's a marine?"

Paul remained quiet, as did BJ.

Tommy stood up, saying, "I might as well leave, come back and pick up the pieces when you two are finished, because it looks like there's gonna be one hell of a brawl."

A weird kind of smile replaced BJ's poke face. "So tell your pal, Paul. You told him you were gonna."

Paul gritted his teeth, and barked, "Enough of this bullshit. I've said all I'm gonna say 'til I know where you stand."

BJ nodded as if in agreement, and turned to Tommy. "Smedley Butler was a famous marine from way back, a hero amongst heroes. I don't suppose his name would mean anything to you. But for us, and for any man who's served the Corps, he's embedded deep in our souls." BJ turned back to Paul. "Feel better now?"

Paul continued his silent treatment. Seeing how BJ liked it.

Tommy, as if he were an arbitrator. "Okay, so our Smedley is, or maybe was, a marine. That's what you're saying, right? I mean, there has to've been millions of marines. What I'm trying to say is... Hell, I don't have the slightest idea what I'm trying to say."

Paul, still with eyes only for BJ.

Tommy, now speaking directly at Paul. "Obviously you think there's something we can learn here that's gonna help us find Smedley."

Never looking away from BJ, Paul said, "Look at what I'm looking at, kid. See what I'm seeing."

Tommy leaned forward, coming into Paul's peripheral vision, and peered at BJ as if he fully expected the big secret to finally be revealed. "Damn it," he said. "You're gonna have to just plain tell me, Sarge. Because I ain't got a clue."

"Look at his eyes. Look at that smile."

Tommy looked back at BJ. "Wait. The weird smile, right? Like Smedley gave me at the Drake." Tommy's face grew contorted. "You mean this is Smedley? No, the guy I saw was white." A second, and he blurted out, "You mean there's two of them?"

BJ laughed, and said to Paul, "You're putting some crazy ideas in the boy's head, ain't you?"

"Crazy, BJ?" Paul said, still holding a straight face.

"You can't be serious." BJ wasn't laughing anymore. The

hard-nosed demeanor was missing, too. "Come on, you can't really think I'd let myself get mixed up in murder."

"Even for the Corps?" Paul said.

Tommy pulled his handcuffs off his gun belt, ready to slap them on BJ. "All I need is your say so," he said to Paul.

Paul pushed Tommy back in his chair. "Relax, kid. I'll handle this." He switching to BJ. "Once, a long time ago, you saved my life. And for that I owe you. I'd do anything for you and you know it. I didn't come here thinking you're part of this, but from the beginning you've been playing games, giving me that, I ain't telling you shit, attitude. So before we go any further I gotta ask. What's to it, BJ? How come all the bullshit?"

BJ, steadily. "First tell me when all this happened?"

"You gonna answer me, or are you gonna start the crap again?"

"Can't you see I'm trying to answer you, you damned fool? Just tell me. When was the robbery?"

Paul formulated a line of questioning in his head. "Okay, here it is. We need to know what you've been doing every minute of every day for the past month. I'm serious, BJ. If I think you're bullshitting, the cuffs go on, buddies or not."

BJ, smirking. "Last couple'a weeks, is that what we're talking about? That makes it easy. Until yesterday I've been out at Pendleton playing war games with the First Division. So unless the Chicago Police is investigating robberies and murders in California, I guess I can't be your man, can I?"

"Can you prove that?" Tommy said, handcuffs still at the ready.

BJ gave Tommy the evil eye. "I ain't lying, boy. Paul can tell you that."

Paul nodded. "No, he ain't lying. But he ain't telling it all, either."

BJ's stoic poise was back, and Tommy said, "Was up to me, I'd cuff the pompous ass and take him to the station. Let him try this stuff from the lockup."

Paul, thinking a new approach might work. "BJ, I know how you feel, not wanting to give up a fellow marine. But this ain't no horse manure bar fight, or a broad looking to get back at her boyfriend. This dude's piling up bodies all over Chicago."

BJ pressed his fingers to his forehead, rubbing.

Maybe Paul was getting close, and he added, "If somebody else dies and you could've prevented it, how you gonna live with yourself?"

BJ looked up, making a smile. Only rather than the tough, marine sergeant sneer kind of smile, it was more a resignation. "You're right, Paul. I've got my suspicions who you're after. But that doesn't mean I know for sure. And I sure as hell don't know how to find him."

"You leave that up to us."

"That's the amazing part. I can understand how you figured out he was a marine, what with the white-side-wall haircut and the rest. But how'd you know I was gonna know him?"

"I didn't know, except when he showed himself to the bell captain, he was wearing highly polished shoes. And they were brown."

Comprehension showed on BJ's face.

"Yeah, that's right," Paul said. "Old Corps, no doubt about it. And you've been in a long time, BJ."

Tommy jumped in. "Wait a minute. Brown shoes? What am I missing here?"

Paul flashed a look at Tommy, and turned back to BJ. "Like the gunny can tell you, for years all the military services wore black dress shoes. That is except for marines, who wore brown. Then along about sixty-one, come a money crunch, and the Corps got switched to black like everybody else. Since Smedley wore brown shoes, I knew he was a marine that had served way back, in the Old Corps."

"Okay, but I've got one more question," Tommy said. The kid was going strong now, probably figuring why not get it all out while somebody was listening for a change. And said, "The sneery smile. The eyes. You gonna tell me every man that's been in the Marines prior to nineteen-sixty is walking around with a grin that could scare you half to death?"

BJ raised his eyes. "Let me answer that one. No, not every marine. Just a very select few, the ones who were drill instructors."

Tommy leaned forward. "You're gonna have to explain better than that."

"You know what a drill instructor is, right?"

"Yeah, so?"

Glancing at Paul, BJ scratched his short-cropped head. "I don't think he's gonna get it."

Tommy's whole body sagged, as if her felt as though he was persona non grata.

Paul said, "I don't know that it'll be any different coming from me, but I'll try." He turned to Tommy. "It ain't like the Marines are this great mystical group of heroes. Not at all. It's discipline, boy, and pride, pride like you can't believe. That's what Marine Corps boot camp is all about whatever anybody tries to tell you. And the men that make it that way are the drill instructors. Drill instructors, they gotta present themselves like gods in front of the boots. Uh, you know, the recruits. You getting me?"

Tommy nodded, but Paul wasn't so sure, and said, "These drill instructors got the meanest faces possible, evil like. And their eyes, like needles that could bore through a mountain. It's all for effect, effect on the boys they're tying to make into marines. And whose lives are gonna depend on the discipline and pride the drill instructors instill in them."

BJ nodded his approval. "That's the look you saw on your boy Smedley, right?"

"I guess," Tommy said, still looking like he was in a fog.

And Paul. "Enough war stories. We need the name of the killer."

BJ shifted. Looking uncomfortable. "Okay. I could be wrong, though." But the sorrowful expression on his face revealed that he knew he was right. "Eric Halverson's his name. You didn't know him, Paul. It must've been around sixty-two, sixty-three. I was with Three-Nine, on Okinawa. That's Third battalion, Ninth Marine Regiment to you," he said to Tommy. "I was a sergeant in a reconnaissance platoon. Halvy was a corporal and served as one of my squad leaders.

"About that time Laotian Communists were having a good old time along the Mekong River, ripping up villages in Northern Thailand. We got sent in. Really wasn't that much to it, except for us guys in reconnaissance. Anyway, Halverson turned out to be a stone-cold killer. Excellent marine, except he was always jeopardizing his troops. I got rid of him."

"What happened to him?" Paul said.

"Relax, Paul. This story's a little long. Halvy went back stateside and finagled his way into DI School. That didn't last long, though. He beat the shit outta some unlucky recruit. Lost a stripe, and was sent back to the Ninth.

"By then we were in Vietnam. That was on my first tour. You came along during my second. Anyway, we were losing men every day. I couldn't be choosy and took him back. Pretty soon he was back to doing what good marines do best, kill and kill some more. He got his stripe back and one more." BJ switched to Tommy. "This one time he found what he thought was a bunch of stragglers out in the open. Without making sure, the idiot set up an ambush. Those stragglers turned out to be a reinforced company of North Vietnamese regulars. He was the only man to make it out alive."

"You never shoulda let him back," Paul said.

"I know that now. But even then I was suspicious. And as long as I was platoon sergeant we weren't gonna leave those boys out there, alive or dead. The long and the short of it was we found the others a good mile from where he said they'd be. Only the radioman was still alive. Barely so, but he lived long enough to tell us Halverson had run, and at the expense of his own men.

"Laos was one thing, but this time I saw to it that coward got court martialed. Problem was the only real evidence we had was the statement from the now dead radioman. It was enough to get Halverson drummed out of the Corps, but no time in jail."

BJ took a deep breath and leaned back in his chair, as if he had just taken a big load off of his mind. "That's the last I ever saw of him. Good riddance, too."

Paul said, "That's it? That's all you know?"

"Yeah. It's not like he came to any of the reunion parties after getting thrown outta the Corps."

"How about his home, his family, wife, kids? I need something to work with."

BJ shook his head. "Uh-uh. He was a lifer marine, married to the Corps. His home was wherever they sent him. As far as family goes, even before this stuff happened we weren't exactly friends, so I didn't know that much about him. I do know he wasn't married. If he has any kids, they're probably wandering around Vietnam looking half American and half Asian."

Paul scribbled into his notepad, and looked up. "So you haven't had any contact with him since the court martial?"

"None. But I do know he got in trouble with the law after he was discharged. It was maybe a year later. I was stateside then, stationed at Twenty-Nine Palms. You know, that shithole out in the desert. A couple'a cops from LA came visiting, and started in asking questions a mile a minute. I thought it was something I'd done 'cause they wanted to know where I was spending my time, with who, stuff like that. And no matter how many times I asked, they wouldn't tell me what it was about."

Paul said with a shake of the head, "That's detectives for you. I'll bet they got around to it, though, didn't they?"

"Yeah, but only after they checked my military records and found out I'd just come back from overseas. That's when they started playing their silly games. They said they'd heard me and Halverson were buddies, that they needed to talk to him, that they'd see to it I'd get jammed up with the Corps if I didn't cooperate."

Paul laughed. "What'd you do?"

BJ flashed his drill instructor eyes. "I busted the nearest one right in the teeth. What'd you think I'd do?"

Paul roared, and slapped hands with BJ. Tommy laughed too, but more as if to go along. Obviously not so sure he believed BJ would have the audacity to hit a cop.

Paul did. "I love it. They fooled with the wrong guy, didn't they?"

"Hell, yeah!" BJ was still laughing. "I knew they hadda be bullshitting. I was the main witness at Halverson's court martial, so how could I be one of his buddies? And jam me up with the Corps? Me, Bobby Joe McCoy? What a crock'a shit that was. They went running to my C.O., told him they wanted me locked up, that I was a nutcase. The old man was a stand

183

up guy. He told them yeah, that they were right. I was a little crazy. Said they'd better clear out before I came looking for them with a grenade or something worse.

"They were gonna leave, too, but I wanted to find out what Halverson had pulled this time, so I met up with them when they came out of H.Q. I told 'em as long as they were straight with me, I'd tell all I knew." He winked. "Which was nothing, of course."

Paul laughed with every word out of BJ's mouth.

"So anyway, I guess Halverson was identified in a series of jewelry robberies."

Paul and Tommy gave each other stares.

BJ said, "I get it. You're after him for a robbery in Chicago."

Paul remained silent, and motioned for BJ to continue.

"Okay, let me think. They wanted to know if I'd seen him, or if I knew where they could find him. Just like you guys. If I'd known anything, I'd've told them. But I didn't. I think they believed me 'cause that was the end of it."

Paul closed his notepad. "And you never heard anything more about it?"

BJ shrugged. "Only when I ran into one of the old Ninth Marines guys. He'd got the same kinda visit from the cops. That's gotta be two, three years ago."

Paul scribbled his phone number on BJ's desk pad. "That's where you can reach me," he said, and got up. "Just one thing more. If it was you after Halverson, where would you look first?"

BJ's face showed surprise at Paul's question, then turned thoughtful. "I haven't got the slightest idea. I'll tell you one or two things I do know, though. Halvy's got one big weakness. He's not much for swimming. Don't get me wrong, he can swim if he has to. It's just, this one time we were all in a chopper that got shot down over a river. He almost drowned getting out. After that, he stayed away from water. Don't underestimate him, though. He's resourceful, and knows how to blend in anywhere. He can strike without warning, usually at the most unexpected time. Look out, 'cause he'll do you in a second if he thinks you're on to him." BJ rubbed his jaw. "I'd be worried for everybody he's come in contact with. He's been trained to leave absolutely nobody behind who could possibly hurt him. One more thing. He used to love to use his Ka-Bar on Charlie. Don't let him get close or for sure he's gonna cut you deep."

Tommy waited until they were back in the car before opening up on Paul. "You know, it took me awhile, but I picked up on almost everything that went on back there. I do have a few questions, though." He waited for Paul's usual rebuff, continuing only after it didn't come. "That story about the LA cops who came to visit, the part where he said he hit the policeman. Didn't you find that a little hard to believe?"

"No, not at all," Paul said, as if it had been the most natural thing in the world.

"Come on, Sarge. Nobody takes a swing at a cop and expects to get away with it."

"BJ can. Maybe only inside the confines of a military installation, but take my word for it, he can."

Tommy, still skeptical. "You're gonna have to convince me."

Paul remained steadfast on his driving. He considered how much he wanted to tell Tommy. A lot of which was private between himself and BJ. He finally said, "You know all the plastic he was wearing on his shirt, the colorful stuff above his pocket?"

"Sure, that's battle ribbons, everybody knows that. Things soldiers get for being in wars."

Paul nodded. "The one on the top, plain blue with a cluster of stars? That's the Medal Of Honor."

"Wow," Tommy said. He sat forward, catching Paul's eye. "Back there you said something about him saving your life. You mean…"

"That's right. Me, and a half dozen more." He looked Tommy straight in the face. "Subject closed."

Chapter 31

HALVERSON READ THE NEWSPAPERS and found a front page article about the girl who had been in the alley when he killed the cop, that she had identified Ditty as the killer. Ha. Just like Ditty had suspected. The article went on to say that she worked as a legal aide, and that she had helped Caldwell in the past. Maybe Halverson had better use his Ka-bar on this broad, just to be safe.

He had her card, the one he'd taken from Ditty, and from it her address. So this morning, after his five mile run, he got into his BMW and staked out her building. That's when he saw the other cop come out, Kostovic, the one who'd tried breaking up the diamond robbery. This cop, whoever he was, might be something Halverson needed to deal with right here and now. Afterwards he'd go upstairs and do the broad. But there wasn't any real need, not just then. Besides, a burning question was still unanswered. When Halverson had done Henry at the Drake Hotel, the cops had shown up. Why? What did they know? And how?

Halverson would follow the cop, see what more he could learn. Predictably, the cop went straight to a police station on the North Side. Halverson drove around the corner, and set up so he had an unobstructed view of the station's front entrance. He didn't think anything worthwhile would come of it, but he'd give it a few minutes, see what happened.

While he waited, he adjusted the radio to Chicago's all-news station. The announcer was reporting morning traffic delays and quips about another loss for the Cubs. Halverson wondered if something had gone wrong on his little sojourn up to Rogers Park last night.

It wasn't long before Paul drove out of the parking lot in a patrol car with the young cop who'd been with him at the Drake Hotel. Halverson waited for a few cars to pass, then got in behind them. They drove in the direction of the Cabrini Green Housing Project, but then made a turn into the industrial area that led back to the river. Peeling off, Halverson drove across the bridge, parking on the opposite side of the river, taking up watch from a vacant warehouse.

Damn. Who were these Task Force cops, and where were they getting their information? Because look at this, there the limo was, the one Halverson had used to rob Randolph Laidlaw. Some black dude had it up on a tow truck. Two other cops were there, too. Dressed like bums, these cops. Not Task Force men, Halverson didn't think. But cops just the same, because the big one with curly hair started fooling around by the limo's trunk. Somehow he got it open. They'd found Halfpint. Only no sign of Randolph Laidlaw. Ditty either. Could their bodies have been removed already? He didn't think so.

One huge question immediately came to mind. Did the cops just happen to find the limo? Under twenty, thirty feet of murky water? Not a chance. No more than they happened to show up at the Drake Hotel just as Halverson was getting rid of Henry. Halverson was missing something. Only, dammit, what?

Only three people knew about the limo. Number one, Halverson himself, and he sure as hell hadn't told the cops about it. Second, Laidlaw. Halverson smiled. Not him, either, not with a bullet stuck in his brain. And Ditty. Halverson's smile turned inquisitive. That kid had nine lives. Somehow he must've escaped from the limo and told the cops everything.

Yes, this was the only answer that made sense. But what didn't make sense was if Ditty was alive and had told the cops everything, then he had to be under arrest. And if he was under arrest, why wasn't it reported in the newspapers?

The key had to be these Task Force cops. Halverson would have to raise them a few rungs on his ladder of respect. He watched across the river with interest.

Not for long, though, because Paul and the young cop were leaving, and in a hurry. Halverson might have lost them had they not stopped at a pay phone. Paul had just hung up, and was jumping back into the patrol car when Halverson pulled out from the other side of the river. They got on a northbound expressway, and were driving like hell, as if they knew exactly where they were going. Ending up at the main gate of Glenview Naval Air Base.

"Son-of-a-bitch. Just who the hell are these guys?"

Hold it. Don't got crazy on yourself. Remember your reconnaissance training. Get in there and find out where you stand.

He pulled up to the gate, and as naturally as possible, said, "I'm with the Chicago Police. Has the others arrived yet?"

"Just got here, sir." The guard said, not asking for identification.

Halverson had to suppress a laugh as he was being explained the directions to Marine Barracks. Then it sunk in. "'Marine Barracks?'"

He drove away from the gate staring blindly, barely able to navigate the wide-open thoroughfare. Only on instinct did he find his destination. Somehow he had enough presence of mind to continue past as the cops were getting out of their car. He pulled up a half block down, hurrying to adjust his rearview mirror as they came around the corner and up the sidewalk to the front entrance.

He tried to learn something by the way they acted. Did they appear as if they had been here before? Not the young one. He looked all but lost the way he straggled behind Paul. But Paul, what about him? Halverson narrowed his eyes on this pain in the ass cop. Look at him, walking straight into the building like somebody who belonged.

That's it, you idiot, came a voice from within. You're looking at a marine.

Which answered so many questions. Paul had been part of the investigation at the Drake Hotel and had to know about Halverson using S. Butler to reserve the rooms next to Shakleford's rooms. Somehow, probably with the help of Ditty, Paul had put Smedley together with S. Butler and came up with Smedley Butler. Easy for a marine.

Still, Halverson couldn't complain. That was the idea, wasn't it? To use famous marines' names as his cover so that eventually the cops would know it was a marine who had fleeced their town? Of course this time the cops were on to him a lot quicker than they were supposed to be.

And Paul, what would he be expected to do after finding out the man he was looking for was a marine? Check with the nearest marines, that's what.

Except they wouldn't know a damned thing.

Halverson figured he'd learned all he was going to learn, and was about go back to the girl's place, get that little job out of the way. Then he thought again. What was the hurry? Why not hang around and see what happened?

This could take awhile. He turned on the car radio, wondering if maybe what he needed to hear was finally on. A loud, pulsating burst of music came on, followed by the deep, sensationalizing voice of the studio announcer.

"THIS IS A SPECIAL REPORT FROM W-H-A-T RADIO, YOUR FIRST WITNESS TO EVERY BREAKING STORY. THERE'S BEEN ANOTHER GANGLAND SLAYING IN THE WINDY CITY." A pause. "IN ROGERS PARK, AT THE BROADMIER APARTMENTS, THERE HAS BEEN A HORRIFIC EXPLOSION. TARGETED WAS A LATE MODEL, METALLIC BLACK CADILLAC—"

Halverson couldn't believe this guy. The damned car was green, and at least fifteen years old. The reporter had seen too many gangster movies, assumed it was black. Well, it's probably black now. Who could tell after plastic explosives were detonated under its front seat?

"—THE CAR WAS DESTROYED. INSIDE WERE THE REMAINS OF A HUMAN BODY. NOT IDENTIFIABLE AT THIS TIME—"

Halverson could just imagine. They'd probably find fingers and toes on the roof of the Broadmier.

"—THE DESTROYED CADILLAC IS REGISTERED TO A MISTER DOMINIC CAPRI, A LONG TIME EMPLOYEE OF THE DRAKE HOTEL. SEASONED DETECTIVES OF THE CRACK CHICAGO POLICE BOMB SQUAD ARE IN THE PROCESS OF DETERMINING IF MISTER CAPRI WAS THE VICTIM—"

Halverson switched to the easy-listening station, satisfied that last night's work had been a complete success. Hadn't been much to it really. A name like Dominic Capri had been easy to find in the phone book. And the car, what a snap that was. As soon as Halverson had seen the Drake Hotel parking permit decal on the back bumper he knew he had his man. Dominic Capri was sent to bellhop heaven—in pieces.

It was close to an hour since the cops had gone into the building. Halverson looked back at the barracks. Finally, there they were. He wished they could see him laughing at them. "What's the matter, boys? Didn't find me, did you? You idiots." He hissed his words through clenched teeth, barely conscious that he had spoken aloud.

Somebody was with them. The uniform was unmistakable, a marine gunnery sergeant. Even from this distance Halverson could see that the gunny had a chestful of battle ribbons. He must have had two, maybe thee tours in Vietnam. Maybe even done Korea, too.

The gunny was walking the cops to their car, jabbering with Paul as they went along. They were slapping each other on the back, having a grand old time. Marines and their war stories. Never know when to shut up.

"Okay, enough talk, Gunny," Halverson said. "Beat it so we can all get outta here."

But they remained, talking.

The hell with this. He'd seen enough, and whipped a U-turn for the main gate, glancing at them as he passed by. At that precise moment the gunnery sergeant turned back toward the barracks, and Halverson looked him full in the face.

"Bobby Joe McCoy! Of all the…"

The shock was almost too much. Halverson could barely keep the BMW on the road. His heart pounded, and he was panting like a dog. Trying to ignore the blood pounding in his ears, he headed for the main gate, repressing the urge to jam the accelerator to the floor.

He checked his rearview mirror. The cops had just turned onto the street. They didn't seem to be in any hurry. And BJ was still standing there, not moving one direction or the other. Forget it for now. Just get your bones outta here. Once you're safe you can sit down and reconnoiter.

The main gate was no problem, never was on any military base. They checked you coming in, not going out. One turn and he was on the road back toward the city.

He used the rearview mirror again. Damn! The cops were right behind, and when he stopped at the first red light they pulled up alongside. Perspiration oozed down the bridge of his nose, dripping onto his chin. He was afraid to wipe it away, afraid to do anything that might draw attention to the cops. Slowly, he turned away so that they could only see the back of his head.

Mercifully the light turned green, and the cops pulled ahead. Halverson took a deep breath, and got going. At the first intersection, he made a left, drove down a block, and parked.

Still on edge, he kept his eyes on the rearview mirror, fully expecting to see the cops come flying around the corner. Even when they didn't, it took twenty minutes more before he could think straight, and then he came to one sure conclusion.

Those two cops knew exactly who he was.

Which made them the enemy.

And any marine knew what to do with the enemy.

Chapter 32

PAUL SAID, "This Eric Halverson. I figure we still gotta chance to find him."

Tommy laughed. "How come I get the feeling your, 'we,' is actually 'me'? As in 'me, the sarge.'"

Paul ignored Tommy, saying, "At least we aren't chasing a phantom anymore."

"Yeah, only we—as in you and me, of course—how do we catch this guy, now that we know who he is?"

Paul, going on, "BJ says Halverson's the kind that'll try eliminating any and all who are a threat to him. Which adds up, him killing everybody he's come in contact with." Paul thought for a second. "He tried doing Ditty once already. No doubt in my mind, given a chance, he's gonna try again."

Tommy said, "If I was Halverson, I'd be long gone from Chicago, Ditty or no Ditty. Maybe we—ha!—should notify the FBI. With their resources, there's a good chance Halverson will be found wherever he goes."

At sixty-five miles per hour, Paul veered off the expressway, all the way from the left hand lane to the right shoulder, in the process cutting off a semi tractor-trailer, and a school bus. Screeching to a halt, he gave Tommy a quick jab in the chest. "I'll work this case, and with no assistance from the FBI. Ain't any other kinda bullshit detective required, either. And that includes Kyle 'the idiot' Debolt."

Tommy threw up his arms. "Hey, that goes with out saying."

The police radio squawked, "Six-six-seven-oh. Come in Six-six-seven-oh."

Still eyeing Tommy, Paul answered up. "Sixty-six-seventy, Squad. What can we do for you?"

"Been trying to reach you for an hour now. Report to Area Six Homicide. Detective Debolt."

Tommy laughed. "'Don't include Debolt.' Wrong again, huh, Sarge?"

Paul got back into traffic, saying, "When we get there…"

Tommy held up his hand. "Say no more. You do all the talking. And me, dummy up."

Paul and Tommy walked into the Homicide Unit's small side door entrance. He hadn't been here since making sergeant, and remembered the first time he'd come through that door. As a new detective he hadn't known what to expect, maybe some badass criminals in a line up, at least one or two Clint Eastwood-looking characters in five-hundred dollar suits, long barreled magnums hanging from shoulder holsters.

It wasn't like that at all, just one large workroom with a small office partitioned off in a corner. Dingy paint peeling from the walls, just like in the Task Force office. An abundance of typewriters were strewn about on plain, Formica top work desks. None of the detectives bore the slightest resemblance to Clint Eastwood.

Today, Debolt was sitting alone, pecking away on a typewriter one finger at a time. When Debolt looked up he had eyes only for Paul, and started out with the same lofty attitude. "The bell captain, Capri. You know, from the Drake. Somebody killed him this morning."

Tommy said, "Sounds like our man's been at work again, huh?"

"Yeah," Paul said. "Damn, I liked that guy. If I knew then what I know now, I would've put Capri into safekeeping."

Debolt leaned back in his chair. Acting smug, he said, "If you would'a been straight with me at the hotel, I'd have this case closed by now."

Paul was not going to let himself get drawn into a shouting match. He produced worrisome eyes, as if to say, I'll be good now, boss. Offering his hand out in reconciliation, he said, "You're a hundred percent right, Kyle. You always were. Whichever way you wanna go, it's good with me."

Debolt blanched. "Well, maybe I came on a little too strong. Just fill me in."

Paul gave him a friendly slap on the shoulder. "You got it, pal. The bell captain gave us a good description of the suspect. I relayed it to NCIC. They had a few names of known offenders who were wanted for similar offenses. I got their pictures, went back last night, and showed them to the bell captain." Paul flicked at Tommy, who was feinting an excuse me look.

Then continuing, "Capri picked out one of the photos on the first try. I just got lucky, I guess."

Paul half expected Debolt to laugh at this obvious lie, but instead the dunce nodded his approval, busily scribbling in his notepad.

"Eric Halverson's the killer's name," Paul added. "I ain't got any leads on him, though. He got thrown outta the service, and hasn't been seen since. So that's where we're at. I guess the ball's in your corner now. You think you'll be able to find this Halverson guy?"

Debolt leaned away from his desk. "Just leave it up to me. I think I know what I'm doing."

Sure he did, and Paul said, "I know you do. But I checked into this Halverson dude. Seems like he don't leave much of a trail."

"Like I said, I know what I'm doing."

Wondering if Debolt might have fallen into some important information, Paul said, "Come on, Kyle. I just spilled my guts. You could at least tell me how you expect to find this guy."

Debolt wagged a finger at Paul. "Sure, and then you'll go out and make the pinch yourself. What you think I am, stupid?"

Tommy, off to the side, rolling clandestine eyes.

Paul said, "You just told me to stay out of it, Kyle. I'm not going against another cop. Especially my old partner."

Debolt's fingers began to drum rhythmically on the keyboard of the typewriter. "Okay," he said. He leaned on his elbows, and motioned them both close.

Paul and Tommy went to each of Debolt's sides, and Debolt, holding his voice to a near, whisper, "While you boys were chasing around like chickens with their heads cut off, I was getting some serious detective work in. The New York PD called. Seems our diamond salesman transferred a big chunk of cash from his company account in New York to a bank here in Chicago. I checked the account here in the city and guess what, there's a second name listed as joint holder. S. Butler. Your Eric Halverson has been using an alias."

Paul chanced a quick glance at Tommy, who was sporting wide eyes for Debolt.

The kid was catching on, and whispered, "No kidding."

194

"Yeah. So then I went over to Motor Vehicles. Bigger than shit they got a current driver's license registration under the name of S. Butler. A new one, and with an address right here in the city. I got a copy of the picture that goes with it." Debolt handed Paul a Photostat copy of the picture.

Paul immediately recognized Eric Halverson's biting eyes from the picture BJ had shown them that morning. Everything else was different. In this photo Halverson had long, blond hair, a bushy mustache, and was wearing steel-rimmed glasses. He dropped the picture into the breast pocket of his uniform shirt.

Debolt held out his hand. "Uh, I need that, but nice try."

Paul smiled. "Sorry, bad habit. The address on the driver's license, did you check it yet?"

"Yeah, no luck. It's a flophouse hotel. If Butler—uh, Halverson, was ever there, he sure ain't now. It was a different story at the bank. There I got lucky. Our guy showed up there the very day Shakleford got pitched onto that UPS truck. He removed the money Shakleford transferred in from New York. The teller remembered him, too. She said ordinarily she wouldn't, but the withdrawal was for over a quarter million."

Debolt was sounding excited, and his voice began to rise. Paul shushed him.

"Yeah, yeah," Debolt said, rubbernecking over his shoulder. He returned to whispering. "Anyway, you know how they make you give them your mother's maiden name and all that other piddley bullshit when you open a new bank account? Well the teller asked Halverson all that stuff. And he had all the answers."

"Did you show her the driver's license picture?"

"Yeah. There I struck out. She said the man she knows as S. Butler looked completely different than the picture. He had black hair, a goatee, and was wearing thick, black-rimmed glasses. I figure he was disguised, 'cause the teller said there was something about the man in the picture that reminded her of Butler. She just couldn't put her finger on it, though."

His eyes, that's what the teller couldn't put a finger on. Paul said, "So you don't have an identification. Where you going from here?"

"I'm still in good shape," Debolt said with his chest puffed out. "All I gotta do is pick up the Caldwell kid. That shouldn't be so hard. When I get through with that son-of-a-bitch, he'll be only too happy to testify against Halverson. I got me a dead banger, no doubt about it. Of course Halverson's gotta be long gone outta Chicago now that he did in the bell captain. But that's okay. I'll just get a warrant, let the FBI do my work for me. Sooner or later he'll get picked up."

Paul slapped Debolt on the back, and raised his voice a notch. "Sounds like you're in business, Kyle."

Debolt said, "Say, Paul. Let's let bygones be bygones. Next time we'll work together instead of banging heads."

Paul forced a laugh. "All my fault. Good luck catching up to Ditty."

Debolt said, "Uh, regarding that floater. The fingerprints came back. He was a big time diamond salesman from New York by the name of…" Debolt checked his notes. "…Randolph Laidlaw. I don't know exactly where he comes into this just yet. You got any ideas?"

"No, not the slightest," Paul said, managing to keep steady eyes.

Tommy blinked as if he'd been hit over the head with a hammer, and hid his face behind Paul. And as Debolt retreated back into the office, Paul turned to Tommy with a mischievous eye. "What'd I tell you? Jesus, what a dumbshit?"

"I know," Tommy said, "but that stuff about New York. What'd you make of it?"

"I got me an idea, but nothing's for sure." He headed for the stairs.

Tommy hurried to catch up. "Well, what's your idea?"

Paul stopped. "Listen, I'd tell you, but I just don't know…"

Tommy's shoulders slumped. "Here we go again with the secrets. I'm sick and tired of this crap."

Paul released a blast of air through gritted teeth. "You know what, you're right. If I did know something, I probably wouldn't tell you. But the fact is, this time, I really don't know. So stop your crying and come on. We're gonna see if Stash and Herman did us any good with Motor Vehicles."

He went down the stairs to the Auto Theft Section.

Stash and Herman were sitting against the wall, facing back toward the entrance. Both had telephones up to their ears, and were talking alternately into their respective phones, to each other, and then back into their phones again.

Herman cupped a hand over his phone, and yelled Paul and Tommy over. Returning to the phone, he said, "Uh-huh, uh-huh." Then to Stash, "What a bunch'a idiots they got down there in Springfield. You doing any better with Records Division?"

Stash waved his partner off, and told whoever he was talking to, "You're gonna have to repeat that. I got this old fart screaming at me. Yeah, Herman, who else?" He laughed, apparently with whoever he was talking to, and scribbled a series of numbers on his notepad. Holding the phone away from his ear, he said to Herman, "Get this," and read the numbers from his notepad.

Paul watched as Herman and Stash went back and forth for five minutes or so, and then Herman hung up. Giving Stash a dirty look, he said, "Old fart, huh? I'll give you old fart right in that big nose of yours."

"Shut your face," Stash said. "I'm finally getting somewheres here." He went back to the phone. "Mary Beth, you're the only one in all of Records Division who knows what they're doing. I owe you a big plate of blood sausage." Putting down the phone, he showed his partner his notepad.

Given his first opportunity, Paul said, "We were just up at Homicide…"

"We know," Herman said. "That fool Debolt, right?"

"How'd you know?"

"When he finally showed up by the river this morning, he was asking all kinds'a questions about how maybe he could get some information from Motor Vehicles if all he had was a name. Since he was so busy, and us being auto dicks, maybe we could do it for him. That yahoo is always trying to get somebody to do his work for him. I was ready to tell him to take a hike when he ups and mentions the name he wants to check. Can you believe it, he's trying to run down S. Butler?" Herman tilted his head at his partner. "Stashu was so shocked he about did a header into the river."

"Yeah, sure," Stash said. "And you were cool, right? Pauly, this old fool grabbed Debolt around the shoulders, told him, 'Anything for you, pal.' My five-year-old daughter would'a seen through his bullshit."

Herman produced a proud smile. "Not Debolt, though."

Relieved, Paul said, "So it was you guys that got him all that stuff from Motor Vehicles. He made out like he did it all by himself."

"That's Debolt for you," Stash said. "But hey, better us than somebody else. This way he got just enough to keep him busy. Meanwhile we got some real work done."

Tommy looked puzzled. "I don't get it. What you mean, just enough?' He's got the bad guy's picture, even if it is a disguise."

The two auto dicks shared a laugh, and Stash said, "We took Debolt down to the local motor vehicles office. I don't think he liked being seen with us smalltime auto dicks, only what could he do? We knew something he didn't. As far as the picture goes, well, we had to give him that. No way around it. But the address… all bullshit."

Paul slapped Tommy on the back, and pointed at Herman and Stash. "These two, they're the kinda detectives I like."

Stash again. "Wait a minute, Paul. It ain't all summer nights and cool breezes. While Debolt was running down the phony address, we took a ride over to the real one. Turned out to be a little costume jewelry shop on Wells Street, over in Old Town. Only trouble is the place burned down a few weeks ago. Seems S. Butler, or whatever his name is, was the victim of an arson. He was robbed the day before, too. Or should I say somebody tried to rob him. Somehow he got the drop on the bad guys with a shotgun. Blew their shit outta the water. Robbery Section loved it. Two wrongdoers down and out forever, and the good guy without a scratch. Robbery says it was a couple'a gangbangers from the Cabrini. They said a third suspect got away. That night is when the place got burned down. They figure the one that got away must'a done it."

Herman interrupted. "My money says Ditty was the third suspect, and somehow Butler blackmailed him into helping with the arson. Was either that or get turned in on the robbery. And then he got him to do the diamond heist. Him and Shoestring, of course."

Sounded right to Paul, except it was probably four robbers to start out with, seeing as Ditty never did anything without Shoestring. Which explained how they got mixed up with a white guy.

Stash, going on. "Anyway, Robbery showed mug shots to Butler, but he couldn't identify anybody. They had no choice but to suspend the investigation."

Herman said, "This dude's definitely got himself a pair of balls."

Paul, thinking out loud. "Okay, that part's a dead-end. How about the insurance company? Did they pay off on the claim yet?"

"That's the first thing we checked. Yeah, they had no reason to think it was anything but a robbery-arson. And Robbery Section backed up Butler's story all the way."

"What'd he get?"

"A big eight-oh. Not bad, huh?"

"Eighty thou? Jesus! he really cleaned up. Chicago's gotta be his favorite town."

Herman smiled. "Not that favorite. He's probably beat it outta here, unless he's crazy."

"Oh, he's crazy all right," Paul said. "But not stupid."

"Far from stupid," Tommy added. "Where was he living after the shop burned down?"

Herman shrugged. "Don't know."

"Don't know? Where'd he have the insurance company send the settlement check?"

"Some bank in Mexico. And from what we've been told, it's next to impossible trying to dig information outta banks down there. Looks like another dead-end."

Paul slumped against the wall. "I gotta think about this one."

"We done for the day?" Tommy said.

"I guess."

"Then time for a beer, I'd say."

Herman said, "You guys go ahead. We got a few more things we wanna check." He returned to the phone.

Paul was glad to find The Alibi empty. He wanted peace so he could think. Didn't happen, because Woody came over and started right in. "Kyle Debolt was in before, for lunch, bragging that he's gonna catch himself a primo bad guy and clear up a good twenty murders across the country. He says Hollywood's gonna wanna make a movie for sure."

Paul looked at Tommy, who was staring down at his beer. Paul did the same, hoping Woody would take the hint and leave them to their misery. But the bartender would not let up. "You guys gotta feel like shit. After all you've gone through and Debolt's getting the credit."

Paul said, "I gotta make a couple'a calls. Let me use the phone, would ya?"

Woody grabbed a phone from under the bar. "Yeah, I know I'd be pissed if…"

Paul dialed, waited, and said, "Kyle? Yeah, it's me. You getting anywhere? Is that right? No shit. Sounds awful good."

Woody leaned his ample belly on the bar. "What's going on? Debolt on to the wrongdoer already? He gonna make the pinch today, tomorrow, or what?"

Paul pointed at the phone. "Uh, sorry. You know, police business and all that shit."

Woody put both hands on his chest. "You bet. Far be it from me to interfere in official business." He started away, then stopped long enough to look over his shoulder. "Uh, make sure you let me know what's going on soon as you can, okay?"

Tommy, waiting until Woody was out of earshot. "You telling me Debolt really know something that counts?"

Paul handed Tommy the phone.

Tommy listened, and said, "A dial tone?"

Paul placed the phone back on its cradle.

"You saved us that time, Sarge. No way was Woody gonna leave us be."

"Dammit," Paul said. "We gotta find the Dittybopper before Halverson does."

Tommy said, "I know one thing for sure. We can't just sit here getting pie-eyed while Debolt takes runs at the guy?"

Paul turned his beer up to his mouth, and gave Tommy an,

I'll have to think about that stare, through the bottom of the mug. Then slammed the empty on the bar, and yelled to Woody for a refill.

Woody came running with two more beers. "So, you guys got yourselves a plan? I know you do. That's what the phone was for, right? You're gonna sweep down on the Cabrini, get yourselves a bad guy. Let me know when you're ready to move. I wanna be there."

Paul and Tommy just stared, but Woody wouldn't quit. "Come on, that's it, right?"

Through it all, Paul kept thinking back to what BJ had told them, that Halverson would eliminate anybody who go in his way. Oh, Jesus, Katie. He picked up the phone.

Katie answered on the first tingle of the first ring, and said an abbreviated "Yes," as if she were agitated about something.

"You okay," Paul said.

"Thank God it's you. Get over here right now. We need you."

"'*We* need you?' What's that supposed to mean?"

Katie shot back, "I've got Ditty here. Only I don't know for how long. He thinks for sure somebody's after him."

"You just hold on to that kid. I don't care how you do it—just do it. We're on our way."

He slammed the phone down, splashing beer onto Woody's shirt, and grabbed Tommy by the arm, dragging him toward the door.

Tommy held onto the bar rail, and sliding its length, slurped down the last of his beer.

Paul finally got Tommy through the door as Woody was heard to yell, "Don't forget to let me know when the raid's coming off. I don't wanna miss this one."

Outside, Tommy ripped himself free. Staggering against The Alibi's front door, he said, "Are you outta your mind? I thought the whole idea with the phone was to bullshit Woody into leaving, not us."

"Come on," Paul said, "that call was for real." He ran for the parking lot.

201

Chapter 33

HALVERSON WAS COMING around the corner when he saw Ditty go bopping into the girl's building. Pulling out his Ka-bar, he raced up the sidewalk, and burst through the door only to find the breezeway empty.

An industrial elevator was cranking up into the building.

Damn! Just a second earlier and Ditty would've been his. Halverson was contemplating his next move when a buzz sounded, and the elevator started down again. Lucky him. Here came Ditty, along with the girl. He gripped his Ka-bar tight. This was going to be good. Damned good. And bloody.

A pair of scrawny bowlegs in Bermuda shorts came into view through the elevator gate. Couldn't be Ditty. Sure as hell wasn't the girl, either. The elevator continued downward, revealing a ridiculous looking Harley Davidson T-shirt stretched over a pregnant-like belly. When the elevator clanked to a stop, Halverson looked into the face of a full bearded man who was as wide as he was tall, which couldn't be more than five foot or so. From the looks of the old geezer, he'd have trouble handling a tricycle, let alone a Harley. But he did dress the role. From his belt hung a chain which draped to his knees. Riveted on the chain's end was a wallet in the style used by motorcycle riders.

"I'm Thad Cornopopolous," the man bellowed. He lifted the elevator's gate. "Landlord around here. You got business in my building?"

"Uh, yeah. With Miss Bartovich. So if you don't mind…"

"I get it. Another wrongdoer. Listen, you hairless piece'a shit. I saw the other guy go up there. Looked like some kinda burglar. That damned Bartovich broad thinks she can turn this place into her own private boarding house for assholes. I guess I'm gonna have to go up there and straighten her out once and for all."

Halverson had no time for this. When Cornopopolous reached to push the up button, he slipped him a quick jab between the third and fourth ribs. Cornopopolous peered down at the Ka-bar's handle as his own blood erased the H on

Harley Davidson. His lips mouthing, "Why?"

Halverson thought he was going to have to cut old Thad a half-dozen times more, considering all those layers of fat. But before he could pull his Ka-bar free, Thad went down like Henry from that hotel balcony.

Halverson hadn't experienced a killing quite so satisfying since the war, but he didn't have time to stand around enjoying the moment. He grabbed old Thad by his motorcycle boots, and, "ugh," lugged him into the nearest corner. Now to the gate. He pulled it closed, and pushed the up button. As the elevator lumbered upward, Halverson formed his plan. As soon as he reached the girl's loft, he'd bullshit his way in, cut that Ditty bastard once and for all. The girl would have to go too.

Then he remembered his training. He could just hear Gunny McCoy hammering safety-first instructions into the platoon, telling them every operation had to be worked out to the last detail before they went into the bush.

He pushed the stop button, making the elevator jerk to a halt. He'd think this thing out. Sure, he had his military issue .45 automatic to go along with the Ka-bar. But who knew what weaponry the kid had ready to use? Ditty had to be scared, and a scared man was dangerous. Plus the girl. Who's to say her cop buddy hadn't given her a gun?

Bad odds any way he looked at it.

What was it BJ always used to say when they had an unknown enemy in front of them? Get back to the command post and reconnoiter. Command post, that's what Halverson needed. But where? Someplace in the building, maybe the basement, or the roof. Too bad he'd had to do old Thad. That big mouth had to know this place like Ditty knew the Cabrini.

He gave old Thad a vicious kick in his flabby side, just for dying so easily. The body rolled against the wall, exposing Thad's Harley Davidson wallet.

"Let's see what the old man's got," Halverson said. He ripped the wallet from its chain.

Thumbing through, he came to a driver's license. So, old Thad's place was on the fourth floor, right beneath the girl's. Worth a look. He pushed four on the control panel.

Seemed like Halverson had aged a year before the elevator delivered him to Thad's loft. He lifted the elevator's gate, and tried Thad's inner door. Unlocked. When he pushed it open, Thad's loft was right there. He pulled his Ka-bar, and leaned inside. In luck again. The place was vacant. What a dump the old man had. One large room. A raggedy sofa and a folding table its total furnishing. Didn't even have a private bathroom. Just a commode hooked up to the far wall, in plain view. Next to it, a modest sink. Next to that, a greasy bathtub.

Which was as good a place as any for old Thad. Halverson dragged the body across the bare wooden floor, depositing it in the bathtub.

Now for a quick reconnaissance. He pulled a pair of surgical gloves out of his back pocket, and slipped them on. You never know, he might have to beat it out of here, not have time to wipe clean fingerprints like he had with Henry's hotel room and the limo. Okay, where to start? A man's possessions told a lot, so the closet came first. Its floor was littered with tools, used paint cans, ropes, pulleys, everything a landlord needed to keep a building up. Hanging from a series of hooks on the rear wall were two T-shirts identical to the one Thad was now wearing, four or five pair of trousers, and one blue suit. No sign of a lady's clothes, which meant old Thad lived alone.

Excellent.

Halverson had found his command post. But damn this place was hot. It smelled musty and stale too, like its dead-ass resident. He went to the rear window, and threw it open, hoping a cross breeze might relieve the stench. It didn't. He shoved his head outside, sucking at the fresh air.

And while he did, Halverson heard faint but distinguishable voices. That's right, Ditty and the girl were only one floor above. He looked up. There, just above, a huge bay window protruded from the rear wall of the girl's loft. Its panels were wide open.

Ditty and the girl were talking again. Going rigid, Halverson strained to hear what they were saying. He couldn't pick out every word, but got the gist of things. The girl was congratulating Ditty for staying alive as long as he had. Ditty wasn't saying anything, Halverson didn't think so anyway.

Maybe he was buying her line of bullshit.

Halverson had better strike right now, before she marched him down to the police station. It would be easy, too. Her loft had to be exactly like this one, with the elevator opening directly into it. She probably had her inner door locked, but that wasn't anything his .45 couldn't handle. Or maybe he would use the staircase. He checked a side door. There it was, except half its stairs were missing, and the rest looked to be rotted through. Okay, so it was going to have to be the elevator. He pulled the .45 and placed his thumb on the call button.

Hold on, don't go jumping into things. Better to wait until they came out. He was on the fourth floor, they were on the fifth. As soon as they started down, he'd have the elevator stop on his floor. And as much as he'd like to use his Ka-bar, the .45 was a better choice under these circumstances. He couldn't wait to see Ditty's face when he pushed that cold-steel barrel up his nose. Would be nothing short of beautiful. Surprise was on his side, too, and he'd have a clear avenue of escape. Everything required for a successful operation.

Even BJ would be proud of him.

He remained at his listening post, more confident than ever in his ability to execute his plan. He still heard them talking, but he couldn't understand a word. They must have moved away from the window.

Wait, maybe this was it. Yeah, they were leaving. He ran across the apartment floor, sliding to a stop by the elevator. He listened for its motor to clank on, but heard nothing.

Relax. As much noise as that thing made, he'd have plenty of notice. He'd take up surveillance right here by the elevator. It was hot, but he was used to that. How many times had he manned listening posts exactly like this in the bush? And here he wouldn't have to put up with dive-bomber-sized mosquitoes.

He sat down and waited, chipping at the wooden plank floor with his Ka-bar knife. Over the next hour, four times the elevator came to life and rose up from the breezeway. But it always stopped on one of the lower floors.

Almost two hours had passed now, and he was starting to think about other options. Maybe he should go with his original idea, take the elevator up to the girl's apartment.

He was still arguing back and forth with himself when the elevator started up again, and this time it ran all the way to the girl's loft. They had called it and were finally leaving. He held his hand over the call button, ready to push as soon as they started down.

The steel door on the girl's loft rattled open, and he pressed his ear to the wall.

Chapter 34

"PAULY, FINALLY YOU'RE HERE." Katie buried herself into Paul's chest, heaving sobs on his uniform shirt.

Hugging her close, Paul said, "I could understand letting Ditty come to the legal aid office. But your apartment? What's the matter with you?"

She only hugged him tighter.

From the elevator, Tommy said, "I guess I was right on about this morning. You know, you and Katie, huh, Sarge?"

"Enough of that," Paul said.

He spotted Ditty standing behind Katie's bed. Ditty's eyes darting back and forth between Paul and Katie. His arms hanging limp at his sides, his hands shaking. Reminded Paul of himself, that first day in combat.

Ditty's voice cracked, and he said, "You gotta protect me, man. He gonna get me for sure, you don't."

This was not the same cocky Dittybopper who ruled the roost in the Cabrini Green. Paul had better choose his words with care. "We're here now, Ditty. You're safe."

"You don't know him like me. He like, like the devil. He knows everything. From him, there ain't no place that's safe."

Katie pushed out of Paul's arms, and went to Ditty. "Tell him what you told me. About the man in the alley, the man who killed Lieutenant Matthews. Go ahead, about Shoestring and everything."

Ditty wiped his hand across his mouth, saying, "I ain't never killed nobody, 'specially a polleese."

Holding Ditty's hand, Katie said, "They know you didn't. Just tell them the truth."

Ditty sank to Katie's bed. "It's just I'm so tired of running." He look at Paul. "Man, put me in jail, so's I can close my eyes without worrying he gonna get me."

Not just yet, and Paul said the first calming words that came into his head. "We'll listen, Ditty. I promise. That's why we're here."

Ditty, with his chin shuttering. "Man, he kilt them all. Every damned one."

Paul said, "We know he did. We think we can find him, too. But we need your help. You help us, Ditty, I'll see the judge goes easy on you."

Ditty covered his face with his hands, sobbing.

Katie, with tears in her eyes. "I know. At least now it's over."

Ditty, between sobs. "It was Smedley what killed Shoestring. He killed that cop in the alley, too. You gotta believe me. What happened after that, I ain't so sure. He took me to the Drake Hotel. We were in a limo." Ditty shook his head. "Don't ask me where he got it. Anyway, the next thing I know, I wake up in the weeds by the Chicago River."

His eyes only for Paul. "You was there, remember?"

"Yeah. When we sent you to the hospital."

"That's right. Man, I was terrified. And when that dummy cop give me a chance, I run for it. Been on the run ever since. And I finish out giving myself up anyhow."

Paul stepped closer, like he would to a scared puppy. "You did the right thing coming here." He touched Katie's hand. "Stay with him while I hash this out with my partner."

Ditty nodded up and down, and let himself be taken into Katie's arms.

At best, Paul had moments before Ditty lost it again. And when he did, no telling if Paul would be able to calm him down. He took Tommy by the arm, and pulled him to the street-side window.

"Me, I'm your partner?" Tommy said, like he'd been waiting for an opportunity to use that one.

Paul wasn't having any jokes, and said, "Get serious, boy."

"Hey, what'd you expect?"

Paul, ignoring him. "Quite a tale, huh?"

"Yeah. It's good to have this over. So now we take him into the station, right?"

"Nope. That's the one thing we don't do."

Squinting, Tommy said, "But you just told him you would."

"I know I did. But I think he'll change his mind. That is after I get through talking to him, he will."

"Talk to him about what?"

Paul had to be as careful with Tommy as he had been with Ditty. He just didn't have a lot of time. "Listen good," he said, "'cause this is important." He stopped, expecting one of Tommy's smart remarks, but when it didn't come, "Ditty wants Halverson dead. More than anything, that's what he wants. Given the right set of circumstances, I think he'll go for a chance at seeing it done."

Tommy's eyes showed understanding. "You're crazy. That's murder and I want no part of it."

"Wait, dammit. I'm trying to tell you something."

"Like hell. I'll take him in. If need be, by myself." He started toward Ditty.

Paul blocked his way. "Hold on. You ain't even heard my plan. We're not gonna murder anybody. We're just gonna make Ditty think we're gonna."

"I don't know," Tommy said. "I smell more trouble from the IID. If we don't bring him in right now, I'll never get back to Oak Street Beach."

Paul's next words were going to turn Tommy one way or the other, and he grabbed his conformation medal through his uniform shirt before saying, "I'll tell you what. We'll leave the final decision up to Ditty. If he puts the nix on it, we'll take him right up to the office. Trust me."

Tommy glared.

Paul held his breath.

And Tommy said, "Before I agree to anything, you're gonna have to get off your high horse and explain this super-foolproof plan of yours."

Paul looked back at Ditty, who was leaning on Katie, still holding himself together. Paul allowed himself a breath, a little one, and said, "I'm just about to explain it to Ditty. Won't that be soon enough?"

"As a matter of fact, no. You tell me right here and now, or it's a no-go."

Paul didn't like ultimatums, especially from a rookie, but he couldn't think of a way around it. "Okay, here it is," he said. "Knowing what you know about Halverson, where you think he is right now?"

Tommy looked at Ditty, saying, "Come on, Sarge, stop the bullshit. Just tell me about the plan." Then he cocked his head. "Wait a minute. That's it. You ain't got no plan, do you?"

"I'm serious," Paul said. "For once think like a copper instead of a damned gigolo skirt chaser. Just tell me, if you were Halverson, where would you be right this minute?"

Tommy's face turned somber, but he said nothing. A long way from being a real cop, this kid. Paul had better help him along, and said, "Put yourself in Halverson's place. The man is just plain good. And why is he so good? Because he chooses his victims carefully, makes a plan and sticks to it. You getting me, kid? Is it starting to sink in?"

Realization showed on Tommy's face. "Oh, Jesus! He's here. He's right here watching and waiting for his shot at Ditty." He ran his tongue over his lips. "And us."

Paul grabbed Tommy around the shoulder so that their backs were to the room. "Calm down, dammit, before Ditty hears you." He whispered into Tommy's ear. "No, he ain't here. Not yet he ain't, or that gangbanger over there'd be one dead piece'a meat. But he'll show all right. And when he does, you and me, we're gonna put an end to that scum-sucking pig once and for all."

Tommy searched out the window as if he expected Halverson to be right there, ready to devour them all.

Paul pulled him back around. "Don't get crazy on me. I'm gonna need you before this is over. We're gonna need each other."

"I don't know about this," Tommy said, eyes on the window.

Paul looked at Katie and Ditty, checking to make sure they were far enough away so that he could talk freely. "Here's what we're gonna do. First you hide my pickup. Halverson seems to know everything else, he might know what I drive, too. Move it at least a couple'a blocks away. When you get back, we'll shut ourselves inside the apartment. We'll have to get rid of Katie. I don't know, we'll just tell her she'll have to stay somewheres else for the night. Once she's gone, you and me'll set up an ambush. There's only two ways in here, the stairs and the elevator. As soon as Halverson shows, we'll have him. It'll be easy."

If Tommy believes that, he'll believe anything.

Tommy, back to eyeing out the window. "I don't know…"

Needed a little more tweaking, so Paul said, "If it was you

got killed, Lieutenant Matthews would know."

Tommy squeezed his eyes shut like he'd been hit in the stomach. "Okay, I'm with you."

Paul produced his best smile. "Great, kid. I knew you'd come through." He flipped around—had to because he couldn't hold the smile a second longer—and crossed the room to where Katie was with Ditty.

To Ditty, he said, "Okay. Everything's set."

"You taking me in now?"

"That's right. Too bad, though, 'cause I'd sure like a chance at that Smedley. The son-of-a-bitch."

Ditty snapped Paul a look. "What you care one way or the other?"

Okay, this was a start, and Paul said, "Don't forget he gunned down a damned good cop. A friend of mine, too."

"How about Shoestring? He was my friend too."

Paul let his voice drop. "I know. Shoestring was a good kid. I had him in lots'a times and he never ratted on a friend."

Ditty looked down at the floor. "Whatchamacallit, Halverson, he deserves more than just jail time."

"Yeah, well don't count on even that happening," Paul said, trying to sound discouraged.

Ditty popped his head up. "What you mean? With me testifying against him, he gotta go away big time."

Paul sat down next to Ditty, rubbing shoulders. "It's your word against his, Ditty. And your word ain't gonna carry a whole lotta weight. You oughta know that, being in court as much as you have."

Ditty jumped up. "Dammit! You mean he could beat the whole thing?"

Paul held back as long as he could, then looked Ditty in the eyes. "Yeah, he could. But not you, Ditty. They got a dead-bang case on you for robbing that diamond salesman. Who knows? Could be they'll put a murder charge on you, too."

"I told you, I ain't kilt nobody!"

Paul flipped his eyebrows. "You got me convinced. Only it ain't me that counts."

Ditty kicked the side of the bed. "I'd kill that slime myself, I had half the chance."

"You really mean that?" Paul said. He got up, standing face to face with Ditty.

Ditty, taken aback. "Yeah, I mean it. Why wouldn't I?"

"I don't know. It's just you said you wanted us to take you in."

Ditty, glaring. "And if I don't?"

Just what Paul needed to hear, but he couldn't relax yet. "Forget it. Let's just get you into the station."

Ditty looked at Paul, then Katie and Tommy. "He'll be here, I know it." He went to the front windows, and spied at the street.

Paul went to his side. "How come you're so sure?"

"'Cause he's got the lady's address. After he killed that cop, you know, in the alley, he made me tell him all about her."

Okay, this was it, and Paul said, "What you trying to say, Ditty?"

Who gave Paul a quick glance, and turned back to the window. "We could get him ourselves, we play it right."

"You mean set up an ambush? I don't know, sounds dangerous."

"I wanna chance at him."

"That, I can't let happen. But I could make it so you're here when me and my partner take him down."

Ditty looked Paul straight in the face. "Good enough for me."

"Okay, then," Paul said. "Maybe it could work. After all, this guy ain't nothing but flesh and blood, like all of us."

Ditty kept his eyes to the street, and said, "You better be right. If you wrong, you gonna be dead wrong."

"I'm right," Paul said, trying to sound confident. "You keep watch. I'll see what I can do."

Ditty nodded, never varying his vigil on the street.

Two down, one to go, and Paul turned to Katie.

Who was sitting on her bed, staring back at him. As soon as their eyes met Paul knew she was going to be trouble. When wasn't she? He was surprised she had remained quiet while he'd been roping Ditty.

Here she came, meeting him in the middle of the floor with a finger sticking in his face. "If I didn't love you so much…

Don't think for a minute I don't know what you're up to."

"What?" Paul said, only because he could think of nothing else to say.

"Keep your voice down, before the others hear you."

"Huh."

"Yeah, you got it, them."

"But…"

"But nothing," Katie said, "And I told you to keep your voice down."

Paul thought he was beginning to understand. He hoped to find out for sure, and as long as Katie kept talking, he figured he would.

But now she was quiet, staring at him with one of her loving smiles. He thought it was loving, anyway. He'd better say something. "I'm only trying to catch Lieutenant Matthews' killer," he said, hoping this was the direction she was going.

"Me, too." She took him by the elevator. "You're crazy if you think you're going to make me leave. Yeah, I heard you with Tommy. Wherever you are, that's where I'm going to be."

"Oh, for Christ sakes!"

"I said I'm staying," Katie said, doing that thing with her eyes, making them blaze.

Paul should have known, and said, "Katie, please. There could be shooting."

"No!" she said, and held his arm ever tighter.

Paul didn't like this, but Katie had him figured perfectly and he knew it. "Okay," he said. "You can stay as long as you promise to keep outta the way."

As soon as he spoke, Paul wished he had not, but instead of Katie exploding, she said, "Okay, I'll hide behind the room divider at the first indication Halverson is coming."

Now Paul figured he himself was being roped. But God help him, this was his only chance to revenge Jack Matthews. "You promise?" he said, holding Katie close.

"What was it you said to Tommy? Trust me, wasn't it?"

Oh, Lord, this girl. Just wasn't any use, and he said, "Okay, but I'm the copper here, so let me do my job, okay?"

She spread her hands wide. "Go to it, country boy."

Typical Katie, having to get in the last shot. But Paul couldn't let that bother him. No, he had to be ready for Halverson. Okay, what was it they had done first back in the Marines? Secured possible points of attack. He walked across the room to the bay window. Didn't look very inviting, a sheer five floor drop to the alley, with nothing but a brick wall adjacent to them. Unless—

He turned to Katie. "Who lives downstairs?"

"There's four floors, which one?"

"All of them."

"Well, there's…"

"Never mind. It's evening now, and they all should be home. Give them each a call. Something short, just so we know they're all okay."

"Why wouldn't they be okay?"

"You said you'd let me do my job."

Katie looked like she was about to take a swing at him. Instead, she snatched the Rolodex from her desk. Three times she called. Paul put his ear close to hers as she made brief conversation. On the fourth call, she gave Paul a long face, and said, "Mister Cornopopolous, this is Katie upstairs. I called because…"

"What's going on up there? You having another one of your do-gooder parties for assholes?"

Katie slammed the phone down. "A first class jerk," she said.

Paul wasn't the least bit interested. "Where's the stairs," he said. "We gotta block them off."

"Not to worry," Katie said. "They're rotted out. Mister Cornopopolous was suppose to fix them a year ago, but never has."

"You're sure?"

She went to a side door. Opening it for Paul, she said, "Go ahead, see for yourself."

He tested his weight on the first step. It splintered, sending kindling down an open shaft. Wasn't anybody going to get to them through here. He walked to the center of the room. Okay, think it out. Really, was there much chance Halverson would show? And if he did, would he be foolish enough to

214

make a frontal assault here in the loft? Well, judging by what Halverson had done with all the other witnesses, he had to go after Ditty too. And if breaking in here was the only way—

No. Halverson probably didn't even know Ditty was here. Still, Ditty thought he did. Paul glanced at the front window where Ditty was staring down on the street. Hell, Ditty didn't think it, he was sure of it. But to break in—didn't make much sense. If it were Paul, he'd set up outside, wait until Ditty came out, and drill him with a high-powered rifle, something like that.

Yeah, that probably was Halverson's plan. But Paul had put this stakeout into motion, and he might as well carry it through. At least until morning. Then, if Halverson was really out there, he'd get the surprise of his life because Paul would have the entire Task Force covering his every avenue of escape.

"Okay," he said. "The way I see it, Halverson's only way in is the elevator. We'll set up in the far corner. From there we'll have an excellent line of fire."

He dragged the mattress and bedsprings from Katie's bed, and set up a lean-to. He put the kitchen table on its side, and placed it in front for extra measure.

"When Halverson comes, I want firepower coming from one source. That's what'll break his spirit, even it don't kill him."

"Tommy, you take the right side. Ditty, you go in the middle. Katie, you come with me on the left side."

Tommy took his station, saying, "It could be at any time, I guess."

Paul said, "Anything's possible, but in the Corps we always waited until just before dawn. It's the quietest time of the night, and the best time to catch the enemy off guard. But the least dangerous way of taking out a man is to snipe him. So stay away from the windows."

Tommy said, "What if…?"

"What ifs ain't gonna get it," Paul said. "Enough talk. You people try and get some sleep. I'll take first watch."

Chapter 35

FOR AWHILE Halverson hadn't been able to hear anything. Then Paul and the girl were talking alone. They must have been by the elevator, because he'd been able to pick up enough to understand what was going on up there. They thought they could ambush him. What a joke that was? And the phone call from the girl. Couldn't have gone better. Now they were lulled into a false sense of security. If Halverson had been able to predict that a layer of wooden planks would be the only obstacle between himself and Ditty, he'd have brought along a pound or so of plastic explosives, set up the best booby trap Chicago had seen since Al Capone. Not only would there not be any Ditty left, but the entire building, those on either side, and any unlucky slob driving by would go up in smoke too. So tantalizing was this notion Halverson thought seriously about making a run to his hideout and bring back a supply from his stash. He couldn't chance it, though. What if all of a sudden Ditty lost his nerve? The cops would have to take him to the police station. No, he'd have to be here continually until the operation was complete.

And it would be complete.

It was dark now, time to make a reconnaissance of his objective. Slipping through the alley-side window, he balanced on the sill, waiting for his eyes to adjust to the shadowy light. Slowly his night vision came into focus, and he stretched up, taking hold on the base of the girl's bay window. Totally confident, he pulled himself up, and like a trapeze artist, dangled from its edge. He had a good idea where they were, but it still took a few seconds to orient himself to the interior. The girl's brass bed sat in front of the window, and directly across from it was the door to the elevator. The view on his right was blocked by her oak wardrobe. That was okay, though. He knew what was there, just the makeshift bathroom. What he mostly needed to see was off to the left; the mattress and bedsprings from the girl's bed. And there it was, propped up against the kitchen table, exactly where he'd expected it to be.

Paul's head bobbed around behind it. The others were out of view. Halverson had hoped to be able to see Ditty. If he could have, that would have been it. One well-placed shot and off he'd go to Mexico, job well done, home free again.

Enough for now, and he dropped down at arm's length, swinging hand over hand to the opposite side of the window. Even if they tried, they couldn't see him, not from this angle. Using his powerful arm muscles, he scaled the bay window, and in seconds was standing erect on its roof. Now, stretching out to his side, he grasped the drainpipe which extended down the building's outer wall. Testing its durability and finding it safe, he took hold with both hands, and stepped into midair. Using his body like a pendulum, he kicked higher and higher, and with a lurch lifted one leg onto the building's roof. Safely anchored, he dragged the other leg up and over. A good twist and he was lying prone on a flat-tar surface.

Crouching low, he kept himself in the shadows.

And began his inspection.

Chapter 36

PAUL SAT IN THE DARK, beginning to wonder if this was such a good idea. Look at what he had to work with. A rookie cop usually more interested in chasing broads, a street thief from the projects, and Katie. God! Katie, loving Katie, but who knew what she was going to do next?

And look at what they were going up against. One scary killing machine who didn't make many mistakes. If fact, so far Halverson's only gaffe had been the use of Marine Corps heroes' names for aliases. Names? Maybe—

He eyed the telephone on Katie's bedside table. What the hell, it was worth a try. He put the phone between his legs, and dialed 411. On came the ever-pleasant monotone with the standard, "Information operator, what city please?"

Paul tried Smedley Butler first, and was not surprised when he struck out. Dan Daley, a two time Medal of Honor winner, was negative also. Then he tried Chesty Puller. What better alias than the legendary general who had led the First Marines, along with BJ McCoy, out of Korea's Chosan Reservoir.

"Chesty?" the operator said as if she suspected Paul to be a teenage prank. "I've heard a lot of names, but never Chesty. If this is some kind of joke…"

"It's Chesty," Paul said. "C-H-E-S-T-Y, you got it?"

"Yes, but…"

"Just look it up, lady."

Paul didn't want to admit he had no idea what General Puller's first name was. Everybody had called him Chesty as far as he knew, right down to the lowliest private.

"No Chesty Puller," the operator said. She sounded happy about it too.

"Okay, how about Ira Hayes?" Paul said, thinking of one of the men who had survived raising the flag on Iwo Jima.

"Sorry," said the operator. "We're only allowed to take three requests per call."

"Lady, I know you gotta job to do. But come on, it's three o'clock in the morning. It ain't like you're getting a whole lotta business."

"Sorry," and the phone went dead.

Paul shook his head, and dialed again wishing he had a phone book. But even if he did, he couldn't chance the light which he'd need to be able to see what he was looking at. Stubbornly, he went through the same routine, and after forty minutes of trying he was still on the phone. When he ran out of heroes' names, he switched to crazy combinations such as Belle Wood and Guadalcanal, thinking sites of historic Marine battles might work. Next came Marine Corps bases: Camp Lejune, Camp Pendleton, Cherry Point, and Twenty Nine Palms. He laughed through Pickle Meadows, but received the same humorless, "Sorry, sir. No such listing."

Challenged to come up with new combinations, Paul resorted to the sub-bases within Camp Pendleton: Camp Pulgus, the home of the Seventh Marine Regiment: Camp Margarita, Fifth Marines. Camp Mateo, First Marines. Camp Horno, Tanks and Marine Corps Schools. He thought he was being unusually inventive when he tried the highway which connected them all together, Basilone Road. How could he have forgotten the hero of Guadalcanal?

Matter-of-factly the operator replied, "Basilone, I have two. Mary, on Sangamon Street. The other, John, on Grant Place."

Paul stammer. He couldn't get himself to answer.

"Are you there, sir?"

He swallowed hard. "Grant Place. Give me the one on Grant Place."

"Here's your number, sir," and the operator read off seven digits.

Paul redialed as fast as his fingers would go, this time to the service which supplied addresses for given phone numbers. "Seven-twenty-eight Grant Place," the operator said.

"Gotta be him," Paul croaked. He placed the receiver back on its cradle.

He looked at his watch. 4 a.m. Time to go on the offensive, and he crawled over to Tommy, shaking him awake. "You up?" he said.

"Yeah, yeah," Tommy said, yawning. He snapped his head at the elevator door. "Is he coming?"

"No, but I need you awake just in case. So don't you fall back to sleep on me."

"I can handle a little thing like staying awake," Tommy said with more than a touch of aggravation in his voice.

"Just mind that you do. That's if you wanna go on living."

"You really think there's a chance he's still gonna try getting in here? I mean it's gotta be close to morning."

Paul shrugged. "Probably not, but we can't let our guard down. It doesn't figure, him letting us take Ditty in without a fight. Could be he's decided his best shot is when we come out."

Sounding hopeful, Tommy said, "You never know, maybe he gave up and left."

"Uh-uh. He's there, I can feel it. It's just he ain't gonna make a move without knowing exactly what his odds are. With us in here, he'd be attacking an unknown target. Bad odds. With us on the street, good odds. Except I got my own little surprise."

"Surprise! What surprise?"

"I know where he's staying."

"How long have…?"

"Never mind." Paul checked Ditty and Katie, who were sound asleep. "Okay, this is for your ears only, got it?"

"Yeah, yeah, go ahead."

"Here's what we're gonna do. It's going on four o'clock. At five sharp I'm gonna call in to communications, tell them what we got. They'll have an army of cops lined up at the front door in no time."

"I don't get it. Halverson's bound to run when he sees a bunch'a cops coming."

"That's exactly what I want him to do. He'll head straight for home, and that's where you'll be waiting. You and every cop I can find available."

"Okay, only if you're right, and he's out there, ain't he gonna see me leaving?"

"Uh-uh. I got my little bag of tricks, you'll see."

"I don't know about this," Tommy said.

The kid was sounding more and more like Paul when dealing with Katie, and he said, "Please don't start that shit again." He scribbled in his note pad, ripped off the page, and handed it to Tommy. "Here's Halverson's address. Now come on, we gotta get you ready."

They went to Katie's closet. Grabbing a house coat, Paul slipped it over Tommy's shoulders.

"Are you kidding?" Tommy said. "No way could I fool my ninety-year-old granny with this thing, let alone Halverson."

"Yeah, you will. The thing covers you all the way to the knees, and it's still pitch dark out there." Looking about the closet, Paul pulled a scarf out, and wrapped it over Tommy's head. "There, even better."

"I'll be dead, Halverson catches on."

"Well, then you're just gonna have to make sure he don't. But think about it. Even if he does figure you for a cop, he ain't gonna up and shoot you. That would spoil his chance at Ditty."

"I don't know…"

"Yeah, I know," Paul said, inspection Tommy's disguise. "Roll up your trousers so they're hidden under the coat." He searched back through the closet. "Here, take Katie's laundry cart, make like you're some old lady going for a wash."

He filled the cart with whatever clothes he could find from the closet floor.

Tommy, looking at himself. "Man, I look like some kinda idiot in this getup."

"No, you don't. You look just like what you're supposed to look like." He handed Tommy the keys for his pickup, and pulled him to the elevator door. Smiling, Paul said, "Be seeing you, kid."

Chapter 37

HALVERSON HEARD the elevator start. Nobody else was up this time of the night, so it had to be them. And here he was on the roof, in the worst possible position. He ran to the front wall, drew his .45, and waited for them to come out. His best chance would be when they were right below, and he took aim at the sidewalk by the front door.

When the door finally swung open, he tightened his trigger finger, took a deep breath, and held it. Out came an old lady, dragging a laundry cart behind her. She was cursing in a whiskey voice, saying something about being sick and tired of having to get up in the middle of the night so she could do her wash without worrying about Cabrini Green hoodlums.

Halverson eased off on his trigger finger, sat back on the cinder roof. And laughed. He'd almost killed himself an old lady. Wouldn't that be great? The gun play would have given away his position, leaving him cornered up on this damned roof. From here on in he'd be extra careful.

Back to his inspection. He'd hoped to find an entry into the girl's loft, and had already checked all four outside walls, thinking a ladder of some kind might lead inside. Nothing of the sort. Looked like the bay window was his only entry point. He'd have to expose himself, but what else was there? All right, he'd stay right here, wait until just before dawn, and go at them from the bay window. Resting back against the facade, he checked his ammunition. Nine high-powered rounds were seated firmly into the .45's clip. He'd like to have more, but that would do.

Making a perfect sight-picture, he lined up the .45's front and rear sights, focusing in on a shiny object lying on the roof some ten strides away. Shiny object? Curious, he lowered the .45, and crawled to his target. Looked like a latch of some kind. If it was—

Taking care to make as little noise as possible, he tried easing it open. Nothing. Again, this time from his knees. It wouldn't budge. What the hell was this thing? It definitely was a latch, and had to lead somewhere. He felt around it with his fingers, finding a seam that ran approximately three feet to his left and right. The seam then turned on ninety degree angles, and ran about six feet along either side. Then another turn, this time directly toward each other, forming one large square with Halverson kneeling in the center.

Of course, you damned fool. It's a hatch. Only it's not going to open, not with your silly ass on top of it.

Slipping to the side, he took hold again, putting all of his weight behind it. A creak, and it pulled free from the roof. Holding his breath, Halverson held it just barely open, imagining where they were in the loft. On his right, he was sure of it, and at the perfect angle. He'd pick them off before they knew what was happening.

No time like the present. Readying his .45, he thrust the lid fully open, and poked his head through. He expected to see directly into the girl's loft, but found nothing but complete darkness. Puzzled, he stepped to the side, and let the moonlight shine through. A layer of plasterboard was exposed two feet below. A false ceiling. Must have been put in when the building was converted into lofts. Down on his knees, he reached in and tested its structure.

Flimsy, at best.

And immediately he knew what to do.

Scurrying to the back wall, he swung down from the roof, coming lightly to rest on the top of the bay window. Just a glance was all he needed. Yeah, there was Paul's head, still behind the mattress. No sign of the young cop and the others. They had to be asleep. Good, it would take him a few minutes to set up. He lowered himself to the fourth floor window, and into his command post.

Now, where was it he'd seen those ropes and pulleys?

Chapter 38

SITTING BEHIND THE MATTRESS, Paul listened as a far off siren cut through the night, whining its warning. Another siren joined the first, then a third, and a fourth. Paul tried to determine where they were going. Jesus, could Halverson have shown up at his apartment on Grant Place already?

No, he doubted that. Really, he figured there was little chance of Halverson leaving here, not without Ditty dead first. Tommy being sent to Grant Place had been nothing but a precaution, because God forbid Halverson found a way in here and successfully pulled off an assault—Paul didn't even want to think about it. But if Halverson did, at least Tommy would be waiting for him at his hideout.

There was a more important reason why Paul wanted Tommy gone. He figured Halverson to show, all right. When he did, Paul would revenge Jack Matthews himself, once and for all. How? Any way it took, but Tommy was not to be involved.

He checked his watch. 4:15. Wasn't gonna be long before daybreak. And God, he was tired. He pushed Katie from his lap, and rested her head on a cushion. Satisfied she was still asleep, he got up, and started pacing behind the mattress. Wasn't much room, no more than four steps from one wall to the other. With Ditty and Katie sprawled at his feet, it was like walking through a mine field of arms and legs. He tried standing in place, and doing arm and leg exercises; squat jumps, arm thrusts, even pushups against the wall. Finally, he propped himself up in the corner, one foot on either side of Ditty's head. No matter how hard he tried to keep his eyes open, they began to droop.

That's when an enormous crash echoed through the loft, followed closely by a shower of plaster from the ceiling.

Paul's whole body reverberated, and his knees gave way, plopping him on top of Ditty.

At the same moment three shots rang out.

Startled, Paul look up at the ceiling, where the plaster had come from. Left behind was a gaping hole. Fumbling in his pocket, he grabbed his sub nose, and taking aim, fired as fast as he could. Before he knew it, he was pulling the trigger on empty chambers.

Again he went to his pockets, this time looking for extra rounds, then realized that as fast as the assault had started, it was over.

All was quiet. Deadly quiet.

"Did you get him?" hollered Ditty, pushing in front of the mattress.

"Stay down, dammit," Paul yelled, not sure what to expect. He reloaded his snubnose.

When he looked back at the ceiling, what appeared to be a two hundred pound sack of potatoes dropped through the hole, landing with a crushing thud in the middle of the room.

Ditty said, "I think you got him," and started toward the body.

Paul put a choke hold around Ditty's neck, and jerked him back behind the mattress. "I told you to stay put, dammit."

He turned to Katie, who was curled at his side, staring up at him. He said, "Both of you, stay right where you're at until I say different."

Katie, grabbing his arm. "But, Pauly. I think Ditty's right. You shot him."

Paul looked at his snubnose. Tiny puffs of smoke trailed away from its barrel, the smell of gunpowder filling his nostrils. "My God," he mumbled. "I guess I did."

"It's okay," Katie said, and caressed him to her.

Paul had to get hold of himself. Katie was probably right, but what if Halverson was still alive? He pried her arms from around his waist, and crawled out into the open floor. Keeping his snubnose trained on the body, he gave it a good shove.

No reaction.

He placed the snubnose's barrel at the base of the body's skull, and trying to sound like he knew what he was doing, said, "You move one inch, I'll blow the top of your head off."

No answer.

He groped in the dark, finding an outstretched arm. Fingering down to its wrist, he checked for a pulse. Nothing, but Paul wasn't satisfied, not yet. He slid his hand up the arm, over the shoulder, then tried pressing his fingertips into the side of the neck like he'd seen emergency room nurses do. Still nothing.

But the body seemed cold, even clammy. Paul was surprised. From his experience working Homicide, he knew it took awhile before a body started showing signs of death. Maybe it was just him, nervous and all. Just to be sure, he ran his hand over the torso, feeling for bullet wounds, injuries, anything to give conclusive evidence. When he pulled his hand away, it was full of sticky, matted blood. None of this made sense. If Halverson had just been shot, his blood would not already be coagulating.

He holstered his snubnose, saying, "Turn on the lights, somebody. I gotta take a closer look here."

Katie flipped the switch on her bedside lamp.

Paul looked at the body face down in the middle of the floor. It was bearing the short haircut worn by marines, with a Ka-bar strapped to its side.

"It's him, all right." Paul got to his feet.

"Let me at the sonofabitch," Ditty said, and scurried toward the body.

Paul tried to grab him, but was too late. Ditty ripped the Ka-bar from its scabbard, and gripping it in both hands, began pummeling the body. "I got him! I finally got him! This is for you, Shoes!" He spat at the body.

"I'm gonna cut those ugly eyes right outta your head, you, you…"

He stopped with the Ka-bar raised above his head, looking horrified into the vacant eyes of—who, Paul didn't know, some old guy.

Ditty mumbling, "What they hell?"

"Ain't me, is it?" came a shout, and two shots rang out.

Paul gaped openmouthed as the first bullet ripped through Ditty's throat. The second splattered Ditty's ear, and he flopped to the floor.

Coming out of his shock, Paul went to one knee, and spun toward the sound of the shots. A silhouette was framed in the center of the bay window, looking like something from a Batman movie. But this was no movie, and Paul dug out his snubnose.

226

He was just about to fire when two flashes illuminated the room for mini seconds. Paul felt as though he'd been hit with a sledgehammer on his chest, and blood was dripping over his eyes. His arms went numb, he staggered. Unable to hold his balance, he toppled onto his back.

It didn't hurt anymore. Not at all. Was just like that day back in Vietnam. Only this time was he going to die. He knew it.

And then nothing mattered anymore.

Chapter 39

PAUL COULD HEAR KATIE CRYING. She was hollering, too, but it was from far off. He couldn't make out what she was saying, not at first, but then her scratchy voice began to grow louder, as if she were approaching. Now echoing in his ears, she said, "I'm a lawyer, the most vicious kind of lawyer, and if he dies I'll have your job, your home, and yes, even your children."

Paul wondered who Katie was talking about. He forced his eyes open. A blurry object was standing over him, and a set of arms were fiddling with Paul's chest. Which hurt something awful.

"Katie, that you?" he croaked.

"He's coming out of it," a male voice said from up close.

"He'd better be," Katie said, and the blurry object was shoved aside. She appeared over him. With her long black hair strewn in her eyes, she said, "You're going to be fine. Just you wait and see, we're going to have at least a dozen Serbian-Croatian children. Okay, Croatian-Serbian children. I'll even move to that little bowdunk town you love so damn much. I don't care, only please, puleeez, keep breathing."

The male voice saying, "Lady, you're going to have to let me do my job."

Katie, draped across Paul's legs. "Jesus Mary and Joseph-Jesus Mary and Joseph."

Paul, more coherent all the time, and with the hurt in his chest becoming a pounding ache, said, "Uh-she'll be good."

"Like hell I will." She faced away. "I want to know your name and address. And by the way, the entire surgery team's, too."

"Lady, surgery's not going to be necessary."

"Huh?"

"That's right. The x-rays show the bullet that hit him in the chest went through and through. And his head, that was just a glancing wound."

Paul, beginning to recall—damn, Ditty was dead. And God, the ache in his chest, even worse.

"He's going to be okay then?" Katie said, sounding unconvinced.

A bespectacled man in a powder-blue gown came into view. "Sergeant, an inch one way or the other—Well, you wouldn't have been so lucky."

Paul, seeing clearer now. "Hurts like hell, doc."

"I know. We're about to give you a pain shot. It'll work quick enough, only along with it you'll be drowsy. A detective has been waiting outside for a couple of hours. He wants to talk to you first."

"Screw him," Katie said.

"No, wait," Paul said, trying to make his brain work. "Tommy, where's Tommy?"

"Right here, Sarge."

An upside down view of Tommy's curly locks came into view. Paul said to him, "Come around where I can see you, dammit." And as Tommy inched sideways, "It's done, right?"

Tommy ran his eyes at the bespectacled doctor, and back at Paul.

Oh, no. Somehow Halverson had gotten away again. "Doc," Paul said. "Can you leave us alone, just for a minute?"

The doctor hesitated. "You have to be suffering."

Paul sucked a breath, and said, "I ain't no hero, doc. It's just I gotta get some business done."

Katie, with tears in her eyes. "Pauly, you can talk about this anytime. Let them give you the shot."

"No, really, I'm okay. Please, doc. Give us a couple'a minutes."

"You're sure?" the doctor said with a syringe at the ready.

Paul managed a nod.

"Okay, but just for awhile," and the doctor disappeared from view.

Paul had a dozen questions, but his chest hurt like the devil. He looked up at Tommy, and through the pain, said, "How come?"

"Katie's right, Sarge. This can wait."

"Now."

"Okay, okay. Not ten minutes after I got to Halverson's place there were these sirens. I figured it was going down back at Katie's loft."

"Halverson's place?" Katie said. "What are you two talking about?"

Paul turned to her. "Please. The sooner we get this hashed out, the sooner I can get that shot." Looking at Tommy, he said, "Yeah, I heard the sirens, too. So?"

"Well, I just couldn't make myself wait, and went back to the loft. You know, thinking Halverson must have tried getting in."

Katie again. "You mean you guys knew where Halverson was living?" Looking angry. "Just how long have you known?"

"Dammit, Katie," Paul said. He winced when a shockwave hit his chest. When it passed, he turned back to Tommy. "Halverson's gone now for sure. And you could've had him."

Tommy, whispering. "I don't think so."

"What's that supposed to mean?"

"After they got you in the ambulance, I went back to Halverson's place. It's a smallish hotel, and his BMW was parked out front. I did a little checking, found out he was up in his room with the lights out. Can you believe it? The dude ups and kills Ditty, shoots a cop, and goes to bed like he's been out to a late-night movie."

Katie, turning on Tommy. "So why didn't you get the Task Force and go in after him?" She looked at Paul. "That was the plan, right?"

"Right," Paul said, disgusted. And to Tommy, "Go on."

"Maybe I should've, but I wanted to make sure it was okay with you, Sarge. I mean, wasn't no hurry, and who knows what kinda guns and whatnot Halverson has in there?"

Rethinking, Paul said, "You did good. I guess I'll let you live. Only tell me exactly how you found out Halverson was up in his room, and asleep."

Tommy smiled. "Uh, there was this girl working the desk, and…"

"Tell me no more."

Katie said, "Okay then, so he's there. Can you guys cut the crap and get the Task Force over there?"

"Not just yet," Paul said, trying to come up with a plan.

Katie, caressing Paul's hand. "He killed Ditty. You too, almost."

"I know, I know," Paul said, picturing Ditty's head being destroyed by Halverson's bullets. "Listen," he said, but wasn't sure how to say what he was thinking. Then the pain again. Fierce, this time. He'd seen good men lose consciousness under the same circumstances. Fearing he might go under at any time, he said, "Katie, you know I love you so. Only give me a break, will ya?"

Surprising to Paul, Katie nodded. Like she really meant to obey his wishes. Yeah, right. Obedience was not a trait he was used to, not coming from Katie, and he found himself staring at her. But he had to keep his head on what was important. "Did either of you talk to Debolt yet, I mean about the shooting?"

Katie, looking suspicious. "I haven't. Why do you ask?"

Paul turned to Tommy. "You didn't, did you?"

"Hell no. I wouldn't say a word to that..." Searching for words.

"... that hemorrhoid."

Paul laughed, he couldn't help it. Katie too.

Tommy smiled, and said, "Anyway, I wasn't there when it actually happened, remember?"

"Good, then nobody knows where Halverson's at but us." He smiled despite his aching chest, and said, "One more thing. Debolt's gonna ask the both of you if you can identify the shooter."

Katie, with eyes searching Paul's. "What's this all about? You know it was Halverson as well as we do."

Paul, feeling his voice cracking. "Yeah, that's right, we know. But Debolt doesn't. Well, he does, but only you and I can testify to it."

Katie flashed at Tommy, saying, "So what's so hard about that?"

Paul gave Katie a sly grin. "That's the one thing we can't do?"

"Why not?"

Paul forced a laugh, and watched to see if Katie laughed too. She did not. Uh-oh, this could be difficult. But that dingleberry Debolt would be in here soon. Paul had to at least try.

Katie, leaning close. "I'm waiting."

"Okay, I'm gonna tell you. But first you gotta answer me a question."

"I'm still waiting."

"Yeah, I can see that. But will you listen?"

"Okay, I'm waiting and I'm listening. So spit it out."

Paul figured he didn't have a choice, and said, "What you want them to do with Halverson when they catch him?"

She produced a straight face. "Hang him by his testicles. I'll even supply the rope."

Paul gave her his best condescending smile. "Only that ain't gonna happen, is it?"

"Okay. They'll just plain execute him. I guess I'll just have to settle for that."

"No, they won't."

"He's murdered five, six, I don't know how many people. Oh, yes. He'll die."

Paul waited a second, letting her catch her breath and another wave of pain in his chest to subside. "Katie, you're a lawyer, or gonna be anyway. Listen to the facts. With Ditty dead, there ain't nobody left to testify against Halverson on any of those murders. He's gonna walk and you know it."

Katie, showing her defiant self. "Except for one thing. Both you and me saw him shoot Ditty. We'll be the difference."

"Are you sure it was him? Be honest."

"Yes, I'm sure. Who else would it be?"

"Nobody else. But you're gonna have to identify him in court."

Katie, looking thoughtful and saying nothing.

"You can't, can you?"

She jutted her jaw at him, saying, "I don't care. I'll identify him anyway."

"Not a chance. Maybe I could get away with a lie like that. Not you, though." The ache was still there, and bad, but he was beginning to get a handle on it.

"Oh, yes I could. Just you wait and see."

"It wouldn't wash. Not in a court of law, simply because as dark as it was, and with all the confusion going on, how could you've been able to see? I sure couldn't." Halverson's image

232

in the bay window popped into his head. "Jesus. How'd he do that, anyway?"

Tommy said, "With ropes and a pulley. Looked like a three ring circus outside that window."

"Christ. Where'd he get that stuff?"

But before Tommy could answer, Katie said, "You're right about court. Any second-year law student would make us out for liars in front of the jury. Easy. But what about fingerprints, he has to have left some, right?"

"I doubt it," Paul said. "Halverson's way too smart for that. Very good chance he'll walk out of court a free man. You don't wanna chance that, do you?"

She looked at him with a suspicious eye. "Just what are you purposing? And don't try any of your dumb lies on me, either."

"All one-hundred percent truth," Paul said, gritting his teeth when a shockwave returned. "Debolt is gonna be in here any minute. I want you to tell him you didn't see anything."

"Pauly, you're hurting. Please, let's talk about this later. Please."

"Now," Paul said. "Will you tell Debolt you didn't see anything?"

"Dammit, you can be a jackass, you know that?"

"Your answer, Katie."

"Just like that, lie to the police?"

"Yeah, and remember, if you tell Debolt you saw Halverson's face, he's gonna put out a nationwide APB. Which doesn't necessarily mean Halverson's gonna get caught. Fact is lots have tried, but ain't nobody got him yet. Meanwhile you and me will be in the same position Ditty was in. And you know what happened to Ditty."

Katie's face showed immediate understanding.

Good. Maybe Paul still had a chance, and he pressed on even though it felt like a thousand needles were jabbing at his chest. "That's right. Halverson might just decide he'll have to eliminate us like he did all the others. He's pretty good at it, too. Just ask Ditty." He let his threat sink in, then said, "Think it out, 'cause once you open your mouth it'll be too late."

Katie started to speak, then stopped with her mouth hanging loose. She stared at her toes. Katie, at a loss for words.

This was a first.

Paul had thought he was getting used to his pain, but it was growing ever worse. He closed his eyes, suffering through another needle attack. Meanwhile he'd let Katie stew for a minute. Saying more would only serve to create an argument. And an argument was the last thing he wanted, especially with Katie.

A minute past, and then another, and another. Paul opened his eyes. Katie wasn't there. Neither was Tommy. Oh, God, they hadn't gone for it, and were spilling everything to Debolt.

"Katie!" he hollered. "Where are you?"

She appeared over him with Debolt at her side. Tommy was just behind.

Debolt said, "Uh-she says we can talk now."

Paul looked at Katie, who had a stoic face on. Oh, man, the one thing Katie Bartovich wasn't was stoic. Well, he'd done as much as he could. Now it was up to her.

She said, "So, Detective?"

Debolt nodded. "I need a description of the offender, uh—" Debolt checked his notepad, "—Miss Bartovich."

Katie flicked once at Paul, and said, "Sorry, but I can't do that."

Paul slammed his eyes closed, hiding his satisfaction.

And heard Debolt say, "Is there a problem I don't know about?"

Katie: "Not really. I just didn't see anything. It went so fast."

"I don't understand," Debolt said. "You must've seen something."

Paul opened his eyes. Katie was looking at Debolt, and with the most innocent of faces. He'd been wrong. She was an excellent liar. And now she said, "Sorry, it's just as I told you. I saw absolutely nothing. Really, I don't know anything, beyond the fact that Ditty was my legal aid assignment. He called and said he wanted to give himself up. Knowing Sergeant Kostovic, I called him. You know the rest."

Debolt looked at Paul. Debolt saying, "That's okay, because you saw the guy, right?"

"Sorry, Kyle. Not me, either. Hell, before I knew it, I'd been shot."

Debolt's clipboard clattered to the floor. He left it, saying, "I just can't believe—I mean, neither of you saw a thing?"

Katie, looking like she was beginning to enjoy this. "Tell me, Detective. Isn't there a strong possibility the killer will come after me now? I mean, we all know it had to have been Halverson, and look what's he's done to all the others. Who's going to protect me?"

Debolt gave Paul a look of defeat, and said, "I've got a lotta work to do." He walked out the door shaking his head.

Paul said to Tommy, "Go find that doctor, will ya?"

When Tommy left, Katie leaned close. "Just you wait a minute, buster. You've got something up you sleeve and I want to know what it is." "No, uh-uh." Paul, said. "You think you wanna know, but you really don't. Trust me."

Katie, with her chin on Paul's chest. "You can pull that, 'Trust me,' stuff all day long on rookie cops. For me, you're going to have to do a little better. Unless, of course, you want to take a chance on seeing a miraculous recovery of my memory."

"The doctor, go help Tommy find him."

"Tell me."

"The pain shot, okay?"

"No way."

"Jesus!"

Chapter 40

HALVERSON, in a tank-top and shorts, loped through the underpass that led to the beach. In full stride, he touched a hand to the new Ka-bar knife which was strapped to the curve of his back. The one he'd left on old Thad's body had been like a loving friend. A sacrifice, having to let it go, but necessary.

He took in the magnificent orange and red horizon, could actually measure the sun as it arced above Lake Michigan, edging up into the pale blue sky. And the water, like glass, not a wave, not even a ripple. Looked like he could walk right out on it.

One mile farther was the breakwater which protruded into the lake from North Avenue Beach. He slowed his gate, straining to see its outermost extension, looking for a special, blond beauty. She wasn't there. Damn. This was the third day in a row he had missed her.

He'd spotted her about a week ago, standing alone on the breakwater, staring out at the lake. The closer he'd got the better she looked, the cheeks of her tight, little ass outlined on a bikini bottom. Firm, golden brown legs, too. Perfectly upturned breasts. And her hair, platinum blond. His favorite, and it curled all the way down to the small of her back. Just looking at her had sent chills through his body, reminding him that he hadn't been with a woman for—for who knew how long?

He'd passed behind her, stopping at the end of the breakwater. Pretending to be resting, he'd craned his neck to get a second look. Unexpectedly, she was looking right back at him, smiling under a pair of oversized sunglasses. From what he could see, her face was a perfect oval, with a cute pug nose, and a pouting mouth.

Also unexpectedly, he had received a pleasant, "What a nice day."

But before he could reply she stuffed her sunglasses into her bikini briefs, and executed an expert dive. Strong arm over arm strokes carried her away, taking her across the inlet. He wanted to dive in after her, but his fear of water overtook him. Maybe he should have met her on the far side. No, he had been right to let her go.

He didn't want to appear too anxious.

He saw her again the very next morning. This time he was ready for her and got in a hello of his own. She had rewarded him with an encouraging, "See you next time," before swimming away. He'd almost dived in that time. But deep water—he just couldn't force himself.

The third morning he got to the breakwater first, probably because he'd been up since three, fantasizing about that sweet body of hers. He'd waited for what seemed like hours, keeping his eyes glued on the beach, hoping for her arrival. And then, from out of nowhere, she came swimming toward him.

That time he thought he had her for sure, and offered a hand to help her out. Only she hadn't seemed to see it, and kicked off in the direction she had come from.

He'd been disappointed to say the least. He hated the thought, but if there was a next time, he'd even dive in after her if that was what it would take. At least then he'd know if he had a chance with her.

To his utter frustration, she failed to show on the next morning. The following day brought the same results. And the day after that, and the day after that.

If she didn't come today, so be it.

But he couldn't help himself, and kept searching the waters for her. No one was out there aside from one small boat. It had one sole occupant. A fisherman, he figured. Anyway, he was so very far from shore, the girl couldn't possibly have anything to do with him.

Halverson continued his run, and reached the far end of Oak Street beach. Turning back for home, his eyes went directly to the breakwater. There she was, standing at the same exact spot where he had first seen her. For a split second he wondered where she had come from. And how was it one minute she wasn't there and the next she was? Then she raised up on her toes and waved to him.

All suspicions were put aside. He had to get to her before

237

she got back into the water. He kicked high, lengthening his stride, pumping as fast as he could. As he came onto the breakwater, she inched toward water's edge. He was sure she was about to dive in.

Waving at her, he hollered, "Wait, I'm coming!"

And she looked around.

Puffing the last few strides, he staggered to a halt at her side. He stood there, bent over, hands on knees, gasping for air, feeling like a damned fool.

"I've been wondering what had become of you," she said from behind her sunglasses.

"You!" he gasped, still out of breath. "How about me? I've been running around here for days trying to find you like an infatuated school boy."

She giggled, and rubbing her legs together like a stripper in a burlesque show, said, "I know."

"'You know?' What do you mean, 'you know?'" Halverson couldn't keep his eyes off those legs.

"I've got a confession to make," she said. "I was attracted to you from that first day. But, well, it didn't seem like a decent way for a girl to meet a man." She gave him a shy smile. "And you're a little older than me. I was afraid you'd think I was throwing myself at you, so after those first few days I stayed away. Not too far away, though. I was watching from afar. Yesterday, when you gave up and started running for home, I even tried to catch up. I'm afraid you were too fast for me."

Halverson finally tore his eyes from her legs. "Where were you? I mean, I looked everywhere."

She offered her hand. "Doesn't matter, my name is Susan Johanson."

"I'm John Basilone," he said. Her hand. So warm. Soft.

"Hello, John Basilone. Glad to meet you."

He pointed at the water. "Please, whatever you do, don't go diving back in. I couldn't stand it."

She gave him an alluring smile. "Don't you worry. Unless you're a serial murderer or something, I'm here for awhile."

No, not a serial murderer, but he'd done his share of killings. For this babe, he had different designs. He'd better start with something light. "Have you lived in Chicago long?"

"Homegrown. And you?"

"Me? I'm from… from Houston. Just finished a business deal in the Loop. I figured why not hang around for a few days, take in the sights? This is one fine town you've got here."

"I think so." She sat down on the edge of the breakwater, letting her feet dangle in the light surf.

Only Halverson wasn't looking at her feet, or listening much, because when she leaned forward, her bikini top fell away from her full chest, exposing two bright red nipples.

She looked up at him, obviously catching him staring down her front. He thought he had blown it, but she smiled like a movie star, and said, "Come sit down. You look like you could use the rest."

Halverson had everything he could do not to drool as he lowered himself alongside her. Not too close, though. Didn't want to scare her away.

Which reminded him. Just being near deep water made his skin crawl.

She patted his shoulder. "Wow! You're all muscle. You must do a lot more than run to keep yourself in that kind of condition."

He delighted in her touch, and this was going so very well. Almost too well, something down deep told him. Come on, relax, he said to himself. You think this living doll is a cop? In the first place, cops don't work that way. If they had something on him, they'd just come out and make an arrest. The FBI? Those guys were different. They might try getting close to him with a girl. But if the Feds had a case on him, which they didn't, they too, would make an arrest. The only question left was why a great looking thing like this would offer herself up to a total stranger.

He said, "I'm a little surprised a high-class lady like you would take a chance on meeting a stranger way out here at the end of nowhere. Muscles or no muscles."

With a trace of hesitation, she said, "You're right, in a way. That's what all those hellos and good-byes were about. And the days I didn't come—Truth is, I was getting up courage to come again." She patted his knee this time, and her hand remained.

Which felt even better than her first touch, but he'd started his line of questioning, and had better finish before he let himself go any further. Trying to sound as if he were making small talk, he said, "Still, you're here. And so far away from everything."

"Not really." She pointed toward the beach. "See those high-rise apartment buildings lined along Lake Shore Drive. They're chock-full of people who spend hour on end with nothing better to do than gaze over the lake with binoculars and high-powered telescopes." She laughed. "I should know, I'm one of them. I'll bet we're being watched right this minute."

Halverson ran his eyes over the maze of Lake Shore Drive windows. She must have a few dollars to be living up there. He may have found himself a nice place to stay for—who knows how long? Maybe the whole winter. He'd see.

She flicked those curly locks over her shoulder. "Now that we're acquainted, what do you say to a little swim, Mister John Basilone?"

"I don't know. I'm not such a swimmer."

"Just a splash. You look like you could use it."

She pulled her glasses off, and plunged in. Popping up a few feet from the breakwater, she smiled at him through long, blond curls. "Well?"

Halverson didn't see any way out of it. He kicked off his running shoes, and slid off the ledge, treading water the best he could. It was cool, exhilarating so, and he felt his confidence growing.

"Nice, isn't it?" she said, her voice trailing off.

He turned to find her backstroking out into the inlet. She lifted one arm over her head and then the other, arching her back, and lifting those firm young breasts out of the water, imprinting her nipples on the wet bikini top.

Didn't he get it? This was all for his benefit. He forgot all the warning signs, his fear of water, and splashed after her.

They swam along, she playfully spraying water at him, he caught up in her loveliness, dodging, and trying to keep up. Each time he started to gain on her, she laughed, and kicked water in his face, forcing him to stop and clear his eyes. As he did, she rolled over on her belly, and with a volley of powerful strokes, swam farther out into the inlet.

He loved how her cute little ass jutted out of the water while the rest of her trim body skimmed along the surface. He struggled after her, and was finally rewarded when she tread water, waiting for him to catch up. As he came alongside, she brushed her hair out of her eyes, and smiled at him.

At long last he was going to get a good look at her face. He rubbed the water out of his eyes, and going back to treading water, blinked them open. She was as striking as he had imagined, equal to the exquisite body she had been showing off for him.

"You're just about the prettiest thing I've ever seen," he said.

But then her face went cold, and she said, "You don't recognize me, do you?"

His every muscle went taut. He might not know her face, but twice he had witnessed that scratchy voice of hers, first in the alley when he had taken out that cop, and again when she was in her loft.

She said, "You're right, I am pretty. The last pretty thing you're ever going to see," and struck out with her leg, kicking him full in the face. Stunned, he sank under the water. Then recovering, he clawed his way back to the surface. Sputtering for air, he brought his Ka-bar to bear, slashing blindly where he estimated her last to have been.

Still unable to see, and not knowing if he'd hit her, he wiped his eyes clear. Gone. He spun around, thinking he must have gotten disoriented while under the water. But she wasn't there, not anywhere. Where could she be?

Had to be hiding under the water. Fine, how long could she hold her breath? Not as long as he could stay on top. He took deep breaths trying to calm himself, and circled, waiting for her to appear. A minute passed, then another. Maybe he had stuck her after all, and in his frenzy hadn't realized it. He checked the blade of his new Ka-bar. Clean, but that

241

didn't mean anything. The water could have washed her blood away.

One way or the other she was gone. Could be she swam away underwater. Easy enough for her, being such a strong swimmer. She'd simply surface long enough to fill her lungs, then go under again. By now she was probably nearing the beach, or the breakwater, whichever direction she had gone.

Oh, Christ! She was sure to run for help. And here he was out in the middle of the inlet, floundering like a turtle. He had to get the hell out of there, but first he had to get hold of himself, and take inventory. Which way should he go? The breakwater, that's where he'd started. It had to be the closest dry land. There it was, but far off in the distance. That bitch, she had lured him hundreds of yards out into the inlet. She must have thought she could drown him with a good kick in the face. Hadn't expected his Ka-bar, had she? It had saved him, and he clenched a grip on it, looking at it like father to his newly-born son.

Okay, okay. Enough of that. Just get back to land. He still had plenty of time. Even if she was already on the beach, it would take her awhile to find a cop this early in the morning.

Under control now, he swam for the breakwater. The Ka-bar made his already awkward stroke even more clumsy, but he was not about to throw it away. It was his only defense.

As he drew closer to the breakwater, his confidence regenerated. He was going to make it, he always had before, and he would this time, too. Once out of the water, he'd throw on his shoes, and make it the hell out of there. He couldn't go back to the apartment, though. If she knew about his morning runs, she knew where he lived, too.

One last stroke and he could glide the rest of the way. He shoved his Ka-bar into its scabbard, kicked, and reached for the breakwater.

And then he felt a sharp tug on his foot, stymieing his forward motion. Bewildered, he tried to shake off whatever was holding him back. Then came another tug, and he was pulled under the water. He forced open his eyes, and looked at his foot. A rope was tethered to his ankle, and beyond it was the girl. She was wearing scuba gear and waving at him, as if to say, now I've got you.

He wanted to cut her right then and there, but needed air, and in desperation struggled upwards, managing to breach his head. One short gasp, and he was yanked under again.

She was going to drown him if he didn't think of something quick. He ripped his Ka-bar from its scabbard, and took a wild swipe at the rope, missing. Again he tried, and again missed. With his lungs about to burst, he grabbed the rope with his free hand, and tried chopping at it. He got in one blow, but the density of the water blunted its effectiveness. Then came another yank, this time intensely so, and he was sucked out of the water.

He got a glimpse of a small boat some twenty feet ahead. It was racing through the water, him in its wake, skimming the surface, being snapped like a whip. After one particularly malicious lash, he lost his grip on the Ka-bar, and watched horrified as it flipped out of sight. Without it survival seemed hopeless, but he struggled on, he had to.

If he could take in even the slightest bit of slack, he might be able to slip the rope off his ankle. Twice the tips of his fingers scraped its coarse fibers, and then fell away. Again, he tried. Yes, he had the rope, but only with one hand. Now with the other—reach, reach, closer, closer. And just as he was about to grab hold the boat made a sharp turn to the right, thrusting him into a vicious spin.

Somehow he held on, and flailing with his loose arm, started to right himself. Then the boat went left, spinning him in the opposite direction. He lost his grip, and was stretched at full extension, getting only wisps of air, hardly enough to sustain him. With little strength left, he gave up. The end was near. He knew it.

Then, just as he was about to lose consciousness, the rope went slack. Battered and dazed, he wallowed just below surface. He didn't have the will to fight, and hoped death would come quick.

The rope tugged on his leg. He was being pulled again. Oh, God, no more. Please. But instead of the torture restarting, he was reeled to the surface. He coughed in what air he could as a pair of brawny arms dragged him toward a small boat. He managed to read "VOLLY'S FLOATING HIDEAWAY" which was painted on it's bow.

Feeling like a newly landed bass, he was flopped over the side, onto a pile of Budweiser beer cans. Someone grabbed his arms, and handcuffed him behind his back. Then a hand slapped him across the face, and somebody said, "Wake up, Halvy. You ain't that bad hurt."

He hadn't been called Halvy since he was in the 9th Marines, and he forced his eyes open, laboring to focus on whoever this was.

At his feet sat BJ McCoy. The gunny was bare-chested, and wearing a pair of swimming trunks.

BJ saying, "With your fear of water, I knew we had you as soon as you jumped in."

Halverson tried to answer, but all he could do was gurgle up Lake Michigan water. He sensed movement off to his side, and spotted the girl lifting herself into the boat. As she did, she kicked him squarely in the groin. The pain was excruciating. He curled up, and turned his back to her, protecting against her next blow.

She said, "Oh, excuse me. Somehow I've forgotten my manners, have I not? Here, let me help you up." Digging her fingers into his ears, she snapped his head forward. He saw her knee coming, but was powerless to avoid the crunch, and a wave of blood splattered from his nose.

"Now you die, you, you..." She pulled at his legs, trying to dump him overboard.

With his will to live rekindled, Halverson kicked her as hard as he could, sprawling her over the side.

She came up, saying, "Now you're definitely gonna drown, slow and painfully, too."

He knew he didn't have a chance. With no other option, he curled into a ball, trying to avoid the inevitable. But when she got back in the boat, BJ shoved her away. "We've got a plan and we're gonna stick to it," he said. "Get us started, and now."

She got the motor going, all the while looking back at

Halverson. "I want to make him suffer. He deserves it, you know he does."

"He's gonna suffer. That I promise," BJ said.

She tried to push past BJ. He held her back, but not before she landed a few kicks on Halverson's legs.

BJ was Halverson's only hope. He yelled, "Keep her away, dammit," and rolled out of her reach.

"Listen to him. Just a few minutes ago he couldn't get enough of me." She turned her bikini-clad bottom to him. "See that, you scum? You thought you were going to get some, didn't you? Well, you're not, not never. I played you just like you played Ditty and all the others before you killed them. Now it's your turn. Just think about that for awhile."

"Okay, that's enough," BJ said. "Get back to the controls before the Coast Guard comes along."

She stood her ground, laughing like the witch she'd turned out to be. "Just look at him," she said, "running his brain a mile a minute trying to figure a way out. Listen, fool, you're mine now, and where you're going there's nothing you can say or do about it."

Halverson figured she was wrong. He'd be safe in jail, and hollered, "Go ahead, take me in. I give up."

Now it was BJ laughing. "Think again, Halvy. We didn't go through all this just to hand you over to the cops."

Halverson lifted his head over the edge of the boat. They were heading outbound. Despair set in as he came to the only logical conclusion. "BJ, please. I'll do anything, just don't drown me."

Who went on laughing. "Being the killer you are, you're gonna appreciate what's coming. Only it ain't what you think."

The girl shoved the throttle all the way forward. They were racing now, and she spun the wheel, banking so that they ran parallel with the shore.

Halverson's nose throbbed. Blood dripped from his chin, smearing on the front of his still-wet T-shirt. His groin ached, and the handcuffs dug into his wrists. He was a total mess, but alive. If he wanted to stay that way he'd better do something quick.

Think. Make yourself think.

Okay, the girl wanted him dead, that was obvious. But BJ had held her off. What was it BJ had told her? That they had a plan. And the girl, she had said something about him going where nothing he said or did would save him. What was that suppose to mean? Maybe the FBI. Sure, he'd been right in the first place, and this was all a bluff. BJ would never kill anybody unless he had to.

Halverson would play it cool. Nobody, not even the FBI, could change the fact that no witnesses were left to testify against him. So he'd got beat up some. No big deal. Once he was in the hands of the Feds, he'd get himself a lawyer. He'd beat the rap. Then guess who'd be laughing.

The girl made another turn, back towards land. She eased off the throttle, and the boat settled into calm waters, gliding toward shore. Halverson looked over the bow. They were coming up on a small, wooden-planed pier. On its end was a bent and rusty sign which read:

WELCOME TO MEIGS FIELD
CHICAGO'S DOWNTOWN AIRPORT

An airport? For what? Not the FBI. Where the hell were they taking him? Trying not to sound too demanding, he said to BJ, "I want a lawyer."

And as they touched land, a different voice said, "This ain't exactly an arrest, asshole, so you don't get a lawyer."

Halverson looked up to see a set of blue jean-clad legs on the pier. Running his eyes upwards, he saw—Uh-oh. The young cop.

Tommy slapped BJ on the back. "Nice job, Gunny. He didn't give you any trouble, huh?"

"Nope. Except I had all I could do to keep Katie off him." Tommy inspected Halverson's battered face, and looked at the girl. "Looks like you got in a few licks."

"I should've drowned the piece of, of— I don't know, filth—when I had the chance."

"This'll work a lot better," Tommy said.

246

Terrified all over again, Halverson was lifted out of the boat. With Tommy on one arm, BJ the other, they marched him off the pier. He searched for somebody who looked like an FBI agent, but found no one. Panicking, he said to BJ, "Come on, tell me what's going on? This is a joke, right?"

"No joke," came a voice from somewhere off to his side.

He looked, and saw a man in a wheelchair. God, they all were here, because it was that sergeant, Paul. That must be it. They were going to let Paul take his revenge. Halverson buckled his legs, straining to pull out of his captors' arms.

They jerked him up, and held fast.

"You can't do this. Please!" he hollered.

"Listen, and hear me good," Paul said. "I've been waiting for this moment from that night you killed Lieutenant Matthews."

Halverson, losing hope. "I confess. Just take me to jail."

Paul looked at BJ. "He's disgusting. Take him away before I throw up on him."

The girl knelt down alongside the wheelchair, and with her arms wrapped around Paul, sneered at Halverson. "Pauly, if you don't tell him, I will," she said.

Halverson twisted so that BJ was between the girl and himself.

"Please," he said. "Whatever it is, don't do it."

The girl laughed. But it wasn't a funny kind of laugh. As though she were repulsed by Halverson. "You're right, Paul, he's disgusting. Not even worth wasting our breath on. And anyway, he'd probably appreciate it more if it came as a surprise."

Paul, face to face with Halverson. "I think that's an excellent idea. Get ready, pal, 'cause we got somebody who wants to meet you, and they came first class." He pointed over his shoulder.

Halverson gawked at a Learjet parked on the runway's apron. "I don't get it?" He looked back at BJ McCoy. "You and me, we fought those little yellow commies side by side. Don't that count for something?"

BJ gave Halverson a push, and he went sprawling toward the jet. "That's right, Halvy. You were one hell of a marine.

But you took it way too far, and now you gotta pay."

Halverson stared at his old marine gunny, trying to understand what was about to happen. And then two men with Latin features came out of the Learjet. Sporting deadpan faces, and dressed in heavily starched khaki's, they led him toward the ramp.

Halverson sensed he was lost if he let them put him in the plane. Struggling against their grip, he looked back at Paul. "Sergeant, I know you're in charge. I'll do anything you want, just don't let them have me."

"Sorry, pal, but you killed a friend of mine, plus bullshitted a lot others to their deaths. Hey, you never know, maybe you can bullshit these guys, too."

Halverson kicked and twisted. "No, you can't!" he screamed, but knew he couldn't be heard over the roar of the Learjet's engines.

They had him on the ramp now, and he looked back at BJ, who turned away. Frustration taking over, Halverson yelled, "Somehow I'll get out of this. When I do, I'll be back to get you all. Yeah, every last one of you."

Chapter 41

THE LEARJET'S outer door rolled closed behind Halverson. He looked about the cabin. It was small but luxurious: leather seats, oaken paneling, a wet bar that stretched across a forward wall. Unlike regular aircraft, the seating was against the bulkheads. That is except for himself. He was placed in a chair immediately inside the outer door, and bound with heavy chains.

Chains? A little overkill.

Wouldn't plain ordinary rope do the job?

He strained to see out the portal windows. There they all were, watching, with Paul in front. So many times he had wanted to kill that cop. That marine.

If he had, none of this would have happened, he knew it.

And then a lurch. They were moving, gaining speed, now rushing, and nose up, they raised into the sky. Soon they were cruising.

Halverson's guards stood mute on each of his shoulders.

He had to start a dialogue, get them talking.

"Listen to me," he said. "I got enough cash we could all fly anywhere in the world, and when we get there we'll live like kings."

The guard who appeared to be in charge said, "*Que lastima, no comprendo.*"

He had to try something else. But what? Wait, all Latins went for women. "I got dozens of broads, all beauties, and every one at my beck and call. Turn this plane for Mexico, and by evening we'll have one for each arm."

The guard shrugged. "No spek de Ingles," he said.

Okay, maybe these two were hopeless, but most Latins were easy to corrupt. He'd wait until he got to wherever they were going. Sitting back, he rested assured that when the time came he'd hit on an idea. Didn't he always?

A light flashed on the cabin wall and the head guard picked up the intercom. "*Capitan Guerra,*" he said, and came to attention. "*Si, Senora. Estamos.*"

Halverson looked at Captain Guerra. "Who was that? Let

me talk to him. Please, so I can—can—please let me talk to him."

The captain spoke to the second guard. "*Abre la puerta.*"

"*Seguro,*" came the second guard's response, and he opened the forward cabin door.

Two women came through. One was fairly young, olive skinned, cute, and wore the same khaki uniform the guards wore. The other lady was middle-aged, slightly overweight. She was light complexioned, definitely not Latin, and dressed matronly, with a frilly blouse buttoned high on the collar. A huge diamond pendant hung from her neck.

"*Sientase aqui,*" the younger lady said. She helped the matronly lady into a chair opposite Halverson.

He'd always been lucky with women, whether they be young, old, beautiful, or ugly, and he forced a smile on them. "Ladies, you have me at a disadvantage. Maybe you could explain."

The younger lady promptly spit in his face, saying, "*Me nombre, Tocita Andujar.* You member me, Meestar Alverson?"

He had to keep his head, no matter what, and wiped his face on his shirt. "No, sorry, but I don't. Please, what's this about?"

"But I tink you do," she said. "*Me esposo*—wha you call 'usband—he was Eduardo Andujar, a very, very good hombre. For you, Eduardo gets shooted."

Halverson had killed a lot of men, some Latins among them. But never an Eduardo Andujar that he could remember. "Ma'am, you've got me mixed up with..."

She held a finger to his face. "I no meexed for nutting. Eduardo, he go Meechigan Avenida. And for that, he get shooted by that boy, Dittybooper. All for you, Meester Alverson."

Halverson came to attention, his shoulders set firmly, his jaw tucked into his neck. And he forced out, "You gotta believe me. Nobody was supposed to die."

She gave her head a violent shake. "Oh, so you no mean to—" She looked at the second lady. "—How you say *muerte* en Ingles?—Meeses Shaykelfort?"

"Murder," the matronly lady said, rubbing he hands together as if she were a witch concocting an illicit brew.

Halverson snapped his eyes at the older lady, at her diamond pendant. "Oh, God, no," he heard himself say.

"Ah, I see he now knows who I am," Essie Shakleford said. "And he also knows the rest, don't you, Smedley Butler? Let me take it from here, Tocita, just so there's no misunderstanding."

She leaned close to Halverson, and raised her voice over the hum of the jet engines. "Sergeant Kostovic and Sergeant McCoy got hold of our embassy in Colombia. The Marines have a security detachment there, and Sergeant McCoy knows the officer in charge. He talked to Tocita's uncle, who happens to be a very influential man in Colombia. It was all easy from there on in. Tocita heard about how you killed my Henry. She called and asked if I wanted to be here. I'm a nice Jewish lady, but you took my man."

"Oh, please," he croaked.

"Yes, please. I'll bet you said please to Henry, too." She turned to Tocita Andujar. "Show him."

Mrs Andujar waved at Captain Guerra, who held a document up to Halverson's eyes.

Halverson, trying his best to keep under control. "I'm sorry, I don't read Spanish."

Mrs Shakleford took the document from Captain Guerra's hand, and pointed at a series of oversized lettering on the top. "You see that, where it says ORDEN DE MATAR? *Matar* is the key word, kind of like *muerte*. You know, murder."

"But—but—I wasn't even there. How can you charge me with—murder?"

"No, no, you don't understand. *Muerte* and *matar* are similar sounding, yet slightly different in meaning. *Muerte* is the Spanish word for murder. *Matar* is the verb, meaning to die."

Halverson squinted at the Spanish words held in front of him. "I still don't understand," he said.

She smiled. "I can see that. Let me explain so that you do. *Orden de matar. Orden*—order. *De*—of. *Matar*—to die. Simply put, death warrant. They do things a bit differently in Colombia."

"What? But…"

Mrs Andujar snapped her fingers at Captain Guerra, who stepped to Halverson's side.

Halverson looked at Mrs Andujar, at Guerra, but got nothing.

Mrs Andujar said, "Now, Meeses Shaykelfort?"

Who put a hand on Tocita's sleeve. "Not just yet." She turned to Halverson. "Sergeant Kostovic made me promise to tell you something. He says, and I quote, 'I don't get mad, I get even.'"

Halverson screamed, "Nooooo!" and jerked against his bindings as Captain Guerra shoved his chair next to the outer door.

Guerra went to the doors control panel. Halverson could only watch as Guerra released the safety bar, pushed a button, and stood back. The door rolled open, and a rush of wind poured through, creating a deafening roar.

Guerra was on the intercom again, shouting in Spanish.

Immediately Halverson felt the plane banked hard left, and he teetered toward the open door. Unable to save himself, he gaped at Mrs Shakleford. "Please, not like this."

With total conviction, she said, "Yes, like this. Just like you did my Henry."

"He was cheating on you, did you know that? You're better off without him."

"Now," she said, looking at the guards.

Halverson looked at Guerra, to the other guard, and back again to Guerra. With wide, unbelieving eyes, he cried, "I have diamonds. I have millions. It's all yours."

Guerra smiled, and replied in perfect English. "Watch the first step. It's a bitch."

Epilogue

AS TOMMY SPED AWAY in Volly's boat, Paul said, "I couldn't wait to spit in Halverson's face. When it came time, I... I froze."

"Me, too," Katie said, and she placed her hands in his.

BJ, looking out at Lake Michigan. "Don't worry, he'll get spit in the face, and that's for sure."

Paul squeezed Katie's hands. "I thought when it was over I'd wanna do handstands. Now..."

BJ turned around, looking at Paul with a firm eye. "You're lucky just to be sitting there."

Paul knew BJ was right, but what if he'd waited for help that first day when he'd seen Ditty and Shoestring in the robbery?

Maybe Jack Matthews would still be alive.

And all the rest, the diamond salesmen, Ditty and Shoestring, maybe—Jesus, there were so many maybes.

Katie stood up in front of him. Even with him sitting, her eyes were only a few inches above his. For a long moment she looked at him, her deep brown tan glistening in the morning sun. Finally, she said, "Leaves you empty, doesn't it?"

"Yeah, that's the feeling."

Katie said, "I could've easily killed him out on that lake. But once we got him to shore... He's still a human being."

BJ, keeping his vigil on the lake. "Once or twice in a man's life, he's gotta do what he's gotta do and to hell with the outcome. Sometimes it ain't easy to live with it." He glanced at Paul. "You've fought a war, been a cop for years, and still you're having a hard time."

"Not the same thing," Paul said.

BJ snapped his head skyward, saying, "Listen."

He pointed at a silvery dot streaking low out of the sky. As it closed on them, Paul recognized the Learjet in which the Colombians had taken Halverson. It passed directly overhead, then roared into the southern sky, swinging its wings from side to side.

"It's done," BJ said, and headed away.

Paul pictured Jack Matthews' face, recalling those fun-loving laughs, the child-like bantering.

Yes, it was done.

And he'd live with it.